Mag

"Plenty of fan..."
—Fresh Fiction

"The perfect blend of dressmaking and intrigue."
—Sew Daily

Pleating for Mercy

"Enchanting! Prepare to be spellbound . . . by this well-written and deftly plotted cozy. It's charming, clever, and completely captivating! . . . Loved it!"
—Hank Phillippi Ryan, Agatha, Anthony, and Macavity award–winning author

"Melissa Bourbon's new series will keep you on pins and needles."
—Mary Kennedy, author of the Talk Radio Mysteries

"Cozy couture! Harlow Jane Cassidy is a tailor-made amateur sleuth. Bourbon stitches together a seamless mystery, adorned with magic, whimsy, and small-town Texas charm."
—Wendy Lyn Watson, author of the Mystery à la Mode series

"A seamless blend of mystery, magic, and dressmaking, with a cast of masterfully tailored characters you'll want to visit again and again."
—Jennie Bentley, national bestselling author of *Mortar and Murder*

"A crime-solving ghost and magical charms from the past make *Pleating for Mercy* a sure winner! The Cassidy women are naturally drawn to mystery and mischief. You'll love meeting them!"
—Maggie Sefton, national bestselling author of *Unraveled*

Also Available in the Magical Dressmaking Series

Deadly
Patterns

A MAGICAL DRESSMAKING MYSTERY

Melissa Bourbon

Ramirez

AN OBSIDIAN MYSTERY

OBSIDIAN
Published by New American Library, a division of
Penguin Group (USA) Inc., 375 Hudson Street,
New York, New York 10014, USA
Penguin Group (Canada), 90 Eglinton Avenue East, Suite 700, Toronto,
Ontario M4P 2Y3, Canada (a division of Pearson Penguin Canada Inc.)
Penguin Books Ltd., 80 Strand, London WC2R 0RL, England
Penguin Ireland, 25 St. Stephen's Green, Dublin 2,
Ireland (a division of Penguin Books Ltd.)
Penguin Group (Australia), 250 Camberwell Road, Camberwell, Victoria 3124,
Australia (a division of Pearson Australia Group Pty. Ltd.)
Penguin Books India Pvt. Ltd., 11 Community Centre, Panchsheel Park,
New Delhi - 110 017, India
Penguin Group (NZ), 67 Apollo Drive, Rosedale, Auckland 0632,
New Zealand (a division of Pearson New Zealand Ltd.)
Penguin Books (South Africa) (Pty.) Ltd., 24 Sturdee Avenue,
Rosebank, Johannesburg 2196, South Africa

Penguin Books Ltd., Registered Offices:
80 Strand, London WC2R 0RL, England

First published by Obsidian, an imprint of New American Library,
a division of Penguin Group (USA) Inc.

First Printing, October 2012
10 9 8 7 6 5 4 3 2 1

Copyright © Melissa Ramirez, 2012

OBSIDIAN and logo are trademarks of Penguin Group (USA) Inc.

Printed in the United States of America

Chapter 1

Forrest Gump's mama always said, "Life is like a box of chocolates. You never know what you're gonna get."

In my family, it was my great-grandmother who had an oft-repeated phrase. Loretta Mae Cassidy always said, "Life is like a mess of buttons. Every time you put your hand in the button box, you find a new treasure."

Wasn't that the truth? A year ago, I'd been celebrating the holidays holed up in New York designer Maximilian's sewing room as one of his seamstresses, sipping eggnog at the company party and singing punch-drunk, Southern-accented, off-key renditions of "Frosty the Snowman" with my roommate and fellow minion, Orphie Cates. Now I was back home in Bliss, Texas, planning a Winter Wonderland fashion show and coordinating arrival times with Santa and his reindeer, trying desperately to communicate with my not-so-dearly-departed great-grandmother, Loretta Mae, and solving the occasional murder.

Sometimes I was tempted to turn on the worn heels of my favorite red Frye cowboy boots and hightail it back to Manhattan, but really and truly, Texas runs through my blood. After all, Butch Cassidy was my great-great-great-granddaddy, and he bequeathed to me a goodly number of genes and the family charm as well.

As I drove through the town square, I reveled in Bliss's abundant holiday spirit. Evergreen garlands wound around the streetlamps. Little brick houses twinkled with white lights. A giant crèche, complete with all the Nativity characters, was on display in front of the courthouse on the square. Storefronts sparkled with holiday decorations, and the strains of Christmas carols sounded everywhere you went.

Bliss, Texas, at Christmastime is like a village straight out of a Dickens story—with Southern flair.

I turned off Maple Drive and onto Mayberry, and smiled to myself. Small-town dramatics aside, this place was magical.

I drove Meemaw's beat-up truck, rumbling past Craftsman-style homes, brick Tudors, and baby Victorians, finally stopping in front of the old Denison mansion. Zinnia James, the wife of Senator Jebediah James, and my biggest fan, had arranged a meeting here to nail down the final details of the Winter Wonderland fashion show. It was the culminating event of the three-day holiday celebration, and I, being one of the newer residents in town, had been roped into taking on multiple roles: decorator, seamstress, designer, and, well, basically Jill-of-all-trades. Whatever Mrs. James needed, I'd help with.

As I entered the historic district, I recalled what Will Flores, city architect, my personal handyman, and the father of my apprentice seamstress, Gracie, had said about the Denison mansion.

The Victorian had been the home of one of Bliss's founding fathers, Charles Denison, back in 1897. Outlaws, gold, and moonshine were all part of the house's history. The Denisons and the Kincaids, the other founding family in Bliss, had been oil and gas partners back in the day.

Until one day in the early 1900s when Justin Kincaid won the Denison mansion in a poker game. The friendship went south right along with the Denisons' marriage. Part of the Winter Wonderland festivities would be the grand reopening of the historic house after decades of neglect.

I made a U-turn, rumbled up alongside the curb, and threw the gearshift into park. Climbing out of the old truck, I buttoned up my coat. "Santa must have left the barn door open up in the North Pole," I muttered.

The clouds in the overcast sky ballooned above me as I looked up at the stately Victorian with its widow's walk and turrets, wraparound porch, and coral and teal color palette. When I was little, the house had been a run-down eyesore, but now the painted lady would reclaim its place as the centerpiece of the historic district. It had eventually been sold to the city by the Kincaids after spending decades on the market with no takers. Too much of a renovation project, I guess, but the Bliss Historical Society was finally wrapping up the transformation and the house had recently been added to the town's historical record.

"Right on time."

I jumped and slammed my hand to my heart. "Lord, Mrs. James! I didn't hear you come up."

The woman was quieter than Meemaw, and that was saying a lot, since Meemaw was currently a ghost living with me in my old yellow farmhouse.

Mrs. James laughed and squeezed my arm with her gloved hand. "Bless your heart, Harlow. I didn't mean to startle you. And let's just stop with the formalities, dear, do you hear? We've been through enough, you and I, that you should call me by my given name."

I swallowed. I was thirty-three, but being a Southerner meant showing respect. "I don't know if I can, Mrs. J—"

"Nonsense," she scolded. "Of course you can. It's Zinnia from now on. Now, we need to get that ugly old sign down." She pointed to the ABERNATHY HOME BUILDERS placard lashed to the wrought-iron fence surrounding the house.

There was no arguing with her. She was stubborn as a mule. "Yes, ma'am, Mrs. Jam—, er, Zinnia." I'd try to call her by her given name, but in my mind she would always be Mrs. James.

"It'll have to be cut off," I said, making a mental note. She fluttered her hand. "Later then."

I pulled my knit hat down over my ears, but they still felt frozen. I'd hand-tailored my rose-colored wool double-breasted coat, fringing the edges of the matching wool belt and lining it with black satin. But on a day like today—blustery and damp—it was more pretty than practical.

Most people believed Texas didn't ever get cold. They were dead wrong. South Texas, maybe, but North Texas? The frigid cold made your fingers numb, chilling you to the bone.

"We're in a heap of trouble if it rains," I said, looking up at the darkening sky. A streak of light bisected the clouds just before a deafening crack of rolling thunder sounded.

Zinnia looked unfazed. "You know what they say about Texas weather," she said.

I did indeed: If you don't like it, wait five minutes and it'll change. "The forecast says it may even snow before Friday."

"And wouldn't that be delightful?" she said, patting her immobile mound of silver hair. "We get a sprinkling of white powder nearly every year. Why not now?" She gave a practiced smile, just wide enough not to crack the thick layer of makeup she wore. Mrs. James was nothing if not the quintessential Texas politician's wife. Eternally, if artificially, young, and eternally optimistic. "A winter wonderland," she said. "We picked the perfect theme. Couldn't have planned it better if we'd had a chat with the good Lord himself."

There were no other cars on the street, and no one was waiting on the porch. "Am I early?" I asked, glancing at my watch. My great-grandmother had taught me to be punctual, but Southern time was often laid-back and imprecise.

"Helen should be along in a few minutes." She looked up at the old house, frowning. "I figured Arnie Barnett and some of his men would be here finishing up."

Barnett Home Restoration had been in charge of transforming the interior of the home while Abernathy Home Builders had done the structural and exterior work. And from what I could see, it had been done perfectly. When I closed my eyes, I could imagine the dirt streets bustling with horse-drawn carriages and the house, in its prime, looking just as it did now.

We passed through the wrought-iron gate and started toward the Victorian's porch steps, but Mrs. James paused, gazing up at the second story. My own gaze stopped at the tiny circular porch on the roofline at the right corner of the house. Texas was far from the New

England coast and there were no ships to watch for, but the widow's walk lookout was ominous, just the same. Another jolt of lightning brightened the sky, thunder booming after it. A chill swept up my spine. I'd never had to worry over a loved one coming home, but my great-great-great-grandmother, Texana Harlow, had when Butch Cassidy had left her, pregnant, and escaped to Argentina.

"Let's get inside," Mrs. James said, pulling me into motion again just as a heavy drizzle started. As we hurried up the front steps and under the protection of the porch roof, I shivered. Snow would give a nice ambience to the Winter Wonderland event, yes, but a thunderstorm? It was risky, at best, to hold a December fashion show outdoors, but between the both of us, we'd tried to cover all of our bases.

Mrs. James turned the knob on the front door—and when she found it locked, she knocked. While we waited, she rattled off the list of everything that would protect us from impending disaster. "Not to worry, Harlow. We have an enormous weatherproof tent, heat lamps, a covered walkway between the house and the tent, extra umbrellas, salt—which, by the way," she said, dropping her voice as if she were imparting a great secret, "I had to get Earl Messer over at the hardware store to order special for me."

"I'd have thought he k-kept some in stock," I said through my chattering teeth. "You d-don't have a k-key?"

"Lost it." She knocked again and then said, "Some, yes. Thirty bags? No."

That made sense. I'd lived in New York for a good many years, but unless it was a hurricane or a blizzard, rain and snow didn't slow folks in Manhattan down one little bit.

But here? When the freezing rain turned to ice on the streets, the whole town shut down.

"The fact that I have all these bags of salt is insurance that we won't actually get any ice, Harlow. It always works out that way. Mark my words."

Even though it didn't make a lick of sense, I thought she was probably right. Anytime I'd bought extra fabric, or a pile of notions, just knowing I was going to have a use for them real soon, they ended up stashed away in a bin just taking up space. Which, in Manhattan, had been precious. I'd shared a tiny loft apartment with Orphie, and we'd barely had room to breathe, let alone hoard swatches of linen and cotton and silk.

"Harlow Cassidy, you're a million miles away." Mrs. James laid her hand on my arm again and I could feel the warmth of her seep through me.

"Just thinking about New York."

"Well, don't do that. You're back home where you belong, just like your great-grandmother wanted." She paused for just a second before adding, "I've been meaning to thank you for taking on so much responsibility with the Winter Wonderland. I couldn't have done it without you."

"Sure you could have, Mrs. J—"

"Phft!"

"I mean . . . Zinnia. I'm grateful for the work." Building a custom dressmaking business from nothing was difficult under the best of circumstances, but in a town as small as Bliss, it was downright scary. I was living from design job to design job, and hemming polyester pants and altering men's suits wasn't near enough to live on.

But Mrs. James, my unofficial benefactor, wanted Buttons & Bows to thrive, so she'd thrown a heap of work my way, most recently asking me to do everything I could to make the Winter Wonderland fashion show a smashing success. "It's your first Christmas back in Bliss since Loretta Mae passed. We need to ring in the holiday with cheer. Working with you is a pleasure, Harlow."

The sky flashed with lightning, another rolling wave of thunder cracked, and a downpour started, buckets of rain gushing from the clouds. I squared my shoulders and shoved my hands deeper into my pockets. "You're right. Weather be damned. This fashion show is going to be perfect."

Despite Mrs. James's heavy makeup, the cold weather made her papery skin even more translucent. It tightened up, pulling taut over her cheekbones. Although she was one of those ageless beauties, the Botox and fillers that I knew she used really did smooth out pesky wrinkles, as I'd recently learned.

She pounded her fist on the door, giving it one more shot. Still no answer. "Why isn't Arnie Barnett or Dan Lee Chrisson here?" she demanded, as if I had the answer to that. I didn't have much personal experience, but I knew that contractors were notoriously unreliable.

I turned and peered up and down the street, trying to see through the sheets of rain. "Mrs. Abernathy's not usually late, is she?" I called over the sound of water banging against the porch's roof.

Her smooth brow furrowed for a second and her voice grew testy. "She is this time. Fifteen minutes now."

Zinnia James didn't like to be kept waiting. Mrs. Abernathy didn't either, so her tardiness was unusual.

But a few minutes later, the beam of headlights coming down the street broke the bleakness of the stormy afternoon. A car screeched to a stop in front of the house and the driver's door was flung wide, a sturdy green and white umbrella popped open, and Helen Abernathy, of Abernathy Home Builders, hurried up the steps to us. "Quite a storm," she said, panting and pausing just long enough to fold up the umbrella, shake it, and plop it into a basket sitting to the right of the door.

She nodded to me, her thin lips curved into a polite smile. "Harlow."

"Afternoon, Mrs. Abernathy," I said, but she'd already turned away, plunging a key into the lock, water cascading off her beige raincoat. She stepped into the house, Zinnia and me on her heels, and she shut the door against the raging storm outside.

"Much better!" she shouted, immediately correcting the volume of her voice. "Much better."

"Stuck in the deluge?" Mrs. James asked, her eyes a little pinched at having to wait.

"The traffic light on Henrietta Street is out," Mrs. Abernathy said.

Huh. "Really?" I said. "I just came over on Henrietta. Not a soul on the street and the lights were working fine."

She leveled her cool gray eyes at me. "You know how it is around here. The power goes out so randomly. It can be on at our house, but the neighbors next door are on a different grid and theirs will be off."

Mrs. James notched her thumb in the general direction of the backyard and Henrietta. "Are you listing a house over there?"

Mrs. Abernathy gave a restrained little laugh. "My, but aren't the two of you inquisitive. We're doing renovations on a place over there, Zinnia. We're working with Arnie and Dan again. They did wonderful work here. It's still in the early stages," she added, "but by late spring they ought to be all set."

She slipped her raincoat off and hung it on one of the hooks on the antique coat tree, pausing to look in the mirror and smooth her windblown blond hair. Her black slacks and boxy cream blouse did nothing for her robust figure. I had a mental flash of her wearing an asymmetrical lavender sweater, buttoned at the top, and instead of the square blouse, a tailored cut with darts and a flared hem.

"Something wrong?" Mrs. Abernathy's voice shook me out of my designing mode and back into the present. She gave me a good once-over, her gaze hitching on the light streak in my chestnut hair, a Cassidy family trait.

"Not a thing," I said, smiling, wishing I could make a garment for her that would soften her uptight demeanor. But my Cassidy charm would never benefit Helen Abernathy if she had anything to do with it.

She frowned, but didn't say anything else; instead, she turned her attention back to Zinnia James. "All the floors were redone—"

"Hand-scraped pecan." Mrs. James ran the tip of her boot over the grain of one plank.

"Just like we discussed."

"I made a list of what still needs to be done," Mrs. James said as we headed toward the kitchen.

We stopped, turning around when the front door blew open, a crack of thunder sounding and the howl of the wind spreading through the downstairs of the old Victorian. Two men barreled in, slamming the door closed and shaking the rain off their coats. "Christ almighty, now that there's a storm," one of them said. Arnie Barnett. I didn't know him well, but I'd gone to school with his wife, Hattie, and her sister, Raylene.

The men surged forward, leaving a trail of water on the floor. Another reason to hope for clear weather. Dan Lee Chrisson, the man who accompanied Arnie Barnett and had worked with him on the restoration, would play Santa right here in the foyer. We wanted happy kids, not kids slipping, sliding, and twisting ankles.

The handle of the front door rattled and then the door flew open again. Speak of the devil. Hattie Barnett stood there, pausing long enough to pocket her keys and call down to someone on the sidewalk. "Wait for me in the car!" she yelled, her voice getting lost in the wind.

I waved to her as she closed the door and then I detoured to the powder room to find a towel. But the pedestal sink and commode were the only things in the tiny water closet—no towels. I finally made it into the kitchen, checked under the antiqued white cupboard, and found a stack of thick blue disposable towels just as the howling of the wind sounded again, followed by a high-pitched screech and a thud.

I hurried back to the foyer just as Arnie grabbed Hattie's forearm and yanked her up from where she'd fallen with one quick movement. "Hattie, are you okay?"

"I'm fine. Why in tarnation is there water on the floor?" she said, glaring at Arnie and Dan. Hattie couldn't have been more than five feet three inches. She didn't look all that tough at first meeting, but we'd been in the same graduating class at Bliss High School, and while she looked sweet as apple pie, she was a spitfire if there ever was one.

"That's going to leave a bruise," I said, unfolding the towels and scattering them on the floor to soak up the rainwater. "We best get a throw rug for the entry here," I called back to Mrs. James.

Hattie arched her back to look behind her, as if she had X-ray vision and would be able to see the black-and-blue mark through her jeans. "Dang," she said.

That pretty much said it all.

Dan Lee Chrisson skirted around Hattie, crouching to help me dry the spatters of water. I vaguely remembered him from Bliss High, too, but he'd been a few years behind me. He'd kept to himself back then, and he still did. Lately I'd seen him around at Sundance Kids, Nana's goat farm, where he was friendly with Maggie, a twenty-something woman who helped my grandmother with her cheese making. He had his head tilted like he was trying to gauge how hurt Hattie was, his gaze directed toward the staircase.

"Did you bring the Santa suit?" I asked him. He'd bought it somewhere in Fort Worth, and I'd agreed to take a look at it, just in case it needed alterations.

He started, bringing his attention back to me. "Uh, yeah," he said, but before I could ask him what he thought of it, he'd turned his head again, intently focused on something else. Whatever was on his mind, he didn't want to talk Santa suits right now.

"What are you starin' at, Dan?" The sharpness in Hattie's Southern drawl drew me up short.

"Nothin', Hattie. Cool your engines."

Her cheeks tinged red and her fists clenched. "Don't you talk to me like that. You have no right—"

"Jesus, Hattie," Arnie said, squeezing her arm. "Give it a rest. It ain't your divorce."

Divorce? I knew Dan Lee had married Raylene Lewis a couple of years back, but had they already split?

My ears perked up at their conversation, but I lowered my head, trying to focus on the cleanup. I had no business listening, but they kept at it and I couldn't help it if they chose to air their dirty laundry right in front of me, now, could I?

Hattie had a look in her eye that I'd never seen before. She jerked free of her husband's hand. "No, it's not, but she's my sister and he . . . he—"

I could practically see the steam billowing from her ears, her dainty nostrils flaring.

"It just ain't right, not with Boone so little." She angled her glare back at Dan Lee. "Don't you go thinkin' that playin' Santa'll make you come off as some nice, misunderstood guy. While you're playing at the North Pole, cavortin' with that no good little elf you're shackin' up with, I'll be comfortin' Raylene."

The color drained from Dan Lee's face, but his voice stayed firm and matter-of-fact. "Me and Ray have been talking, Hattie, or didn't she tell you that?"

Hattie stood stock-still, staring at him, and if her eyes could have shot daggers, Dan Lee Chrisson would have been dead. "No, you have not."

"Yeah, we have. It's our business, not yours."

"She's my sister. That makes it my business."

"She's a grown woman—"

"Unlike your little friend," she shot back.

Dan Lee's neck turned red, the color spreading up to his cheeks. "Dammit, Hattie, things ain't always simple."

"Marriage is. You love someone, you get married, you stay married. Doesn't get much simpler than that."

Dan Lee's lips parted and he breathed in like he was readying himself for a response, but then he seemed to think better of it and closed his mouth.

Hattie plowed on. "You have Boone, or did you forget about him?"

"'Course not. I know what it's like to not know your parents. I'm not a fool, Hattie. I'm gonna give Boone everything I never had."

"Except parents who are married."

Dan Lee looked like he had another comeback, but this time he kept his mouth shut, just shaking his head instead.

"Never mind her," Arnie said as he grabbed Hattie's arm and started pulling her toward the kitchen, but she swung around, pointing and scowling at Dan Lee. "Mark my words, Dan Lee—hurting Raylene was a mistake."

Yikes. I sat back on my heels, stunned into silence. I'd known Hattie a long time, but I'd never seen her riled up like that before. Guess her sister being hurt so badly had brought out the mama bear instinct in her.

"Sorry, man," Arnie said to Dan Lee as he came back into the foyer. "She has to be loyal to Ray, you know—"

Dan Lee threw up a hand. "You've been real fair, Arnie, but you don't have to pick sides. All the time telling me she's gonna keep me from seeing Boone and . . ." He paused, just long enough to let loose an uncomfortable laugh. "Look, ain't nothin' gonna stop me from being with my boy, so maybe you should stay out of it. Don't wanna cause no trouble with you and Hattie."

There didn't seem to be any more to say after that, so Arnie headed to the parlor to start gathering up his tools, and Dan Lee headed upstairs to try on the Santa suit for me.

"Tell Hattie to lock up when she leaves," Arnie said to me from the archway. I nodded, but the only thing I could think was I suddenly regretted our choice for Saint Nick. I didn't want any drama from Dan Lee's divorce putting a damper on the winter festival. But there was nothing to be done about it now.

As I went into the kitchen to throw the towels in the garbage can, I heard the low rumble of Dan Lee's voice. No one else was upstairs, so he must have been on the phone. A few words floated down to where I stood. "Everything's gonna be fine, Mags," he said, and then he said good-bye and seemed to end the call. Overhearing that bit of his conversation, presumably with Maggie from Sundance Kids, reminded me to keep an open mind. Just because he and Raylene weren't good together didn't mean he was all bad.

I leaned against the restored wood counter when I saw that Mrs. James was in full instruction mode. "Harlow Jane, the decorations need to be finished the night before the fashion show. We don't want to leave a single thing to chance. I'll have some folks coming in with the portable heaters, your friend Josie is making the wire-rimmed bows to be placed at the end of each row, and . . ."

She went on and I listened, making mental notes of all the tasks to be done over the next few days. The Winter Wonderland would be in full swing, but I'd be entirely focused on every last detail of the fashion show, making sure the designs were perfect.

I gave Mrs. James an update on the ensembles I was making for the fashion show, while Hattie and Mrs. Abernathy chatted. "I still don't quite have Josie's figured out, but I will," I said, hoping it was true. My pregnant friend was throwing me off my game.

"We'll be out of here today," I heard Hattie say, with a barely audible "Thank the Lord" under her breath.

"The widow's walk railing?" Mrs. Abernathy said. "Has it been fixed?"

"Arnie tightened the bolts again yesterday, but he said they're stripped. He's replacin' them today. It's the last thing he has to do."

Mrs. James nodded, satisfied, then covered a few more items before clapping her hands and turning to face all of us. "It's going to be just perfect, ladies! I can't thank you enough for all you've done to make the Winter Wonderland a smashing success."

A door slammed from somewhere in the house, reminding me that I had one thing to take care of before I could get back to my sewing. "I'll just be checking the fit on the Santa suit; then I have to get back to my shop. Lots to do!" Maybe too much, I thought, but I knew that seeing the kids sit on Santa's lap and watching the magic of the fashion show unfold would make it all worthwhile.

When Mrs. James went out the kitchen door to check on the tent and Mrs. Abernathy headed to the parlor, I was left in the kitchen with Hattie. "It's too bad about Raylene's divorce," I said.

"Yeah, too bad," she said. "Having a baby's supposed to be a joyous and happy time. They were a new family." She fell silent for a spell before adding, "I don't get how he could just up and leave like that. You think you know someone . . ." She trailed off, shaking her head.

"Sounds like he plans to be there for the baby, though," I said.

"Yeah, so he says. He's always talking about the number his parents pulled on him, but you know? They mighta been crappy parents, but they stayed married, and that's more than Dan Lee was willing to do. He got himself a nice little girlfriend, and she's at his beck and call. And Raylene don't want her baby anywhere near either of 'em. She wants full custody. Dan Lee doesn't have the sense of a cockroach if he thinks we're not goin' to war over it."

I couldn't say I blamed Hattie for sticking up for her sister, or Raylene. I came from a long line of strong, single women. Aside from my grandmother, none of the Cassidy women had hung on to a man for very long, and we were fine with that. Maybe Raylene and Dan Lee weren't meant for each other, but I couldn't see a woman giving up her baby without a fight.

There wasn't much more to say and we were both busy, so Hattie left a couple of minutes later. "I'll be back. Gotta get the cleaning supplies to finish up in here." She was still limping from her fall, and appeared distracted, but I imagined working kept her mind off worrying over her sister and nephew. It was exactly what I would do. Immerse myself in my sewing, getting lost in my own world.

From somewhere nearby another door slammed, and then Mrs. James's voice echoed through the creaky house. No matter how much the place had been refurbished, it was a century old, after all.

After another few minutes, Dan Lee still hadn't reappeared. Where was he? I was starting to get impatient for him to come down and show me the Santa costume. "Two more minutes," I muttered. That was all the time I was going to give him before I snuck out and headed home, leaving him to fend for himself in his red velvet suit. The sewing projects at my little yellow farmhouse beckoned.

Chapter 2

Mrs. James stood at the base of the staircase, her hand resting on the wood banister. The front door opened, the wind howled, and Mrs. Abernathy and Hattie practically blew inside. "That's an old story," Mrs. Abernathy snapped.

"If you say so—"

Another gust of wind flung the door toward the wall. Hattie gasped, dropping the plastic tote full of cleaning supplies and lunging to catch it before it hit the floor. She quickly closed the door, shutting out the storm.

I wrapped my coat tighter against the cold, but it didn't seem to make much difference. No matter how much insulation and updating an old house had, it was still drafty and held on to a chill.

"Pshaw. Enough old stories. This town is full of them." Mrs. James's sharp tone pulled them both up short. "Come up here, Helen. I want you to see the bathtub."

Mrs. Abernathy sidestepped into the parlor, picking up an old quilt that had fallen to the floor. She folded it, hung it over a chair, and came back to the foyer just as Hattie disappeared into the kitchen lugging her cleaning supplies. Mrs. Abernathy climbed the staircase to the second story while I drummed my fingers on the banister. Where in the devil was Dan Lee Chrisson? Truth be told, I couldn't skip out without an inspection of the Santa suit. I was nothing if not a perfectionist.

"You, too, Harlow," Mrs. James said.

I peered up and started to say, "Oh, it's okay—" but I figured if Dan Lee wasn't coming down to me, I'd just go up to him. "Sure," I said, and I fell in behind them.

The click of our heels against the newly redone steps as we mounted the wood stairs echoed, the rolling thunder outside getting louder as we ascended. I looked down over the railing and into the open space below, wondering if the spirit of Charles Denison, or his wife, Pearl, was hanging around this old place. But there were no signs of any ghosts. Loretta Mae Cassidy, my great-grandmother, was a ghostly presence in my old farmhouse, purely a Cassidy thing, I knew, but still, sometimes I wondered if other houses had spirits that lingered and tried to stay connected to the living.

"Quite a place, isn't it, Harlow?" Mrs. James said from behind me. "I've never seen it looking so lovely."

It really was. "Mmm-hmm." From what I remembered, the Denison family had long since left Bliss and no one had seen hide nor hair of them for decades. Would they be pleased to see their house brought back to its original glory?

Mrs. James and Mrs. Abernathy paused at the door to the bathroom. A brand-new claw-foot tub replica was the highlight of the big square room. "Perfect," Mrs. James said. She went in to take a closer look, stopping to examine the pedestal sink, the ornate mirror, and the silver vanity looking glass and brush set on display atop an antique dresser.

I was more enamored with the silk dressing gown hanging from a crystal knob on the back of the door. I moved closer to fawn over the details: hand embroidery along the yoke and a shirred front panel with fine, hand-embroidered scalloped edging. When worn, the dressing gown would be sensuously open from the breastbone tie to the waist, with a cherry blossom damask pattern in the silk skirt. It was beautiful.

"Found that tucked away in a secret closet," Mrs. James said. "I just love old houses. So many nooks and crannies. You never know what you'll find hidden."

I followed Mrs. James and Mrs. Abernathy back into the hall. "The walkway to the tent will start just outside the kitchen," Mrs. Abernathy said, but Mrs. James interrupted. "I want to see the widow's walk. If it's not fixed, we'll need to lock the door and keep people off."

Mrs. Abernathy shook her head. "The rain . . ." But she trailed off as Mrs. James headed for the second flight of stairs and started up.

Mrs. Abernathy turned back to me with a thin smile. "To the widow's walk," she said, then turned on her heel and followed.

Good thing I'd left my coat and hat on, since we'd be stepping back out into the cold.

Mrs. James turned the crystal doorknob and pulled. A gust of freezing wind shot through the opening. I folded my arms over my chest as I pushed forward, outside, and braved the cold. Mrs. James had her jacket on too, but Mrs. Abernathy shivered.

Out on the small platform, Mrs. James immediately stopped short. She slowly turned to look at Mrs. Abernathy. "Look at that railing. What in the devil? Where is Arnie Barnett?"

"Should I call Hattie?" I offered, peering through the door to get a better look at the problem. "If it can't be fixed in time, we can make sure the door is locked."

"He'll fix it. With the amount of time he and his workers have spent here, nothing should be left undone," she said tersely.

Mrs. Abernathy shoved past me. I followed, nearly plowing into her as she came to an abrupt stop. Suddenly I realized that the railing wasn't loose at all. An entire section of it was missing, the jagged edges of the painted wood all that remained. Just below the flooring, where the roof sloped downward, shingles were torn off. The white tent where the fashion show would be held covered the majority of the yard. A narrow enclosed walkway led from the house, connecting it to the tent. My gaze kept going down, down, down, and then hitched suddenly on a patch of red and black peeking through the leggy winter brush, half hidden along the side of the walkway.

I pointed. "What's that?"

The women leaned forward to see what I'd spotted. Mrs. Abernathy let out a high-pitched choking sound. Her hand flew to her mouth and she turned her back on the sight.

I peered through the downpour, trying to see what had upset her. "What is it?" I shouted over the rat-a-tat-tat of rain on the roof and the booming echoing in the sky.

Mrs. James pressed in next to Mrs. Abernathy. "Is that a boot?" She leaned farther over the gaping hole in the railing.

A boot? My heart shot to my throat. "No," I said and tried to get a better look, just as Mrs. James's foot slipped on the wet wood. She lost her balance and lurched into Mrs. Abernathy. Mrs. Abernathy careened forward, grabbing hold of the ragged end of the railing.

"Help!" She teetered on the edge of the widow's walk. Mrs. James had regained her balance and gripped the other woman's arm. I stepped to the right, trying to edge my body in front of hers to stop her from falling, but her foot slipped out from under her. Her body jostled into mine, knocking me forward as she fell backward. She landed with a thud on her behind, but her legs stretched out in front of her, kicking my feet out from under me.

I felt myself flying, my legs in the air for a second before they crashed against the roof, tearing shingles away. Someone screamed. Me? Mrs. James? I couldn't tell.

Rain pelted my face. The back of my head thudded against the roof and everything went fuzzy. And then I was falling, headed straight for the red mound below.

Faces flashed like an old-fashioned picture show. Meemaw. Nana. Mama. Granddaddy. My brother, Red. Gracie Flores. Will.

The people who loved me and who I loved . . .

And then I crashed. It wasn't the hard, bone-breaking collision of a body against the ground, but a soft landing against something pliable, almost like a trampoline, and it cradled me, cupping my body as I sank into it.

"Harlow!"

I tried to shake away the clouds in my head, peering up at Mrs. James's horrified face. Her arm was stretched over the broken railing, as if she were still trying to catch me.

Just as I caught a glimpse of Mrs. Abernathy behind her, her back pressed against the door, I lurched, the fabric of the tented walkway that held me giving way. It pitched and a second later I was sliding, then falling, until I hit the ground.

Right next to the lump of red we'd seen from above.

I gasped for air, afraid to move. Blinking away the veil of fear from the fall, I peered up at the widow's walk. Mrs. James and Mrs. Abernathy were gone.

Everything was fuzzy, but I tried to take inventory. I wiggled my toes in my boots. Moved my fingertips. Shifted my hips. Everything seemed to be working. Finally, I turned my head, just a touch, to look at what I was lying next to. Or rather, who.

I registered the fur-lined coat, the red and white hat, and the black belt. Dan Lee Chrisson hadn't come back downstairs for me to fit his Santa suit because he'd slipped off the widow's walk and—

My gaze traveled down the length of red until I saw black boots twisted awkwardly, and a wave of nausea filled my gut. Poor Dan Lee Chrisson was dead.

Chapter 3

Nurse Jude Cranford, a forty-something woman who lived in her nurse's scrubs and Dansko clogs and whom I'd become tight with over the last several hours at Presbyterian Hospital, navigated my wheelchair through the corridor. She prattled on about the storm outside, how she lived just down the street from my grandparents, and how she was glad she'd taken the extra shift, since she got to meet me, because normally she worked Labor and Delivery. "Four days a week, twelve-hour shifts," she said. "But I love the ward, and it's good for J.R. to wash his own clothes and cook his own meals — not a bad thing, what with how he smells, what with running the farm."

I shifted my aching body to take the pressure off my bruised hip and continued to half listen to Jude. At the mention of the pregnancy ward, my To Do list suddenly shot to the front of my mind. Finalizing my plans for my friend Josie Kincaid's maternity outfits for the Winter Wonderland fashion show was at the top of it. I'd left her creations for last in case her baby bump grew. Which it had. She was five months along, but when she'd come for her last round of measurements, her belly had grown several inches.

Nurse Jude wheeled my chair past the information desk, heading straight for the automatic double doors. "So what really happened?" she asked me. "Was there ice? Did you see that poor man fall?"

"No," I said, wishing, not for the first time, that none of us had lollygagged in the foyer. Maybe we'd have seen Dan Lee Chrisson go onto the widow's walk and could have stopped him. Or saved him. Maybe then something would have turned out differently.

"He was going to play Santa at the festival?" Jude asked.

"He was," I said, my mind suddenly spiraling. Not only was the poor man dead, but the kids wouldn't have a Santa.

We approached the doors and they whooshed open, a wall of brittle cold pushing against us. I pulled my coat up over my lap and the scene from earlier replayed in my head. My chest tightened as I remembered the rush of the air against my face as I'd fallen. I'd had the fleeting thought that I would be joining Meemaw a lot sooner than planned.

I closed the door on those thoughts, thinking instead that I needed to touch base with Mrs. James to make sure the tent was fixed, find someone new to play Santa at the event, and ... what else? I'm sure there were other things that needed doing, but for the life of me I couldn't think what they were. The edges of my mind felt fuzzy, some of my thoughts out of reach.

Mama and Nana had left me with Jude while they went to bring Mama's Jeep around to the pickup area. They arrived and were out of the car in seconds flat as they saw me, each of them taking one of my arms and pulling me up to standing. As Jude moved the wheelchair out of the way, Mama gave me a good once-over and said, "Bless your heart, Harlow Jane." Her hand fluttered toward me for just a second before she pulled herself together, swallowing hard and throwing her shoulders back. Tessa Cassidy was a tough cookie, but having her only daughter fall nearly to her death had forced a crack in the veneer. "You sure you're okay, baby?"

Nana scoffed. "She fell from a roof. Of course she's not okay." But she lowered her chin and with her next breath she said, "Now then, Ladybug, you're gonna be just fine, you hear me?"

The Cassidy women weren't known for their over-abundance of emotions. What with hiding our magical charms since . . . forever, we'd had to learn to be restrained. But Mama and Nana both looked about as strung out as I'd ever seen them. My eyes welled, but Jude clearing her throat broke the moment. "The doctor's given her the green light to go home. She just needs to take it easy. Probably should steer clear of the widow's walk over at the Denison place," she added with a chastising smile.

"You think?" I said with a little laugh. But truth be told, I knew I'd have to go back to the mansion soon. Although it could wait until tomorrow, assuming the raging storm didn't knock the whole of Bliss off the power grid. Which would be bad. No power would mean it would be next to impossible to work on Josie's ensembles and get them done in time for the show.

Mama and Nana fussed over me, helping me into the Jeep. I waved to Jude. She raised her hand and gave a little nod. The second Mama drove off of the hospital grounds, she peered at me in the rearview mirror and Nana whipped around to face me. "What in tarnation happened?" Nana practically barked.

I stared at them. "What do you mean?"

"How did you fall? That's what I wanna know," Mama said at the same moment Nana said, "You attract death like honey attracts a bee. Do you know that, Ladybug?"

"Whoa, what are you talking about?" I threw up my hands, grimacing at the shooting pain in my side. The doctor had given me the green light to go on home, but the painkillers hadn't completely taken away the throbbing that the fall had inflicted on my body.

The rain changed direction and Mama hit a slick of water. The Jeep skidded and then lurched. I careened against the door, righting myself with a grimace as she straightened the car out.

Mama went on as if nothing had happened, heaving a sigh. "Hoss says those screws were stripped and that railing was an accident waitin' to happen. He's comin' by to talk to you tomorrow." She paused weightily. "And that boy of his—" She paused, gritting her teeth like she could hardly stand to utter his name. "His boy Gavin had the audacity to say how strange it is that you're connected first with Nell's death, next with Macon Vance, and now with Santa Claus."

"The only unnatural deaths Bliss has had in who knows how many years," Nana spit out. "Girl, you gotta stop gettin' yourself involved in stuff like this."

I stared at them both. "It's not as if I'm asking for folks to up and die around me. And I certainly didn't have anything to do with Dan Lee Chrisson falling from a roof. Why in the world does the sheriff think it wasn't an accident? Dan Lee kept to himself, from what I know."

"He didn't say," Mama muttered, turning her gaze back to the road, the windshield wipers slapping as they tried to keep up with the downpour. I stared at the back of their heads. From the outside looking in, I supposed it did look suspicious. The sleepy little town of Bliss had been just fine until I'd returned home. Now we were two murders in—three if what Sheriff McClaine and Deputy McClaine suspected was true and Dan Lee had been pushed off the widow's walk.

"I hardly knew the man," I said, more to myself than to them, and instantly, all the other people who'd been at the Denison place danced through my mind. Mrs. James and Mrs. Abernathy had both been working with Dan Lee, and Arnie and Hattie knew him well. Could anyone else have come and gone while none of us had been looking? I had heard the door slam once or twice, and Hattie had been talking to someone. Raylene, perhaps?

"Well, I knew him. Maggie's been mighty sweet on him, and she's beside herself. Hasn't been back to the farm since she found out, and she practically lived there, you know," Nana said, shaking her head sadly. "I don't think she's coming back to work, bless her heart."

My head pounded. Even in the protection of the closed-in Jeep, the cold was suddenly bone-chilling. Why did Dan Lee Chrisson have to die, and why, oh why was I involved in yet another murder?

Chapter 4

The Cassidy family story goes way back, all the way to the days of famous outlaw Butch Cassidy. No one ever said outlaws were a faithful bunch. And I'd recently discovered that, thanks to Butch's unfaithfulness, the Cassidy clan included other Bliss residents—namely Sandra and Libby James, the daughter and granddaughter of Zinnia.

Butch's long-ago legendary wish in an Argentinean fountain had given good fortune to his descendants in the form of magical charms. Namely: What Meemaw wanted, she'd gotten, including me back home in Bliss. Nana could communicate with her goats. Mama could make plants grow or wither away and die, depending upon her mood. And me? I'd recently discovered that when I designed outfits for people, their deepest desires were realized.

Sandra and Libby James, descendants of Etta James and Butch by way of Senator Jebediah James, were also charmed.

Until now, I hadn't had the occasion to experience their charms firsthand, but I'd woken up the morning after my fall from the widow's walk to the soul-comforting scent of biscuits baking in the oven, gravy simmering on the stove, and my favorite Extra Bold Dark Magic coffee running through my coffeemaker.

I stepped gingerly down the stairs, taking it nice and slow, pausing and regrouping at the landing. I'd been sore the night before, but now I was stiff, too. And black and blue under my black stretch workout pants and long-sleeved gray thermal tee. Fuzzy socks with skid-resistant soles completed the outfit. A designer's look it wasn't, but for practical post-fall recovery? Perfect.

"We're here to help," Sandra, my half cousin, announced as I hobbled into the kitchen. "I don't really sew, and neither does Libby, but we can cook and clean and help you with whatever you need while your mom and grandma help you with the dresses you have left."

"Thanks—," I began, but Libby piped up.

"And the Santa suit."

The smile that had been forming on my lips, the only part of my body that wasn't aching, froze. "What Santa suit?"

A visible shiver passed over her. "If I was a kid, there's no way I'd sit on Santa's lap if his suit had blood on it."

I swallowed. "Blood?"

Sandra took the tray of biscuits out of the oven, plopped one on a plate next to an over-easy egg, and ladled white, peppered gravy on top until the biscuit and egg were practically floating in it. She set it down on the pine table, pulling the chair out and gesturing for me to sit.

"The impact from the fall," she said, darting a worried glance at Libby.

Death was never easy, but the demise of Santa Claus, even if he was just playing dress-up, felt particularly bad.

"I figured you'd whip up a new one," she said.

People who didn't sew seemed to think a seamstress could simply bat her eyes, as in *I Dream of Jeannie*, and voilà! An outfit would be ready. Yes, I could make a Santa suit. It was just yards and yards of velvety red fabric trimmed with white fur. But it was one more thing to add to my To Do list. The same To Do list that was already the length of my left arm.

"I suppose I can," I said finally. I'd have to take some measurements, do a fitting or two, but I could pull it off. "But we don't have a replacement Santa yet," I went on, taking a bite of gravy-smothered biscuit and egg.

We all turned as heavy-booted steps came from the back porch, the Dutch door swung open, and my protégée, Gracie Flores, rushed in. And then, as if the universe had heard my unasked question and was providing an answer, her father, Will, stepped over the threshold.

Long before I ever set foot back in Bliss, Meemaw did a fancy behind-the-scenes two-step with Will Flores. The deal they agreed on was that if he did handyman work for her, I'd give sewing lessons to Gracie whenever I returned home.

The handyman work continued, and Gracie's sewing lessons had turned into an apprenticeship. The girl had talent. She was interested in draping, pattern design, and the intricacies of the fashion world, and having her around after her school day and on weekends made my days feel pretty complete. She could read fabric as if the cross grains were words on a page. The result was that the Floreses spent nearly as much time in my farmhouse as they did in their own house out on Hickory Creek Road.

All Meemaw's doing.

Will stopped in the doorway, his gaze quickly landing

on me, an unspoken thread of concern passing between us. A burst of emotion welled up in me at the expression on his swarthy face. His lips pulled into a frown above his goatee, and he pushed back the Longhorns cap he wore. It seemed as if he was ready to say something, but then he looked at the others in the room and closed his mouth, stifling whatever it was he'd wanted to say.

But the second Gracie laid eyes on me, she rushed forward, her brown-flecked green eyes puffy and red-rimmed. "I'm sorry we didn't come to the hospital," she blurted, swiping her fingers under her eyes and brushing her dark hair back from her face.

I fluttered my hands, waving away her concern. In all my years away from Bliss, I'd only ever been close friends with Orphie Cates. My jobs in fashion had kept me so busy that I didn't have any time to form a real social circle in Manhattan. Now I looked around my kitchen with the distressed pale yellow cabinets, the butter-colored replica appliances, the deep white farmhouse sink, and the large red-and-white-checkerboard-patterned curtain on a pressure rod below the sink—and the people who were part of my family, both by blood and by choice.

Sandra was plating more biscuits and eggs. Southern hospitality meant feeding whoever crossed our threshold. Libby made another cup of coffee in one of my black and gold Maximilian mugs.

"I'm fine," I said once I knew my voice wouldn't tremble. "Truly."

"Did you really fall off a roof?" Gracie blurted. In true teenage fashion, the girl cut to the chase.

"I sure did. Guess I can check that off my scuttle list." I laughed.

Gracie's brows pulled together. "What's that?"

"You know, a scuttle. A bucket. Like a bucket list. Things to do before I die. Falling off a roof—" Holding an imaginary pencil, I made an invisible mark in the air. "Check."

Sandra glided across the kitchen, sliding the two plates of biscuits and gravy onto the table. I breathed in the ribbon of scent from the food until a calmness settled over me. Her gift. Her cooking accentuated a person's emotions. Thankfully, right now all I wanted was to feel calm, and Sandra's food filled me with a sense of ease I hadn't felt since the fall. I knew that with each bite of the biscuits and gravy, I'd find more and more tranquillity. As long as nothing else happened to stir the pot.

Will, on the other hand, looked like he was getting more agitated. This was the thing about the Cassidy charms. They weren't always a blessing. Just the aroma of the food Sandra had made heightened Will's emotions, and right now he seemed to be pretty worked up over my fall. His hands clenched and he finally stepped inside, sucking in a deep breath before he said, "You could have died."

"Right," Sandra said. "She's lucky she lived to tell the tale."

"Yes, she is," Will said. He still hung back, shoving his hands in his pockets. I got the feeling he wanted to move closer, to inspect my injuries, make sure I was okay, but he stopped himself, letting his shoulders hunch in as he leaned against the molding at the door.

"It was an accident—"

"Doesn't matter. You're damn lucky," he said. "I'm going over to that house today to see exactly what happened."

I shook my head. I didn't want him spending his time at the Denison mansion. "Don't the police have it cordoned off, or something? Are we even allowed in?"

"They were in and out of there. I'm pretty sure Mrs. James got the senator to pull a few strings and make sure the Winter Wonderland festival and fashion show could go on as planned."

"You don't have to go, Will. The railing came loose. Hattie said it had been giving Arnie and Dan trouble," I said. "I slipped is all." Maybe it was denial, but I didn't want to believe something sinister was behind Dan Lee's death. Bliss had seen enough of murder in recent months.

"But it shouldn't have come loose," he said.

"Dad." Gracie stretched out the word, her message clear. She wanted him to drop it.

Sweet girl. When I'd first met her, it had taken all of five minutes for her to grab hold of a piece of my heart. Already I knew she wasn't ever letting go, and I didn't want her to. She was like a little sister, or a close friend . . . or even a daughter.

But Will wasn't going to be placated by Gracie. His normally mischievous, sparkling eyes were dark and brooding. "You fell off a second-story roof, Cassidy," he said, and suddenly he pushed away from the wall and strode to where I sat at the table. He flipped his baseball cap around to face backward and bent down beside me, laying a hand on my knee. Then he touched his fingers to my cheek. "You're lucky to be alive."

"I'm fine," I said, part of me wanting to convince him that I wasn't shaken up from the fall, and a smaller part of me wanting to lean against him and feel safe.

Before I could do either, the pipes in the ceiling moaned. Which could mean only one thing: Meemaw was nearby. My great-grandmother had gotten what she wanted when I returned to Bliss—it was her Cassidy charm—and while her passing had made that happen, she hadn't let go of this life yet. Her ghostly presence had lingered in the old farmhouse, flipping pages of books, causing warm patches of air to encircle me, and occasionally trying to materialize, but mostly she just made the pipes creak. It was her most reliable means of communication. Right now she was probably worried about me, too, and that concern might well work her into a ghostly tizzy. Not something I wanted to deal with at the moment, since only Nana and Mama knew that my house was haunted.

"Mrs. James called while you were sleeping," Sandra said. "She's awful worried about you."

I made a mental note to phone her later, to reassure her that I was fine and to let her know that I would still be able to finish everything for the Winter Wonderland festival.

The bells on the front door of the house, which doubled as the entrance to Buttons & Bows, jingled, the hard clomp of cowboy boots sounded against the scraped pecan wood floors, and Deputy Gavin McClaine and his father, my mother's boyfriend, Sheriff Hoss McClaine, appeared. They traipsed through the front room of my shop, up the three steps to the little dining area, and through the archway to the kitchen. "Well, well," the deputy said. "Got yourselves a nice little party here." He nodded to me. "Harlow. Good to see you up and about after your tumble yesterday."

Gavin McClaine had an ego the size of Yosemite Sam's ten-gallon hat and then some, and while he said the right thing, his words dripped with sarcasm. He seemed anything but glad to see me up and about, mostly fallout from the fact that he didn't like that his daddy and my mama were sweet on each other.

Will stood and leveled his gaze at the deputy. "The same fall killed a man. I'd say that was more than a tumble."

The deputy folded his arms over his chest, eyeing Will's UT hat. Gavin was an Aggie, a natural rival to a Longhorn, and the scowl on his face made it clear he didn't like the burnt orange Will was sporting. "I reckon you're right," he said. He let his gaze slip to me for just a second as he added, "Harlow always was a little bit charmed."

Oh Lord, there it was. We all worked so hard to fly under the radar and keep our charms mostly to ourselves. None of us wanted to be on the receiving end of a witch hunt. But try as we might, people saw the flowers Mama grew, and they witnessed Nana's connection with her goats. The rumors were there, and Gavin had dropped more than a few hints about my family's gifts. What I didn't know was if he was just spouting off, or if he really knew something about our magic.

Hoss, bless his heart, had a mite more sense under his cream-colored suede cowboy hat than his son had under his black one. The sheriff ran his thumb across the tuft of hair just below his lower lip, but stopped to pat the air with the palms of his hands. "All right, now. Let's just simmer down. Harlow, your mama was worried sick. Glad to see you're all right."

The sheriff and I had had our share of run-ins years ago. Tipping cows and outrunning trains in the dark were not just rural activities done by country kids in the movies. They were real-life happenings in a small town like

Bliss, and my brother, Red, and I had done our fair share of troublemaking. But we'd reached a truce, which was more than I could say about me and Gavin. "Thank you kindly, Sheriff," I said.

For a good while, I thought I'd lost all my Southernness, but bit by bit it crept back into me. You could take the girl out of Texas, but you couldn't take Texas out of the girl. "What can I do for you?" I asked as Libby handed a mug of coffee to Will and another to Gavin. The sheriff shook his head at her, so she went back to her plate of biscuits and gravy.

"Have a few questions for you. Figured it'd be a mite easier on you if we came here instead of having you come on down to the Sheriff's Department."

The Sheriff's Department was a converted Baptist church just a hop, skip, and jump away from Buttons & Bows, but the idea of walking there, or trying to climb into my old truck, sent a shock wave through my body. I didn't think I could walk to my workroom without grimacing from the pain.

"Mighty peculiar that you happened to be in the vicinity of yet another dead body, don't you think, Harlow?" Gavin hadn't taken his eyes off me, and now he set his lips in a hard line. "Mighty peculiar."

"More bad luck," I said, although to be truthful, I didn't think he was that far off the mark.

Hoss sent his son a look that said to zip his lips, and then turned back to me. "We have reason to believe that the railing on that widow's walk was tampered with, Harlow. Did you know Dan Lee Chrisson? The deceased," he added.

And we were off to the races. "Depends how you define the word 'know,' Sheriff. I've met him a few times.

He's been working on the renovations, and I've been there working on the fashion show plans."

"He was playing Santa at the festival, is that right?" Gavin sounded more like he was cross-examining me than doing a friendly post-accident follow-up.

"Right. He'd tried on his Santa suit so I could check the fitting and do any alterations."

Gavin gave a single nod. "Mmm-hmm. Like I said, peculiar."

That was it. Hoss's son was officially a thorn in my side. And from the pulsing vein on Will's temple and the strain in his neck, it was clear the annoyance didn't stop with me.

"Gavin McClaine," I said before Will said something to get under the deputy's skin, "do you want me strung up for murder?"

"Just simmer down, Harlow," Gavin said. "It's far more likely to be the ex-wife or the girlfriend, but you know I have to ask. You were one of the last people to see him alive. We've questioned the senator's wife and Helen Abernathy. We've talked to the Barnetts. We've interviewed a few folks who live on Mayberry. So far, no one knows much of anything."

"And did you hear that Arnie had been having trouble with the railing?"

"Stripped screws," Gavin said. "Yup, we heard that. The question is, how'd they get that way?"

You could have heard a sewing pin drop in the kitchen. Sandra, Libby, Gracie, and Will listened with rapt attention, watching us more intently than die-hard Mavericks fans watching the NBA play-offs.

"Maybe they were just bad." I said it, but I wasn't sure I believed it. I knew enough to understand that screws didn't just strip themselves. They'd been turned and turned and turned enough to lose the threads. The question was, who kept unscrewing them in the first place?

Gavin snarled, and I could tell that he didn't believe my unlikely scenario either. "Let's take a walk through the events. Chrisson changed so you could do a fitting, or whatever. Where did he change?"

"He went upstairs, so in one of the bedrooms, I guess."

"And where were you?"

"Downstairs. In the kitchen."

Gavin made some notes in a little black notebook before he leveled his dark eyes at me. He didn't have his dad's oddly amiable, grizzly bear looks. No, Gavin was lanky, angular, and looked like he was ready to laser me with an invisible beam. "Why do you reckon he went out onto the widow's walk. Why'd you, for that matter?"

I felt everyone's eyes on me, as if I could supply all the answers and let Bliss go back to being a sleepy little town. But with growth, which had been happening slowly but surely around here, came problems. In this case it was an unfortunate death. "I don't know, Gavin. I. Did. Not. Know. Him."

"He went to school with us."

"Years ago."

"What's your best guess, Harlow?" he asked, not willing to cut me even the tiniest bit of slack.

I pushed my plate back, my appetite all but gone. "Maybe to check the screws? Same reason Mrs. James and Mrs. Abernathy went out, to see if the railing was finally fixed."

Hoss, with his pure Southern charm, patted the air again. "Okay now. He's just askin', Harlow. No need to get riled up. Did you happen to see Raylene while you were there?"

Oh boy. Gavin had said it was likely to be the ex-wife or the girlfriend, but did they really suspect Raylene of having something to do with Dan Lee falling?

Libby, Gracie, and Sandra had been looking at the sheriff, but now their eyes were back on me. "Hattie and Arnie were there, but no, I didn't see Raylene." I thought about telling him what Hattie had told me about Dan Lee leaving Raylene and their custody battle, but I decided it just wasn't my place. It sounded to me like poor Raylene had been through enough without me sending the sheriff—or worse, the deputy—after her. Although she already seemed to be on their radar.

Hoss McClaine nodded, looking satisfied. I didn't put much stock in that, though. He was smooth as molasses, but underneath, he was sharp as a cactus thorn—and Gavin was just thorns all the way. "You let me know if you hear anythin', y'hear?" Hoss rumbled, the pad of his thumb passing over the soul patch under his lower lip once more.

I didn't know Hattie or Raylene well anymore, but I couldn't imagine either of them messing with the railing's screws so Dan Lee Chrisson would fall. Unless someone had followed him out onto the widow's walk and actually pushed him—

No. I shoved that thought right out of my head. Bliss was a quaint Southern town where ordinary people didn't become murderers. "Yes, sir, Sheriff. I sure will," I said.

Chapter 5

I'd learned to drape fabric long after I'd learned to use a pattern, but now I relied on the art of draping whenever I started a new dress design. I could see a garment take shape in my hands. The feel of the fabric, the flow of a line in a piece of cloth, and the inspiration that comes from color and texture all help me create just the right piece.

When I was employed at Maximilian, patternmakers and drapers worked with sketches, interpreting the designs. I'd fitted plenty of women for garments, mostly models, but in my spare time, I'd learned to refine my eye of detail, balance, line, and proportion. I'd learned to coax fabric into doing what I wanted it to do. I'd developed the courage it took to take a draped design and turn it into something real. Something tangible. Something inspirational.

One thing I'd never done was make a Santa suit. In fact, aside from mending and one plaid shirt I'd made for Will, I hadn't handled men's clothing at all.

"I don't know about this," Will said. He stood on the milk crate that I was still using for a fitting platform, looking down at me, none too happy about what he'd been roped into doing.

"You'll be great, Daddy," Gracie said, batting her eyes at him.

He angled his chin down. "You think so, huh?"

She grinned. "I know so. You're saving Christmas."

"Yeah, right," he said, but I heard the smile in his voice. "You sure you're up for this?" he asked me.

"I'm fine. Getting back to work'll be good."

"Falling off a roof is not like falling off a bike, Cassidy. And now you're going to make something else—"

"If you're going to play Santa, I have to make you a suit."

"I can head into Fort Worth and try to find one."

I flipped open my sketchbook, pushed my glasses up the bridge of my nose, and peered at him. "It's not like there's a Santa store, and anything at one of those party places is going to be—" A shudder passed through me at the very thought of the cheap, thin polyester fabric, plastic belt, and black booties. That's what Dan Lee Chrisson had been wearing and I wanted Will to wear something that was miles away from that. I shook my head. "No. Kids need to sit on the lap of a real Santa. If necessary I won't sleep for three days, but I'll find the time to make the best Santa suit you've ever seen."

"I know you will, Cassidy," he said, giving in, but one side of his mouth quirked up. He never looked completely innocent, what with his dark olive skin, his goatee, and his mischievous grin, but when he smiled, his eyes lit from behind and I always felt like I was getting a glimpse into his soul.

I wondered if making a Santa suit for Will would make his deepest desires come true. I'd made him the one shirt, but as far as I could tell, his life hadn't changed as a result of it. As I jotted down "Chest," "Inseam,"

"Arm Length," "Waist," "Neck," my mind wandered. Maybe my charm worked only with women.

Gracie bounced through the French doors separating the front room of Buttons & Bows from the workroom, which once upon a time had been Meemaw's dining room. She grabbed a cloth measuring tape from around the neck of one of the dress forms. "You look like you're in pain, Harlow. Want me to take the measurements?"

I nodded, cringing at the very thought of crouching down to measure Will's inseam. I picked up my sketchbook to hand it to Gracie, but I stopped, suddenly feeling the heat of Will's gaze on my back. I looked up at him. His gaze was glued to me, waiting, as if how I answered Gracie was a test. Something brushed against me and I jerked, my fingers loosening. Before I could stop it, the sketchbook fell with a thud onto the hardwood floor. I whipped my head around, looking for evidence of a ghostly presence. And then I saw it. The sleeve of a blouse hanging from the wood-slatted privacy screen gently moving as if a breeze had passed through the room. Which it hadn't.

Meemaw.

So she was up to her antics, playing matchmaker between Will Flores and me. Again. Or still. "I don't think so," I muttered. I didn't need my ghost of a great-grandmother making love connections for me. Getting me to move back to Bliss and orchestrating Gracie and Will's presence in my life had been enough.

Gracie sucked in a sharp breath. "I—I'm s-sorry. I didn't mean—"

"Not you, Gracie!" I glared in the direction of the innocent blouse before gingerly turning to face my protégé, softening my expression when I looked at her. "I'm not going to let any aches and pains stop me from doing my job, that's all."

She breathed out a relieved sigh. "Oh, phew. I thought . . ." She trailed off, waving her hands in front of her face. "Never mind." Her smile brightened. "What can I do to help?"

"I'll measure, you write."

I started toward my runaway sketchbook, but Gracie scurried in front of me and snatched it from the floor. She handed me the measuring tape, found the page I'd started, and tapped the pointed tip of a pencil against the paper. "Ready."

I shuffled back to Will. With my hands on my hips, I looked up at him. "Are you ready to play Santa?"

"I'm reprising the role," he said.

Gracie piped up. "He played Santa every year when I was in elementary school. All my friends have pictures with him in a furry white beard."

I tilted my head to one side, considering. "So you're experienced? But you don't have the Santa costume?"

He chuckled. "Uh, no. It belonged to the school."

"It wouldn't fit him now, anyway," Gracie said.

I looked Will up and down. Usually when an old outfit didn't fit, it was because someone had gained weight, but Will Flores didn't look like he had even an ounce of extra padding. He looked like a cowboy Cassanova, with a Rhett Butler smirk and just enough of a down-home accent to make a girl melt. "Oh?"

"I was pretty young when Gracie was little," he said. He patted his stomach. "I've filled out."

In mighty nice ways. I walked behind him to hide the blush I was sure had tinged my cheeks. Darn Meemaw for knowing just what I found attractive in a man, even before I realized it myself.

One by one, I took measurements, calling out the numbers to Gracie, who scribbled them down. "What kind of fabric will you use?" she asked after I'd finished the shoulder to waist and waist measurements. She was like a sponge, absorbing every detail of everything I did in my workroom.

My cell phone beeped from the cutting table in the center of the workroom as a text came in. I reached for it, raising my eyebrows as I read the message. *How are you?* From Zinnia James. Whereas my mother didn't know thing one about sending or receiving texts, Mrs. James had taken to communicating this way with me quite often. She was a twenty-first-century Southern matron if there ever was one.

Doing fine, I texted back.

Gave us all quite a scare.

My fingers flew over the touch pad. *No need to worry.*

Spare no expense, came the next message.

I quickly typed a response. *For what?*

Will Flores. Santa suit. I'll drop a check off today, she responded.

I stared at the phone for a beat. How in the world did she know Will had stepped in to play Santa and that I was making the suit?

Yes, ma'am, I texted, thinking that maybe Meemaw wasn't the only one who knew what I needed before I did. Did I wear my every thought on my sleeve?

I didn't have an answer to that, so I went back to Will. With Mrs. James footing the bill, inexpensive, cheap-looking material wasn't necessary. "Red velvet upholstery fabric for the coat, pants, hat, and bag," I said, answering Gracie's question. "We'll trim the bottom of the pants and arms, up the center of the coat, around the collar, and the brim of the hat with a winter white long-hair fur fabric. And the belt will be black vinyl." I eyed my sewing machine, hoping it could handle the heavy-duty fabrics. Once business really started to boom, I would invest in an industrial machine. "The kids will love it," I added, leaning forward to wrap my arms around Will's waist. My cheek brushed against his stomach as my left hand grabbed hold of the tape measure, and a jolt of electricity pulsed through me.

I sucked in a quick, stabilizing breath before rattling off the number, dropping the measuring tape, and bending down to take the inseam. I stretched the cloth tape from the top of Will's shoe to the crotch, my hand trembling just a touch at how intimate this process was with someone you were sort of dating. It would be like him measuring my chest, keeping the tape measure snug as he brought the ends together at my breasts.

I swallowed, and once again I felt heat spread from the soles of my feet to the tips of my ears. I quickly took a second measurement from crotch to the back of his heel, telling Gracie the number as I moved my hands safely back to my own space.

But as I stood and wrapped the cloth tape around his neck, our gazes met and he smiled, and darn it if that twinkle in his eye didn't tell me that he knew exactly what was going on in my head.

"Bend your elbow and put your hand on your hip," I said, looking away. I stepped behind him again and measured from the middle of his neck, around the shoulder and elbow, ending at the wrist bone for the sleeve.

The clatter of dishes and chattering in the kitchen distracted me as I did the final measurement, wrapping the tape measure around the fullest part of his hips. "Done," I said after I'd told Gracie the number.

"Or just getting started," Will said, that sparkle still in his eyes. "I'll have to do a fitting, won't I?"

I leaned against the stool at the worktable, nodding. "I'll go into Fort Worth today to get the fabric. You'll have to find black boots and white gloves. And suspenders. I can do an elastic waist, but with the padding, suspenders will look better. Can you do that? Oh! And a beard. And make sure it's not a cheap one." He barely nodded as I continued. "I'll buy a pattern for the coat and can make one for the pants. It'll work for pajama bottoms, too." I gulped. "If you ever, you know, wanted me to make you some, I mean."

"You're in no condition to drive to Fort Worth," Will said, stepping down from the milk crate. The thunderstorm had lagged during the night, but was back full force. If I hadn't known better, I would have guessed that Meemaw had done it, but she didn't have control over the weather. At least I didn't think she did. "And just so you know, I'm going to make you a platform. That crate is dangerous."

"I'm fine to drive," I said, "and you don't have to make a platform." Although I knew he could probably whip one out with hardly a smidgen of effort. I looked up at the dress pulley he'd built and installed for me a few months ago during the Margaret Moffette Lea Pageant and Ball. I'd conceived the idea, but he'd executed it. Beautifully. Anytime I worked on a gown or a wedding dress, I no longer had to worry about the train or skirt of it dragging along the floor. It stayed on the pulley at the ceiling when I wasn't working on it.

Gracie handed me the sketchbook and I passed through the French doors, leaving the workroom. I held on to the railing as I mounted the three steps leading from the main room of Buttons & Bows, cringing with every step I took, a steady pounding in my head.

Behind me, I heard Gracie whisper something to her dad. He answered, the low rumble of his voice wrapping around me like a warm blanket. Or maybe that was Meemaw.

Rain pounded against the windows. "You plan to drive to Fort Worth in your old jalopy?" He looked outside as another bolt of lightning flashed, shaking his head as he surveyed the ancient truck I'd inherited from Meemaw. "Uh-uh. I'm driving you," he said. "No argument."

I turned, ready to refuse again, but the concern in Gracie's eyes and the firm set of Will's jaw stopped me. "Okay," I said without further argument, and ten minutes later, we'd said good-bye to Sandra and Libby, I'd flipped the CLOSED sign hanging just outside the front door to my shop, filling in the chalkboard space—BACK AT 3:00—and Gracie, Will, and I hurried through the rain to Will's truck. Before long, we were traveling down Loop 820 toward the Berry Patch in Fort Worth.

Chapter 6

"Hard to believe Dan's dead," Will said as we took the Hulen Street exit off the highway, the windshield wipers barely keeping up as they slapped the rain off the glass.

Gracie sighed from her seat in the extended cab of the truck. "He was a nice man."

"Did you know him well?"

"I met him a few years back. He did some work with the Historical Society every now and then. A real history buff. Liked the old outlaw stories, just like you," Will said with a wink.

I angled my chin down and gave him a little smile. "I am kin to Butch Cassidy."

"That you are."

I turned, trying not to grimace from the stiffness in my bones. "It's awfully sad," I said, returning to the subject of Dan Lee.

"I saw him all the time at the Denison mansion. He was a good worker. Whenever I inspected the historical elements of the house for the city, he was there." He shook his head sadly. "It's a shame."

Will pulled into the parking lot of Heritage Square across from Hulen Mall and parked in front of the Berry

Patch. He covered Gracie and me with an oversized umbrella and we hurried inside. Immediately, I felt like a
contestant on *Project Runway*. I didn't want to spend
more than a half hour in the store. We also had to stop
by J&D Interiors for the velvet upholstery fabric, so the
clock was ticking. Will and Gracie trailed behind me,
talking about Dan Chrisson's tragic fall, then shifting to
discuss the records Will had been tracking down so the
Historical Society could officially include the Denison
mansion in the town's directory of historic buildings.

Just last month Madelyn Brighton, one of my new
best friends and the city of Bliss's official photographer,
had taken pictures of my old farmhouse to include in the
directory, as well as in a calendar for the upcoming year
and a book about Bliss's history and unforgettable characters. It was rumored that Bonnie and Clyde had hidden out in my backyard after they'd gone on one of their
rampages.

Bliss had no shortage of outlaw history, and Dan Lee
wasn't the only one fascinated by it. Folks came from all
over to take ghost tours of the historic buildings on the
square, and the old outlaws would have a place of honor
once the new museum opened in the courthouse.

I hurried up and down the aisles of the store, scooping
up a pattern, snaps, buttons, thread, batting to pad Will's
midsection, and other notions for the Santa suit project.
I pointed to a bolt of the perfect white fur. "Will you
grab that?" I asked Will.

He carried it, along with the black vinyl for the belt,
to the cutting area. At the checkout counter, I spied a
copy of *Victoria* magazine. The cover's headline said
HOLIDAY BLISS in bold lettering. Red drapes created the
backdrop and a gingerbread trifle was prominently pic-

tured. Next to it lay an assortment of Victorian-era ornaments and decorations.

Holiday bliss . . . it echoed our hopes for the town festival. An omen? Good fortune? It didn't matter. The
magazine spoke to me, and I couldn't pass it up. I added
it to my pile and, ten minutes later, we left the Berry
Patch and headed to J&D's on Main Street. "What else
do you have to do for the fashion show?" Gracie asked
once I'd bought four and half yards of red velvet fabric
and we were on our way back to Bliss.

"I'm finishing Josie's outfits," I said, and then added,
"And hoping she doesn't get any bigger in the next few
days."

Gracie laughed from the backseat. "Holly said she's
ODing on Chubby Hubby."

I peered at her through the vanity mirror on the
truck's sun visor, a question mark in my expression.
Holly was Josie's niece, but I didn't get it. Josie was nuts
for Nate, but the guy wasn't chubby, so . . .

"Ben and Jerry's," Gracie said, answering my unasked
question. "Chubby Hubby. Holly said Josie is dreaming
about fudge and peanut butter pretzels."

"Oh boy." Good thing the fashion show was just days
away or I'd be pulling some all-nighters to make sure
Josie's clothes fit her come runway time. There was only
so much waist I could let out to accommodate a growing
stomach.

We spent the rest of the ride talking about the Winter
Wonderland festival. "I'll help decorate," Gracie said.

"That would be fantastic," I said, making a mental
note to myself.

"Is the house all finished, Dad?" she asked. "Did they
fix the railing?"

Will darted a glance at me, then at her through the rearview mirror. "Shh."

"What?" she said, and I could almost hear the shrug of her shoulders in her tone. "I'm just saying. Someone needs to fix it, right?"

"It's okay," I said. "She's right. Let's stop by, Will. We should make sure it's repaired before the festival. Either that, or make sure that door is bolted shut. I don't have a key, but maybe someone's there."

"We don't have to, Cassidy," Will said.

"I'm fine."

"You had a big scare. If you're not up to it—"

I gritted my teeth, twisting in my seat enough to face him. It was the best I could do under the circumstances. "Will Flores, I am not an invalid. It was an accident, the hospital released me, and I'm just fine, thank you very much, so if you'll stop pussyfooting around me and acting like I can't do anything, I'd greatly appreciate it."

He arched an amused eyebrow at me and I took stock. With my glasses, curly long hair with the crazy blond streak in it, and yoga pants, I was hardly the epitome of a tough Texas woman. But he just nodded and said, "Yes, ma'am," not bothering to hide the little half smile tickling his lips.

A few minutes later we took the first Bliss exit and drove down a country road leading to town, finally passing through the square with its quaint shops. The Opera House, Villa Farina—the best Italian bakery this side of the Rio Grande, Seed-n-Bead—the bead shop Josie owned and operated, Two Scoops—the old-fashioned ice cream parlor with red and white awnings and curlicue chairs, and a little antique shop were only some of the businesses ringing the courthouse in the center of the square.

I breathed in the scent of the small town. The rain had finally stopped and the blue sky brightened the whole place. Visiting Fort Worth, or Dallas, or even Austin, where I'd gone to college, was a treat, but being back in Bliss made me realize just how much the little town had become home to me again.

Two minutes later, Will parked behind a ragtop Jeep on Mayberry, right in front of the Denison mansion. On the wet sidewalk, Gracie tilted her head back to look up at it. "Is that where you fell from?" she asked, pointing to the far right corner of the roof.

A shiver wound through me at the visual reminder, but I threw my shoulders back with as much strength as I could muster and anchored my sore body, planting my feet on the ground. "Sure is," I said. I led the way through the little gate and up the porch steps, trying the handle on the front door. Locked.

"I was afraid of that. No one has any reason to be here."

But Will had pulled out his key ring and slid a key into the lock.

I stared. "How did you . . . ?"

"The city offices have keys to all the houses on the historical registry."

That one simple sentence sent my mind into a tizzy. The sheriff and deputy had said the screws on the railing might have been tampered with, which meant someone must have been able to come in and out of the house. Who else had a key? I ran through the possibilities. The workers on the construction crew had to be able to get in and out. And I remembered Hattie bursting in that day. Calling down to someone on the sidewalk. Pocketing her keys.

My heart thumped in my chest. The deputy had his eye on Raylene, but Hattie's last remark to Dan Lee shot to the front of my mind. *Mark my words, Dan Lee—hurting Raylene was a mistake.* Could Hattie have come into the house without her husband and loosened the screws of the railing on the widow's walk? Did she want to get back at her sister's ex-husband that badly?

Will held the door open and let Gracie and me pass into the foyer as he said, "You're off on a rabbit trail again, Cassidy."

I blinked, coming back to the moment. "Hattie has a key."

"Right."

"But why?"

He gave me a look like I'd lost my marbles, but answered anyway. "Because they did the restoration. Helen Abernathy has one, too, since Abernathy Home Builders did the renovations."

Another memory flashed in my mind. Mrs. James and I had had to wait for Helen Abernathy to show up before we could get inside the Denison mansion because—

"Mrs. James lost her key."

"Right," Will said again. "She came by my office a few days back to see if we had an extra copy." He pulled a small paper envelope from his pocket and held it up. "Had one made for her, but I haven't seen her to give it to her."

"Maybe she didn't lose her key," I mused. "Maybe it was stolen. Which means maybe the sheriff is right. Maybe the screws really were loosened on purpose."

"Or maybe she really did lose the key and nothing sinister is going on," he said as he closed the door.

"Maybe." But I suddenly didn't think so. Still, it didn't

hurt to look at the other possibilities. "Did Helen Aber-nathy know Dan Lee Chrisson?" I asked.

"Why?"

I pushed my glasses up to the top of my head. "If the sheriff is right, someone had to loosen the screws—"

"Hoping that Dan Lee would just happen onto the widow's walk, lean against the railing, and fall to his death? Not really a foolproof plan, if you ask me."

He had a point, but I still felt as if I were on to something. I couldn't think of a single reason why Helen Abernathy would want Dan Lee dead, though. The man had lived and worked in Bliss, but as far as I'd heard, he hadn't ruffled any feathers.

Gracie prowled around, peeking into the parlor, running her fingers over the diamond-shaped fabric pieces of a neatly folded antique quilt done up in a Lone Star pattern. She moved on to the secretary desk, rolling up the cover and riffling through a stack of old books.

"Gracie," Will said with a hiss. *"No toques."*

My high school Spanish was rusty, so I didn't know what he said, but Gracie snatched her hand away from the books as if her fingers had burned from their touch. Her shoulders lifted and her cheeks tinged pink. "Sorry. All this old stuff is just so . . . so cool."

She was right, only I couldn't appreciate the intricacies of the antiques and the history of the house at the moment. My thoughts were crowded with the nightmare of the fall from the roof, and worse than that, I worried that the loose railing had been intentionally tampered with. But Will was right. Loosening screws on a railing was hardly a foolproof plan for murder, unless—

I gasped. "What if someone pushed him?"

Gracie whirled around, but Will held his hand out to

her. "Just simmer down." He turned to me. "You're assuming the sheriff and deputy are right. That someone tampered with the railing. But that doesn't make sense."

I didn't agree. "It does if they planned to sneak up behind him and give him a good shove."

His eyebrows pulled together, and I could tell he couldn't argue that point. "Okay, but Dan Lee was a pretty decent guy, far as I know. Why would anyone do that?"

It all came back to motive. Who would have wanted him dead? Other than Raylene and maybe Hattie, neither of whom I wanted to believe could have been involved, no one had a reason to kill Dan Lee. At least none that I knew of. I had no answer to Will's question.

Gracie had gone pale, so I pushed the thought of murders and motives out of my mind and turned to her. "You'd love this old dressing gown I saw yesterday." I ushered her toward the stairs, gritting my teeth against the stiffness in my body and the sore spots where bruises ran up and down my side, using the handrail to climb up behind her.

Will was suddenly right beside me, his hand on my lower back. "Cassidy," he said softly, "you sure you want to go up there after what happened yesterday?"

"I'm not going onto the widow's walk. I'll never trust another railing," I said lightly, trying to make it sound like a joke. But it came off tinged with fear, and I wondered how much truth was behind the words.

As I blinked, I suddenly saw myself on the widow's walk again, and then I was falling, falling, falling. I stopped for a second in alarm and put my hand on Will's arm, looking up into his smoky blue eyes. "Would you check the railing on my porch? Make sure it's not going to split in two like the one here?" There were steps leading up to it and it wasn't high off the ground, but I was spooked.

He laid his hand on mine and squeezed. "No problem."

At the landing, I led Gracie and Will to the bathroom with the claw-foot tub. Behind the door I pointed out the silk dressing gown. Gracie brushed her fingers over the skirt, closing her eyes. I'd done the same thing, wanting to isolate just my sense of touch as I felt the quality of the fabric. She angled her head slightly, a strand of her dark hair tumbling down her forehead. I watched her, amazed at how attuned she was to the fabric. Her eyelids fluttered as if she could absorb the history of the garment just by touching it. "I can almost see who wore this," she said softly.

Will nosed around the bathroom, finally gesturing to me that he was going to wait in the hallway.

"Did it belong to the woman who owned the house?" Gracie asked as he started to leave. Her question made him stop.

"Which owner? There have been a few."

"There have? I thought Justin Kincaid won the deed to the house in a poker game," I said.

Will leaned against the doorjamb, hands in his jeans pockets. "Right. So there was Vanetta and Justin Kincaid, but before that was Pearl and Charles Denison. They were the first owners. Far as I remember, the Kincaids let Jeb James's grandmother live here for a spell. The senator lived with her as a boy. Or so the story goes."

I stared at Will. I'd been in this house a handful of times, most often with Zinnia James, and she'd never mentioned that her husband had lived here as a child.

More secrets. It seemed I uncovered one everywhere I turned. Bliss was bursting with them.

Gracie's fingers tightened on the silk skirt. "This dressing gown belonged to Pearl," she said. "I'm sure of it. She was the first owner, right? So it has to be hers. I can almost picture her in it," she added, her eyes fluttering closed, a slight smile curving her lips.

Sweet Gracie. She was a sixteen-year-old romantic at heart. We went on to look in each room, marveling at the attention to detail. "Barnett Restoration did a great job," I said. From the ceiling molding to the windowsills to the hand-scraped wood floors, the house had been brought back to the glory it had known when it was first built.

I paused at the staircase, drawing in a deep breath and bracing myself for the pain of descending. "Before we go, I want to check out the runway in the tent," I said.

Gracie pointed to the door at the end of the hallway. "Is that the widow's walk?"

As I nodded, Will bypassed the staircase and went for the door, Gracie on his heels. "Since we're here, I wanna see this railing," he said in what I imagined was his official architect voice.

I followed him. "No, let's go see the runway," I said, but he was already turning the glass doorknob. Pulling the door open. Stepping out.

I reached my arms out to stop him. "Will—"

A woman screamed.

Gracie screamed.

I clapped my hand to my chest. And screamed.

A dark-haired woman gaped at us from the center of the widow's walk.

She screamed again, her arms airplaned, and she was suddenly off balance.

"No!" I yelled, reaching for her from where I stood, still inside the doorway. Will lunged, blocking me, and the next second, he was hauling her inside by her limp arms.

She crumpled to the floor in a heap, her brown skirt settling around her legs. I crouched by her side, my heart still in my throat, as much from nearly reliving my fall from yesterday as because of this woman's near miss. "Are you okay?"

She gasped for air, her hand against her chest. "I— I'm—I think so." Her gaze skittered from me to Will to Gracie and back to me. "You s-scared the livin' daylights out of me," she said, her heavy accent making each vowel sound extend into two syllables instead of just one.

"You scared *us*!" Gracie said, her voice jittery. "Who are you? What were you doing out there?"

I wanted to know the very same things, but I'd planned to be more tactful about asking. Leave it to a teenage girl to cut to the chase.

"I—I was just . . . that is, I . . ." She paused, her eyes wide, looking like a deer in the headlights. She hemmed and hawed before her shoulders finally sagged and she said, "I needed to see . . . to see . . . where he died."

We all stared at her, and suddenly I recognized her. She had the same rosy cheeks as Hattie, and their hair was nearly the same Miranda Lambert–blond. The biggest differences were this woman's Marilyn Monroe shape and her dowdy clothes. This had to be Raylene Lewis, Hattie's sister and the ex-wife of Dan Lee.

Will crouched next to her, holding her hand. "Are you . . ."

She placed a trembling hand against her plump chest and I had a sudden vision of her in a cheongsam, an embroidered brocade fabric making the traditional Chinese gown interesting, and a body-skimming fit reminiscent of a sheath dress. I'd never made anything like a cheongsam, but I couldn't shake that it was the dress for this woman. Maybe it was her curves. "Raylene Lewis," she said. "Dan . . . he was . . . was my . . . my—"

"Ex-husband," I finished for her.

She gulped down her tears, nodding her head. As she brushed her hair away from her face, I registered her red-rimmed eyes and her sunken cheeks. My heart went out to her. Even if a divorce was ugly, death was worse. The man she'd created a child with and had once loved was gone.

She looked at me, a hint of recognition flickering over her. "H-Harlow? Harlow Jane Cassidy?"

"It's good to see you, Raylene," I said. Bliss was a small town and I'd been back for a good many months now, but there were plenty of people from my childhood I hadn't yet reconnected with.

"I heard you were back." Her eyes glazed over as she spoke, and I could feel her pain.

"I'm so sorry about your . . . your . . . about Dan Lee," I said, knowing that none of my words would ease her pain.

She spread her arms wide, gesturing to the house at large. "H-he was obsessed with this place. He wore Arnie down until he finally let him work on the renovations." She chattered on, her words carried on her grief-filled, nervous energy. "We used to t-talk about buying this house and turning it into a bed-and-breakfast. He researched some of the best bed-and-breakfasts in Texas, and I knew I could do better than those. I've always wanted to have a little gift shop with homemade j-jams, pickled okra, and canned peaches." She stopped, her gaze jumping around. "I can just see this place decorated up for holiday teas. Petit fours, cucumber sandwiches, and cranberry white chocolate scones. But now? He went crazy. Do you know that?" Her voice took on an angry edge and sounded laced with venom. "Off the turnip truck, and I don't know what to do."

Her rambling faded and she sniffled, running the back of her fisted hand under her nose. She buried her face in her hands, sobbing. "I may n-never . . . never . . ."

She broke down sobbing again.

"I'm awfully sorry, Raylene." I took her hand and helped her up, leading her away from the door. My shoulder blades unclenched as we moved farther away from the widow's walk. We stopped at the top of the stairs just as the front door slammed and someone sprinted up the steps. "I heard a scream all the way outside!"

Hattie. She skidded to a stop as she saw us and put her hand on Raylene's shoulder. "Baby, are you okay?"

Will met my gaze for a second, to make sure I could handle Raylene and her grief, I think. I gave him a quick nod and he moved back onto the widow's walk. Raylene watched him, her red-rimmed eyes wide, before turning to her sister. "No. I'm n-not even close to bein' okay."

Hattie gave her a sympathetic hug. "I know. I'm so sorry, Ray." She gave her sister another squeeze, pulling her even closer. "I told you yesterday, Harlow. Dan Lee put Ray through hell, and now that lyin', cheatin' — "

"Hattie!" Raylene jerked free of Hattie's hug.

"It's true!"

"Okay, but we don't gotta air all our dirty laundry," she said tersely.

"But everythin' has changed," Hattie said. "He — "

"Stop," Raylene said, and this time she grabbed Hattie's arm.

"But — "

Raylene squeezed, and Hattie jerked her arm free. Raylene started for the stairs, but Hattie's frown deepened. "That banister was the last thing on Arnie's list of repairs. If only he'd gotten to it before Dan Lee went out there."

"But he didn't," Raylene said.

"It was an accident," Hattie said, but her cheeks had gone pale.

Not according to the sheriff and deputy, I thought grimly, my aching body reminding me that I might well be the innocent victim of a sinister crime. "The sheriff isn't so sure," I said. I didn't want to say too much, but I figured it wasn't a huge secret at this point.

"Arnie tightened all those screws three times. Three times," Hattie said with emphasis. "He was going to change 'em out, but he said it would hold fine till he got to it." She paused, as if she were imagining the scene in her mind. "Oh Lord, Arnie's fingerprints are all over this place. What if the sheriff thinks . . . ?"

She heaved, falling forward and resting her hands on her knees as she caught her breath. A second later, she looked up, pushing strands of her ash blond hair away from where they'd fallen in her eyes. "What if they think it's *his* fault?" she asked, her voice barely more than a whisper.

"They won't, Hattie," I said, but they felt like empty words because I knew they were thinking Raylene had something to gain if Dan Lee wasn't around anymore. People I knew from high school days couldn't be murderers. The very idea sent my stomach reeling. I didn't trust Gavin's detective skills for a second. He wanted an open-and-shut case, no matter who he pinned to the wall.

Hattie's eyes welled with tears. "Can you imagine? If our kids hear people think their dad killed Santa Claus— not that he didn't deserve it, the son of a bitch, but still—"

Raylene grabbed her wrist and gave it a shake. "Hattie, get a grip! Arnie didn't kill Santa Claus. It was an accident."

"But what if it wadn't?" she said in her heavy drawl, dropping the "s," as so many Southerners do. "Think about it. Things come in threes. Bliss has had two murders this year. First there was that bridesmaid that done got herself killed. Then the golf pro. And now this. You know what small towns are like." She looked at me. "You were there at each one—" Her eyes narrowed and she backed away.

My head had started to pound again. I could practically see what Hattie was thinking. It would be the same thing half of Bliss would ponder when they found out I was at the scene of another death. Either I was cursed ... or I was involved.

Maybe both.

There was nothing to do but pretend I didn't see the doubt and suspicion on her face. "Hattie," I said, "are you sure Arnie tightened the bolts?" Maybe it was an accident after all.

She nodded. "Positive." Her forehead puckered. "We came to do a few last-minute chores the other night. I— I came up to the widow's walk to look at the Christmas lights. It's got a great view of the square. The railing was a little loose, so I called him up there. He tightened them right in front of me, said they'd hold till he could switch 'em out, and that was it!"

After a few seconds, Raylene raised her gaze to me. "I'm awfully sorry for your loss," I said, squeezing her hand. I'd lost Meemaw not that long ago, and the fact that her spirit hung around the old farmhouse didn't wipe away the empty feeling of knowing I would never see her again.

Will came back inside, slowly closing the door behind him, cutting short any more offerings of comfort. His face was grim as he met my gaze and flicked his eyes to the side. I got the message. He wanted to talk to me— privately.

"If I can do anything to help, you just let me know," I said, my heart going out to Raylene. "I'll be right back, y'all." Gracie, Hattie, and Raylene headed downstairs, a stark contrast to one another. Gracie held her head up high, her graceful neck and easy posture making me think of a model on a runway. Hattie had pushed away her worries about her husband being targeted for the loose screws and stood straight, shoulders back and chin up. She seemed to know that Raylene needed her, and she held her sister by the arm, walking by her side with each and every step. And then there was Raylene, bless her heart. Her shoulders slumped and her legs looked like they'd buckle any second.

"Harlow."

The sharpness in Will's tone, not to mention the fact that he'd used my given name instead of my last name, made me turn away from the stairs and hurry over to him. "What's wrong?" I said, but from the hard line of his lips and the darkness in his eyes, I almost didn't want to know the answer. I backed away, waving my hands in front of me, fingers spread. "Oh no . . ."

"I'm pretty sure Hoss and Gavin are right. That railing didn't just give," he said, his voice low.

"What are you saying, Will Flores?" I heard my mother's voice coming out of my mouth, with her Southern indignation and her use of a person's first and last names. I gathered up my gumption, not daring to believe he could be saying what I feared he was saying, but I jammed my hands on my hips and looked him straight in the eyes. "It had to have been an accident!"

His look told me he felt sure it wasn't.

I gave it one last-ditch effort. "Will, it's an old house."

"I want to show you something," he said, and he took me by the arm, steering me back to the widow's walk.

I shook my arm loose, but followed him out onto the porch, stepping slowly and gingerly, and steering clear of the edge. He pointed to the bracket that had attached the railing to the house. It barely hung on by two loose screws.

"What about it?" I said, hoping against hope that the screws had pulled out of the wall from the force of Dan Lee's fall against the railing.

As Will crouched down, pointing, my nerves tingled from being in the exact same spot I'd been in the day before when I'd fallen. My bravado evaporated into the wintery afternoon, and I clamped my hand down on his shoulder as I moved behind him.

He tilted his head back to look up at me. "You okay, Cassidy?"

"Yup," I said, realizing that my hand had tightened, the cloth of his shirt clenched between my fingers. I released it, smoothing the wrinkles out of the fabric. "What are we looking at?"

"The heads of the screws." He pointed. "Look."

They looked like ordinary screws to me, and I told him so.

"Uh-uh. The head of that one," he said, pointing to the one on the right, "is ground down."

To see any better, I'd have to come around to Will's side, closer to the gaping hole where a railing used to be. Which wasn't going to happen. Instead, I stayed behind him, putting both my hands on his shoulders. As I leaned down over him, the same warmth I felt whenever Meemaw was near seeped into me. "What are you saying, Will?"

I felt his body tense, as much from the question as from me being so close to him. The warmth evaporated, replaced by a cold chill. I stepped back, away from the edge of the porch, away from him, away from the loose bracket. I knew what he was going to say.

"I mean," he said, standing up, "that this was no accident, and from the way the railing was ripped out with such force, I'd say you're right. Someone pushed Dan Lee Chrisson to his death."

Chapter 7

My friend Josie was perched on the stool in the work-room of Buttons & Bows, her golden olive skin glowing, her walnut hair shimmery. A pint of Ben & Jerry's ice cream sat on the cutting table next to her. She stared at me, wide-eyed. "Murdered?"

I dusted the windowsill, waving my duster at the goats lined up at the fence line between my property and my grandparents' goat farm. Not that they could see this far, but somehow I got the impression that they knew I could see them. "Hoss and Gavin seem to think so," I answered, "and Will is convinced that the railing was tampered with."

"Well," she said, "if Will's convinced."

We were long past junior high, so I ignored the teasing and continued. "Hoss said there were no fingerprints on the doorknob to the widow's walk, which is strange. Not even Dan Lee's were there, and they should have been."

She licked a spoonful of ice cream, waiting. "So?" she finally asked.

"So," I said, putting the duster in the corner and picking up a piece of fabric and a thick metal washer, "there should have been fingerprints. Dan Lee's, definitely. Hattie said she'd been out there to look at Christmas lights a few nights back, so hers should have been there. It was wiped clean."

"Poor Raylene," she said, resting her hand on her belly. "I can't imagine what she's going through. I might be big as a house, but Nate would never up and leave me and his child."

I scolded her with a wave of my hand. "You're not big as a house," I said.

"Um, yes I am, and I'm not going to be in the fashion show."

I dropped the heavy washer I'd been turning into a fabric-covered pattern weight and stared at her. "Josie Sandoval Kincaid, what did you just say?"

"Look at me, Harlow!" She turned, propping her elbows on the cutting table, dropping her head into her hands. "A fashion show? Nothing will look even halfway decent on me."

I came around to her and rubbed her back. Pregnancy had made her curvier than she'd been, and she looked vivacious and glowing. "Josie, you're pregnant."

"That doesn't mean free rein to gain a hundred pounds—"

"First of all, you haven't gained a hundred pounds, and second of all, that little baby inside you must just need peanut butter and pretzels," I said.

She nodded, barely, but didn't look entirely convinced. Her cotton maternity top pulled up over a pair of light blue maternity jeans, the dark navy stretchy panel partially exposed. "Whoop, there he goes again," she said, staring at her stomach as if she had X-ray vision and could see the little baby growing inside her. "It feels like little flutters. Like a butterfly's inside flapping its wings. Thank God there is a baby in here, or I think Nate would turn his back on me."

Oh boy, her insecurity over her changing body was making her loopy. "Don't be silly," I said, although worry settled into my gut. This was not the fun-filled, confident Josie I knew.

"I'm only five months along and . . . and look at me!"

I did, and while she had a pretty good baby bump and was already moving more slowly, she was still gorgeous. "Meemaw always used to tell me that when you're pregnant, you feel fat for nine months, but a lifetime of joy takes over once that baby is born."

Her face cleared for just a split second, but then her frown returned. It would take more than one of Loretta Mae's bits of wisdom to get Josie out of her funk. So I did the thing I did best; I walked to the portable clothes rack in the front room, riffled through the garments hanging there, and pulled out a maternity blouse I'd made for her. I came back into the workroom carrying the three-quarter sleeve empire-waist tunic, perfect for her to wear over black leggings.

"Oh, Harlow, your magic isn't going to work on me," she said, eyeing the blouse.

I froze for a second, staring at her. My magic? Josie didn't know about my charm! Only Madelyn Brighton, who happened to be a die-hard paranormal groupie, had figured it out, and I wanted to keep it that way. I felt better knowing that the Cassidy secrets were safely under wraps.

"None of your creations can bring my figure back," she said, and I realized she hadn't meant it literally.

I released the breath I'd been holding. "It's not sup-posed to," I said. "Try it on."

One eyebrow rose skeptically, but she maneuvered off the stool, took the hanger, and disappeared behind the garment-strewn privacy screen. A minute later, she emerged from behind the oversized distressed-wood win-dow shutters, her belly leading the way.

She didn't bother to look in the oval floor mirror, in-stead just throwing her arms out to the side in resigna-tion. "See? I look like a house."

My shoulders sagged. She was right. The blouse made her look more pregnant than she was, and the sash belt didn't sit under her breasts as it should. "It's okay!" I said, sounding more cheerful than I actually felt. "I have something else I've been thinking about. Come back to-night, okay?"

I'd had two other designs knocking around in my head, one of which I'd partially finished, but neither of them had struck me as just the right one for her.

In the back of my mind, doubt was slowly creeping in. Was my charm somehow failing me? Normally, I had a crystal clear vision for a person—like I'd had for Ray-lene Lewis. But the maternity garment for Josie had me stumped. Nothing explicit came to mind, and making a pregnant woman feel sexy and beautiful had its own set of challenges—which I hadn't conquered yet.

"Harlow, I'm not sure I can bear it. I know how hard you're trying, but—"

"Trust me, Josie. I'm going to make you something spectacular for the fashion show."

And, I decided at that very moment, I was going to make the cheongsam I'd envisioned for Raylene. I would start it after the new year and give it to her to symbolize the hope for a new beginning, assuming she wasn't put away for murder, of course. I might not be able to take away her sorrow over losing her ex-husband, but surely a beautiful garment would help her figure out how to move on.

Chapter 8

Josie gathered up her jacket and purse, tossing her Ben & Jerry's container in the garbage can as she left. "Gotta check in at the shop," she said.

"So you're not staying for the Santa doll class?" I asked her.

"Oh yeah. I'll be back. Just want to check the order that came in."

Once she left I was alone with yards of red velvet and white fur and forced to face the fact that I had no ensemble for Josie's fashion show debut and couldn't stop worrying that someone in Bliss had pushed Dan Lee Chrisson to his death. And I had almost suffered the same fate.

I wanted nothing more than to believe that Hattie and Raylene had nothing to do with it, but the more I thought back over the events leading to his death, the more the finger pointed straight at them. Hadn't Hattie said Dan Lee would be sorry?

Anger, betrayal, and revenge were powerful motivators. But it was time to focus on my sewing work. I laid out the red velvet, spread the pajama pants and robe pattern I'd picked up in Fort Worth on top of it, and weighted the thin beige tissue paper down with my pattern weights. There were no design elements to work into the pants, and even if there had been, I didn't have time. I had to get the Santa suit done.

Using my firecracker-red-and-white floral-handled Ginghers, I cut without thinking, wondering, not for the first time, what made a man leave his wife and child. It had happened to my mother. He'd left Mama with two mouths to feed and not a single dollar to help us along the way. We hadn't seen hide nor hair of him since.

It had happened to Raylene, too. Had her anger gotten the better of her? Or had Hattie taken things into her own hands? Either way, a man was dead, and I felt most sorry for the little baby who was left behind with no daddy.

Fifteen minutes later, the pant legs were pinned together and I sat at my Pfaff and stitched. The whir of the machine was like a cup of Pecan Plantation coffee and a hunk of corn bread—soothing, right down to the marrow of my bones. Surrounded by fabric and buttons and patterns and trims, I felt as if there was nothing I couldn't do, no obstacle I couldn't conquer.

But the feeling was a lie. I couldn't save people from their own sadness or despair. I thought of the long, slow road Raylene Lewis had ahead of her. I couldn't get her through her grief any faster, if it was grief she was feeling.

And I couldn't summon up my charm at will, no matter how much I wished I could. The tunic I'd designed for Josie hadn't made her see how beautiful she was with that baby growing inside of her.

Butch Cassidy's legacy was failing me at the moment, but there was one thing I could always count on. Mama and Nana. I heard them coming through the kitchen door. They had showed up right on schedule, ready to help me out with my To Do list. Over the next hour, I focused on Will's Santa suit, Nana worked on Josie's blouse, and Mama took over cutting out the pieces for the Santa dollmaking class slated to start at Buttons & Bows in less than two hours.

"Maybe you should cancel the class," she said after she cut the tenth set of fronts, backs, arms, cowls, and hats.

I looked up from the piece of foam I was cutting, but my eyes were drawn to the window leading to the backyard. The winter had made the bushes and trees barren, but Mama and her concern for me were making the wood wither. Most of the time, her charm made things grow, but if her emotions ran wild or stress settled over her, her charm backfired. Sort of like my charm could help a person realize a dream, even if the dream would end in heartache. There was a good side and a bad side to the Cassidy blessing.

"I'll be fine. I have three people coming, and they already paid. That's close to six hundred dollars," I added. The dolls were not cheap to make, what with all their expensive trimmings, and would be three times as much if I tried to sell them retail.

I was making ends meet with the boutique, but teaching classes gave me that extra little breathing room.

"Darlin', you set up the class before you decided to make more than one outfit for Josie, before Santa fell from the roof and you took on making a new suit for Will, and before you nearly fell to your death. I've been watchin' you and you're walkin' mighty gingerly."

"I'm fine," I said again.

They worked in silence for a few minutes, not our typical Cassidy behavior. Finally, Nana cleared her throat. "Well, let's see one," she said. "Do you have a sample?"

"Of the Santa doll? I sure do." I ignored the aches in my body, scooted over to the antique secretary desk just outside the French doors of the workroom, and picked up one of the sample Santa dolls I'd made. I turned it for them both to see, smiling. It was modeled after a hand-made doll my great-great-grandmother Cressida Cassidy had sewn and that I'd loved as a child. I'd taken the basic structure and created a base, adapted the pattern to include a cowl, used heavy upholstery fabric for the body, and used tassels and trims and buttons to adorn it like an old-fashioned Saint Nicholas.

I'd made several samples, in two different sizes. Two of them were here at Buttons & Bows, and I'd given Josie one to put in Seed-n-Bead. I planned to set at least one out at the Denison mansion during the fashion show.

"They're kind of artsy," Nana said. "My grandmother would have loved them."

"Ah, so artsy in a good way?" I clarified. Her smile said it all, and I could tell she was remembering the doll her grandmother had made.

Mama laid out the last length of scrap upholstery fabric on the cutting table, spread the homemade pattern pieces on it, and set pattern weights on top. "Last one," she said as she started cutting.

"How's Maggie doing?" I asked Nana. I hadn't heard much of anything more about Dan Lee Chrisson's death around town since I'd run into Raylene and Hattie at the Denison mansion. I still couldn't shake Hattie's words from my head—telling Dan Lee he'd be sorry he hurt Raylene—but another thing had crossed my mind. Maybe Dan Lee and Raylene were doing more than talking, and if so, could Maggie have found out and confronted Dan Lee on the widow's walk?

"I gave her time off," Nana said. "She's beside herself. Can't hardly talk straight on the telephone, and when I stopped by her apartment to drop off her tote bag and a few things she left behind in the stalls, she wouldn't let me in the door."

So she hadn't skipped town. "But she's fine? She's not hurt, or anything?"

"Just heartache. I saw her car at the farm as I came over here, but that's the first I've seen her since Dan Lee met his Maker." Nana cocked her head to one side. "What are you gettin' at, Harlow Jane?"

Good question. "Nothing, Nana. Nothing at all."

I deposited my thoughts about Maggie in a little corner of my mind. Maybe I was reaching, trying to get my mind off of Hattie and worrying that she might have had something to do with Dan Lee's death. She had a key, so she could have loosened the screws, and if she wasn't an expert with tools, she could have stripped them. She'd been at the mansion that day, and she could have snuck up and shoved him into the loose railing.

So could Raylene, I reasoned. If she'd been waiting for Hattie in the car, she could have snuck into the house, skirted upstairs, and taken care of Dan Lee once and for all.

It was easier to believe that Maggie, who I didn't really know, and not two women I'd gone to school with, was the murderer.

I tested the size of the foam by holding it against my stomach. It stretched past my sides and up to my chest, but was plenty round. "You can wear that next Halloween and pretend to be pregnant," Nana said, a little twinkle in her eye. "Since I might never get any real grandchildren out of you. Then again, you are making it for Will . . ."

"Nana, bite your tongue. It's a jolly belly, not a pregnant tummy, and you know perfectly well why I'm making it."

"My point exactly," she said, drawing her fingers across her lips as if she were closing an imaginary zipper.

I took the high road, choosing to ignore her. Will and I had gone out a few times, and I saw plenty of him, but we certainly weren't getting hitched or having children anytime soon.

"I think this'll fit him just fine," I said, mostly to myself. Will was taller than I was by a good five inches, which made him over six feet, so the piece of foam I'd cut ought to make him look good and jolly.

I grabbed the cotton casing I'd made to house the fake belly, working the spongy foam into it. Two pieces of elastic hung from one side of the shell, and two pieces of Velcro were attached to the other side. The final step would be having Will try the belly on so I could cut the elastic to the right length. It had to fit snugly. A belly that slipped out of place was no good in my book.

I used safety pins to tighten the belly around one of the dress forms. Next I wrapped the waist of the pants around it and clipped it to hold the pants in place. They looked kind of sad, hanging there with no legs to fill them, but I didn't have time to dwell on it. I moved on to stitching the inseam of the red velvet pants and finishing the enormous waist. I'd cut the pants large enough to fit around the fake stomach, but looking at the pants now, I wondered if I'd added a bit too much girth.

I could have Will come over now before I went any

further, but the class would be arriving before long. No, I decided. If I had to adjust, I'd do it later. I stitched, pulling out the pins from the waist casing as I went. A few minutes later, I tossed the pants aside and moved on to Santa's jacket. I'd cut the pieces and had it all pinned together. It was a simple pattern. Now it was just a matter of stitching the seams and adding the closures and fur trim. Easy as pie.

Except that the bells on the front door of my shop chimed and a gaggle of women meandered in. It was time to make some Santa dolls.

I hightailed it out to the front room as Michele Brown, a transplant from Houston, lifted her hand in a wave. Her mass of curly mahogany hair fell past her shoulders. She pushed it aside as she bent to set down her sewing machine. "We're a few minutes early," she said. "Hope that's okay."

I nodded, smiling. "It's fine."

Mama and Nana waved and offered a friendly Texas howdy, then went straight back to work.

"Couldn't hardly wait to get started on the dolls," the portly woman beside her said—Diane, Michele's sister, I remembered. They'd seen my sample Santa doll at Seed-n-Bead and had signed up for the class then and there, according to Josie.

When I'd met them the first time, I'd instantly seen Diane in a long caftan with a slit neckline decorated with embroidery and three-quarter sleeves that flared at the end. In my mind, the full cut complemented her full figure.

Michele, on the other hand, had thrown me for a loop. I'd pictured her in contemporary nun's apparel: a simple headdress instead of the traditional starched white cotton wimple, a nondescript skirt that fell to mid-calf, and a white blouse.

A third woman brought up the rear, closing the door with a bang and then striding toward me. "Olive Madison," she said, stretching her arm out. "Pleasure to meet you."

"Harlow Cassidy," I said. She squeezed as she shook my hand, and if she'd been staring into my eyes and pursing her lips, I'd have thought she was trying to get a message across. But she smiled and I realized that she was just rodeo strong. She could probably wrangle a bull if she ever had the need.

I pulled my hand free, rubbing the crunched bones, and pointed to the dining room. My two extra sewing machines sat on the table, close to two portable tables filled with all the trimmings for the dolls. "We'll be working in there."

Michele hauled her machine up the three steps and set it at an empty space. "Just give me a minute, and I'll be right with you," I said, heading back into the workroom.

"You sure you don't mind us bein' early?" Diane asked sheepishly, her words slow and as Southern as they come. "We figured it would be better to be early than late, but it it's not convenient—"

I waved away her worry. "It's fine! We're just finishing up a few projects. You can take a look at the samples—" I pointed to the small Santa doll on the desk next to the French doors and to the large doll I'd put on the coffee table in the seating area. It stood next to a little basket filled with fabric scraps and next to my lookbook—a collection of my designs, from both my time at Maximilian's and my solo projects.

Diane and Olive made a beeline for the lookbook, but Michele stopped to peek into the workroom. She stepped across the threshold and, as if drawn forward by an invisible rope, headed straight for the dress form. She gently brushed her fingers over the red velvet, then poked at the soft foam belly.

"For the Winter Wonderland festival?" she asked.

"Yes."

"That lovely Will Flores is going to play Santa," Nana said. "Isn't he a peach for filling in at the eleventh hour?"

Mama and Michele both nodded. "He doesn't have any young children, does he?" Michele asked, squeezing the hollow pant leg.

Nana and Mama both turned their eyes to me and I felt a slow red heat creep up my neck. "Hush," I said, but the sound of my voice was drowned out by the clanking pipes above us.

Michele dropped the velvet and stared upward. She took a step back, gaping at the dress pulley contraption clinging to the ceiling. "What was that? Is it going to fall?"

"No! I put gowns on that so I can adjust the height and do handwork, hems and beading." *Meemaw, hush*, I silently implored. "That's just some old pipes groaning," I added.

Something squeaked, sounding an awful lot like laughter. I turned and stared out the window to the backyard. The gate between my property and Nana's goat farm swung back and forth, a creak sounding with each swing.

It stopped just as suddenly as it had started, and all I could think was that Meemaw was having a little too much fun with her playful haunting. She'd brought me back to Bliss and had brought Will into my life. But since she couldn't stare me down and ask me what in tarnation I was waiting for, she flitted around in her ghostly form scaring the bejeebers out of my customers.

Michele hadn't noticed the window or the gate, but she didn't look convinced that the pulley above us was stable. She backed out of the workroom and joined Diane and Olive in the seating area. A love seat snuggled in one corner near a matching sofa. I'd brought a red velvet settee and a rustic coffee table made from an old door into the grouping and used it as the consultation area of the boutique.

I started back toward my sewing machine, but stopped short, staring. The machine was zipping along on its own, the motor purring as the side seams of the jacket were sewn together.

Bless her heart. She had good intentions and was just trying to help out.

Nana and Mama grinned, looking completely content, and the sudden sensation of the four generations of Cassidy women together in one room sent a wave of prickles over my skin. When Meemaw died I'd never thought I would see her again—which, technically, I hadn't—since she was a ghost and all and hadn't taken on an opaque figure. And I certainly never thought we'd all of us be together in one room. But here we all were. And sewing, to boot.

Working with fabrics and cloth, designs and notions— it was the thing that connected me to all the women in my history. Our stories were woven together, intertwined and inseparable.

"That's a fancy machine you have there," Olive said from the threshold of the workroom.

I whipped my head around to face her. The sewing

machine stopped. Meemaw had enough sense not to advertise her presence, thank heavens.

I placed Olive at fifty or so, give or take, but her height, cropped ginger hair, and the confidence she exuded made her almost ageless. Her elegant black slacks and forest green sweater set, a string of pearls around her neck, probably helped too.

I laughed, passing it off as best I could. "Sometimes the pedal sticks," I said vaguely.

She nodded, but I couldn't tell if she believed me or if she thought something otherworldly was going on. I didn't wait to find out, instead surging forward and ushering her back to the dining room. Just then, as if on cue, the bells jingled, the front door opened, and Mrs. Eleanor Mcafferty waltzed in.

Chapter 9

We all stopped and stared. I'd been under the impression that Mrs. Mcafferty would never set foot in Buttons & Bows. She'd been friends with Nana and Zinnia James once upon a time, but they'd had a falling-out the size of the Grand Canyon over my granddaddy's affections and who knows what else.

She ran her hand over her hair, a few of the blond-highlighted strands lifting from the contact. She cleared her throat. "I saw a flyer about a dollmaking class," she said.

I tried my best not to gape. "You . . . you're wanting to make a Santa doll?"

"If it's not too late to sign up," she said. She paused at the steps to the dining room, turning to take in the shop. "I haven't been here in ages," she said. "Not since . . . well, not since I was a young woman."

Nana's lips quivered. She and Mrs. James had made amends, but as far as I knew, there was still some bad blood between the two of them and Eleanor Mcafferty. "It's been a good long time, Eli," she said.

The other women in the class all seemed to sense that something important was going on. They stood by, quietly watching, as Eleanor Mcafferty solemnly lowered her chin. "It sure has, Coleta."

And just like that, with two simple sentences, the feud between them seemed to slip away. Nana moved forward in her stocking feet and took Mrs. Mcafferty's hand. "She knows it didn't mean anything," Nana said.

"It happened before they were married. She'd been so sweet on Dalton, I never imagined her with Jeb, but then they got together—"

There was only one Jeb, at least that I knew of, in Bliss. And only one Jeb in the circle of friends Nana and Mrs. Mcafferty had been part of.

Senator Jebediah James. Zinnia James's husband.

So that's what their falling-out had been about. Zinnia had crushed on my granddaddy Dalton before he'd married Nana, and Eleanor had been sweet on Jeb before he'd married Zinnia.

Good Lord, what a hot tangled Southern mess.

"You and Rudy fell fast and hard, Eli. He's been good to you," Nana said.

Mrs. Mcafferty nodded, but the color hadn't returned to her face. "He has. Never batted an eye about—"

She broke off, turning to face the other women in the shop as if she'd just remembered they were there. "I'm so sorry, ladies. Old history." Her Southern accent separated the syllables of the words like bacon grease and black coffee separating in a bowl of red-eye gravy.

She brought her gaze back to me. "I'd like to make a doll," she said. "If that's all right with you. I know I didn't call ahead, but I thought—"

I shooed away her apology. How she and Nana had mended fences in a minute flat had my head spinning, but I wasn't going to question it. I led her up the steps to the dining room. "We're just getting ready to start."

Inside, I rushed through silent thanks that Gracie had no plans to come by the shop today. She'd found out recently that the Mcaffertys were her grandparents, but that had to be one of the best-kept secrets in Bliss. I'd heard it from Zinnia James—who knew everything about everything—and Gracie had figured it out, but no one else seemed to know who her mother was. From what Mrs. James said, Mrs. Mcafferty didn't have a clue that Gracie was her granddaughter.

Mama scurried off to the workroom to gather another Baggie of materials for Mrs. Mcafferty, and before long, everyone, including Nana, was seated around the table. Mama escaped back to the workroom to finish the hem of Josie's blouse.

I held the sample Santa up and was talking through the steps we'd be taking over the next several days, when the bells on the door of the shop jingled again.

Madelyn Brighton strode in, looking smart in South American–inspired gauchos she'd found at a thrift store in Fort Worth. She'd paired them with a full-sleeved blouse and had a definite Argentinean cowboy look going. All that was missing was a wide-brimmed hat and the bolero jacket and she might have looked like a heavyset black Jacqueline Kennedy from the sixties.

"Cheeri-o," she said in her very British accent, the same accent that I'd had trouble understanding at first, but that now always made her sound chipper to me. Except for right now. The cheeri-o fell flat as she looked at the table, the sewing machines, and the boxes of trims. "What's all this?"

"Dollmaking 101." Olive piped up from the table. "Plenty of room." She whispered something to Diane, and then they both scooted down.

"You know you've always wanted to make a Santa," I said, ushering Madelyn to the table.

She arched one brow at me. "Have I?" But whether or not she really had, she took her camera out—Madelyn was never without her camera—before tossing the favorite Epiphanie camera bag aside and taking the spot Olive and Diane had opened up for her.

She immediately snapped pictures of the two samples. "So I can see what my doll is supposed to look like," she deadpanned. Next she turned the Nikon on her classmates. Diane made an effort to turn her back, but Madelyn snapped away. Michele waved her hands in front of her face, blocking any attempt Madelyn made at getting a decent photo. But Olive posed, throwing back her shoulders, angling her head to the left, and lifting just one side of her lips in a mischievous smile.

"Nicely done," Madelyn said, looking at the digital screen on the back of her camera. She wagged her finger at the sisters. "You two. There's nothing wrong with having your picture snapped, you know."

"There is if you haven't primped first," Diane said.

Michele shook her head at this, sending her sister a scolding look. "The sisters prefer very few photographs."

Diane scoffed. "You're not a nun—"

"Did I say I was a nun?" Michele said, lifting her gaze to her sister.

"You sure talk about it enough."

The hairs on the back of my neck stood up. Hadn't I just envisioned Michele in a nun's habit? "Are you planning on—" What was the right terminology? Joining up?

Crossing over? "Taking your vows?" I asked as I unclasped the lids to the containers of trim, laying out some of the loop and tassel fringe.

I'd had no idea you could be in your forties and join a convent. My holy trinity was Mama, Nana, and Meemaw.

Michele chuckled. "No, I just like messin' with my sister. Although," she added, the corners of her mouth pulling into a frown, "I live a chaste enough life."

My head was spinning. "So you're not joining the convent?"

"She probably will one day, just you wait. Either that or she'll end up like the Lafayette sisters."

"We'll end up like the Lafayette sisters," Michele corrected. "I don't see a husband in your bed either."

But I'd pictured her in a nun's habit. Either she was going to become a nun, or my charm was going haywire. I turned to Nana, but she and Eleanor had their heads bent together as they whispered. Catching up on years of estrangement.

Michele had blushed the color of a ripe strawberry from all of the attention. "Come on, now, let's make some Santa dolls!" she said. "I want to set mine up at our Winter Wonderland table."

Diane explained to Madelyn and Olive, "There's going to be a section of the tent dedicated to crafters. You can rent a table and sell your wares. Michele makes gorgeous felt hats and beads."

"I'm hosting a table," Madelyn said. "I want to add a few more photographs, but otherwise, my portfolio is together. I'm featuring the pictures I took at the Margaret Moffette Lea Pageant and Ball a few months ago."

Nana and Eleanor glanced up at the mention of the

pageant. The brouhaha between them had happened years ago at the very same pageant we'd just had in Bliss.

"There's a stunner of Libby James," Madelyn continued, "and the one of Gracie Flores and Holly Kincaid is gorgeous."

I couldn't help but beam. I'd designed the gowns Libby and Gracie had worn, stitching confidence into every seam, weaving poise into each pleat, and breathing the vision of their futures into the layers of fabric. The Cassidy magic had surrounded them—especially Libby, since she was part of my family. I knew that whatever Madelyn saw in the photographs was enhanced because of my charm.

"Seed-n-Bead will have a table, too," I said, although since Josie was in the fashion show, she wouldn't be running it. "Villa Farina is catering the pastries, and Pick-a-Lily will have a table and is doing the centerpieces for the buffet table. And of course Santa will be there."

"I still can't believe that man fell from the roof. Such a tragedy," Olive said. "He worked there, isn't that right?"

I nodded. "With Barnett Restoration."

She shook her head sadly. "Such a shame."

Michele threaded her sewing machine with the black thread I'd provided. "I heard he left his wife and baby for a younger woman."

And the gossip was off and running. "Lots of marriages don't work out," I said, pushing my glasses up the bridge of my nose. The last thing I wanted during our festive dollmaking class was to start slinging mud about other townsfolk, but then again, maybe one of them knew something about Dan Lee that would stop me from wondering whether Hattie had anything to do with his death.

"I heard Raylene was holding a pretty good grudge against him on account of his philandering," Diane said.

No Southern hedging here. Diane had cut right to the chase. "Was he philandering?" I asked. "I ran into Hattie and she mentioned he had a girlfriend, but I thought maybe that happened after he left Raylene."

Nana stopped whispering with Mrs. Mcafferty and piped up, defending Maggie. "You got that right, Ladybug. It happened after."

Diane didn't back down, though. She met Nana's gaze head-on. "You're the goat woman, right? Sundance Kids, is that your place?"

Nana nodded, just once. "Yup."

"I heard the girlfriend works for you over there."

"She's a fine cheese maker," Nana said. "And she's not a homewrecker."

"If you say so." Diane went back to threading her machine, but I wasn't so sure she believed my grandmother's endorsement of Maggie. I hardly knew her, so I wasn't so sure I believed it either.

Or maybe that was just my wishful thinking that someone other than Hattie and Raylene was involved.

"Hattie's a nice girl," Michele said, as if she'd read my mind and wanted to put me at ease. "I see her at church most Sundays. But she was a hot mess at the Denison place the other day. I heard that her and Raylene showed up and Dan Lee was there and it just wasn't pretty."

"The day he died?" Olive asked, finally finding a way to join the conversation.

Michele hunched over her machine, squinting as she tried to thread the needle. "That's right. The day it stormed."

My heart sank to my stomach. So Raylene *had* been there.

Michele peered up at Diane. "Isn't that what Martha Crenshaw said?"

Diane nodded. "That she did. Said she thought she saw Raylene on the porch, then when she looked again, she was gone."

"So Raylene didn't go inside?"

Michele flattened her palm against her chest. "I wasn't there, Harlow Jane, so I wouldn't know. Mrs. Crenshaw told me that she'd been talking to Arnie Barnett over at the hardware store and he told her how heated his wife got."

"She's not normally like that," Diane said. "Sweetest thing you ever did see, but you mess with a woman's sister, and you better watch out. Dan Lee shouldn't have cheated."

"But did he cheat?" I asked again. "And even if he did, that doesn't mean he deserved to die."

All eyes turned to me. "'Course not, Harlow," Diane said. "All I mean is that if Hattie was stirred up, it was because Dan Lee up and left Raylene."

"It's too bad Dan Lee didn't love Raylene like Arnie loves Hattie," Diane said. "They're forever going on dates to all those gun and coin shows down in Fort Worth. I see them around the square, holding hands. I heard that he even went with her to the Dallas Design Center," she added, whispering the last part as if she were revealing a big secret.

Nana used the scissors she held to slice through a square of heavy tapestry. "I'm sure he does, and I know she's a peach, but y'all just remember, none of us are inside their marriage, just like we weren't inside Dan Lee and Raylene's. That man is dead and someone's to blame, but I don't reckon it's Maggie Pagonis."

As if Nana had asked them to utter silent prayers, the women all bowed their heads. "God rest Dan Lee's soul," Michele said as she touched her index and middle finger to her forehead, chest, left shoulder, then right shoulder.

Our voices pooled together as we muttered, "Amen."

"Who's going to play Santa for the kids?" Olive asked after a moment of respectful silence had passed. She leaned to the right, trying to get a better look into the workroom. From here, you could barely see the Santa pants hanging from the dress form.

"We have a replacement lined up," I said.

"He's perfect for the job," Nana said, looking up and winking at me.

Mama came out of the workroom. I imagined she'd heard the whole conversation we'd just had, but if she had, she didn't let on. "The hem is done," she told me, "and I finished stitching Santa's jacket. I didn't want to mess with the fur—"

"Knowing how persnickety you are," Nana said to me. Her eyes twinkled, and she looked happier than I'd seen her since she and Zinnia James had made up. She stood, giving Mrs. Mcafferty's hand a pat. "See you later, y'all. I'm off to Fort Worth. Need supplies for a new type of lotion I'm working on tomorrow. Pomegranate. Don't you be a stranger," she added.

Eleanor Mcafferty smiled wanly. "I've missed you, Coleta." They both seemed to slip into reminiscing for the briefest moment before Nana headed through the kitchen. At the Dutch door, she slid her boots on. "How do I get me one of them tables at the Winter Wonderland, Ladybug?" she called to me.

"For your goat products?" Michele asked. "That will be wonderful!"

"They'll do really well there," Mrs. Mcafferty added.

Diane bobbed her head. "Mmm-hmm. Pomegranate lotion. Intriguing."

I gave Nana the sponsor form, and poof! she was gone to tend to her babies. Mama, however, picked up one of the sample Santa dolls and turned it over in her hands. "I want to make me one of these," she said, marching over to the table to take Nana's vacated seat. She folded her hands like a perfect little schoolchild. "What do we do first?"

I gathered the gallon-sized Baggies with the pattern pieces for the dolls and handed them out, instructing them to pin and stitch the body first, then the arms. Next came the filling. "Take little bits at a time so it doesn't get lumpy. Each doll will use almost an entire bag of batting," I said, demonstrating.

"Dang, a whole bag?" Olive asked, staring at the stack of bags next to the staircase.

"Yup. It takes a lot of fluff to make old St. Nick." I kept stuffing the shell of a body I'd prepared. Before long, it was filled, but I took tufts of batting and worked them into every nook and cranny of the doll, filling the Santa out until he was nearly rock solid.

Michele had opened and closed her mouth a few times, like she wanted to ask me something but wasn't quite sure how to broach the subject. Finally, with her doll halfway stuffed, she just blurted it out. "Is it true," she said, looking at me, then at my mother, "that the Cassidy women are magically charmed? Because—"

I felt my face go hot. "W-what?"

Mrs. Mcafferty and I both sputtered, and I remembered the pact she'd had with Nana and Mrs. James. She'd probably kept the secret all these years.

"I read a story online, but . . ."

"But what, for pity's sake?" Mama snapped, her patience all but gone. She'd guarded the Cassidy secret better than Nana's dogs guarded her precious goats. The idea that all would be revealed meant she'd have some explaining to do to Hoss McClaine, for starters, and to the whole town, truth be told. They all knew we were an eccentric family, but peculiar they could handle. If it turned into something they'd perceive as witchery in the very big brass North Texas buckle of the Bible Belt? I wasn't sure we could expect much tolerance.

Michele hesitated, darting a glance at her sister. "I—I don't think you can always trust what you find on the Internet. It's probably not even about y'all."

Behind Michele, the sheer drapery panels fluttered. The pot of lavender Mama had brought me a few months back sat on a little corner plant stand. It bloomed no matter what, but now the stalks arched, the tips of the flowers reaching toward the table. A reaction to Mama's surge of emotions.

God almighty. The Cassidy women and our charms had always flown under the radar in a don't ask, don't tell kind of manner, and it was better that way. Madelyn had been the first outsider I'd ever told, and that was only because she was part of the North Texas Paranormal Society and had heard rumors about a magical family. But a story? On the Internet?

Michele studied her Santa doll as if stuffing it just right was suddenly the only thing she cared about, but I could almost see her ears twitching. "It's probably noth-

ing," she said again, but my head felt as if it were filled
with batting thicker than the dolls we were making.

"Of course it's nothing!" I managed to say, laughing it
off. I couldn't get any more out of them without clueing
them in that maybe there was something to the story, so
I signaled to Mama to drop it. We swallowed our worry,
hard as it was to do, and went back to the Santas.

The rest of the afternoon passed painfully slowly as I
handed out the muslin ovals with their hand-painted
Santa faces, we glued the flat, fabric-covered bases onto
the bottom of the bodies with Fabri-Tac, and even as I
instructed the women on picking out just the right pieces
of faux fur, loop tassels, ribbons, and other trims.

Finally, I ushered the group out, their Santa dolls scattered on the dining table for them to finish at the next
class.

The second the door shut behind Olive, Diane, Michele, and Eleanor, I spun around to look at Madelyn,
the only paranormal groupie I knew. "Do you know
what they're talking about?"

Her gaze met mine, but her brown, gold-flecked eyes
were clouded. "No idea, love," she said.

I pushed aside the pile of scrap fabrics that had wound
up on the computer desk and plopped down in front of
it. Not even the sudden warm air encircling me, which I
knew was Meemaw trying to bolster me up, could take
away the icy sting I felt at feeling my family secrets
threatened with exposure.

Michele had brushed away whatever she'd seen about
the Cassidy clan, but she'd read something that had
sparked her interest.

Mama hovered behind me on one side, and Madelyn
stood on the other as I moved the mouse, bringing the

screen to life. My fingers flew over the keyboard and after a few clicks, I found it.

Dread crept from the soles of my cowboy boots all the way up to my hair follicles as I read the headline.

Charmed Family Makes Magic in Bliss, Texas

I skimmed, looking for our names, details about our charms, and any other identifiers. Our names weren't there, but plenty of other details were, including what the inside of Buttons & Bows looked like. *Descended from an outlaw. A streak of blond hair. Magical, unique "gifts."*

God almighty. I went from cold to clammy, sweat beading on my forehead. Mama put her hand on my shoulder and squeezed. "Everythin' will be okay. You have to know to look for it. Nobody—but nobody—will believe it, if they're even able to find it," she said, but I could hear the doubt in her voice. Stories got around, and if Michele, who was just an ordinary woman in Bliss, had read it, who else had? More than that, had any of them told other people?

I wanted to spend my time finishing everything on my list for the fashion show and the other Winter Wonderland events, and maybe, by some miracle, figure out who had wanted something bad to happen to Dan Lee Chrisson. Finding out what my hometown would do if they found out the truth about the Cassidy women was one thing that was not on my To Do list.

Chapter 10

My mind was whirring and I was ready to jump out of my skin.

And from the odd looks Mama and Madelyn were tossing my way, I wasn't hiding it too well. "Are you coming down with something, Harlow?" Madelyn asked, touching the back of her hand to my forehead.

"No, no. I'm fine." I started gathering up the scraps of trim the women had discarded.

"Sugar," Mama said, "are you sure?"

I stopped what I was doing and turned to look at Madelyn and my mother. "Sure of what?"

"Maybe you're havin' some latent effect from that fall, or somethin'?" She looked me up and down. "Sure you're okay?"

I waved her hand away and scooped up another handful of scraps. "I told you, I'm fine."

"Then, sugar," she said, lunging forward and grabbing hold of my arm, "why in heaven's name are you throwing away all that good trim?"

"What?" I looked at her, baffled, and then looked at the loosely woven basket I used as a garbage container. It was overflowing with mounds of loop fringe, cording, tassel fringe, and everything else that had, a minute ago, been organized in the different bins sitting on the folding table.

I gasped. "I . . . I did that?" What had I been thinking? I gave myself a mental thump on the head. Of course I hadn't been thinking. Not about fabric, anyway.

The second the words left my lips, chaos hit. It was as if someone lifted the garbage can and flung it straight up into the air. Mama, Madelyn, and I stood still as statues as the fabric scraps flew around the dining room, circling like a tornado of fripperies and fringe. And then, as if someone had turned off the power, the swirling stopped cold and the trim fell to the floor.

I snuck a look at Madelyn, holding my breath. She knew about Meemaw's otherworldly presence, but that didn't mean she wouldn't be freaked out by a demonstration. But she looked enraptured by the magical moment, her cinnamon-colored skin flushed and a dash of pink on her cheeks. "Fantastic," she whispered.

The front door opened, the bells on the knob jingling. We all three whipped around to see Will standing in the doorway, his toolbox in hand, a stack of air-conditioner filters under one arm.

"Hey," I said, swallowing my nerves. Will didn't know about Meemaw—or any part of my magical charm. If he'd arrived ten seconds earlier, he would have gotten a good gander at my family's gifts in action.

"Hey, yourself," he said, taking in the mess all over the floor. "What happened here? One of Coleta's goats escape again?"

That was a good guess, and safer than the truth, but I couldn't quite bring myself to lie, so I sort of moved my head in a noncommittal half nod, half shake.

He set his toolbox down and laid the filters next to it, out of the way, and then looked around. A new central air and heat system was one of the few changes Meemaw had tackled in the old house, but I was eternally grateful she had since I lived and worked in the same place.

"Any other damage?" If it was odd to him that the chaos was confined to just the dining room, he didn't comment.

"Nope."

When I didn't offer more detail, he stepped back outside and brought in the ladder he'd left on the front porch, then shut the door behind him, walked to the steps leading to the open dining room, and put his hand up on the railing between the two rooms. "I just heard something awful," he said.

The coil of nerves in my stomach tightened.

"What'd y'hear, sugar?" Mama asked him.

Will turned his Longhorns cap around to face backward, but barely got a sound out before the bells on the door rang again. But this time the string of silver flew off from the force of the door bursting open. Raylene stumbled in, her face pale and drawn.

Will dropped his hand from the banister and moved aside as I rushed forward. "Raylene?"

"Good Lord," Mama said in a hushed breath behind me. "She looks like she's seen a ghost."

"Who's that?" Madelyn whispered to her.

Mama responded, but I ignored their whispering as I focused on Raylene. "What is it? What's wrong?"

She staggered over to the green and gold paisley damask sofa. Mama and Madelyn beelined to either side of Raylene, and I perched on the edge of the coffee table, knee to knee with her.

"M-my baby," she stammered. "I—I didn't know where . . . where else to go. Y-you said you'd help. The . . . the sheriff—"

The hairs on the back of my neck stood up. My vision of her in the embroidered brocade cheongsam had been so clear when I'd seen her at the Denison mansion, but now all I saw was a blur of gray. My eyebrows lifted in question as I shot a quick glance at Will, and from the way his left eye pinched slightly, I had the feeling that whatever he'd been about to tell us, we were going to hear from Raylene.

"Is Boone okay?" I asked Raylene. "What about the sheriff?"

Her hand had grown clammy and her face drained of all color. She looked paler than a ghost. "I—I shouldn't have come. What can you do? What can anyone do?" she wailed.

She started to rise, her gaze skittering from me to Mama to Madelyn, but she suddenly fell back, as if she were pulled, and I had a fleeting thought that Meemaw wanted her to stay put. Raylene, bless her heart, buried her face in her hands.

Mama rubbed Raylene's back, making soothing *shhh shhh shhh* sounds, but she raised her gaze to me.

I shrugged helplessly.

"Come on, love," Madelyn said through Raylene's cries. "You're here. What in the bloody hell could be so bad?"

I caught Madelyn's eyes and shook my head, frantically trying to communicate telepathically with her, but of course that didn't work since I wasn't capable of telepathy and neither was she. The one thing we both knew was that something was definitely wrong. Raylene had already lost the father of her child. What more could happen to the poor woman?

Raylene's shoulders heaved. "My . . . my . . ."

Before she could get an entire sentence out, the front door swung open. Josie sidled in, leading with her pregnant belly. She glanced at us, but quickly turned left instead of right and headed straight up the three steps to the dining room. She'd missed the entire dollmaking class, but leave it to her to show up in the thick of a new drama.

She skirted around Will and his ladder, aiming for the kitchen. "Tell me you have some fried okra," she called over her shoulder.

The girl had the maternity cravings bad. She didn't wait for an answer; instead, a second later I could hear her clanging around the kitchen, on the hunt for something else when she realized a bowl of fried okra was not at the ready.

I turned back to Raylene's tearstained face. She'd angled her body on the sofa and was turned, staring into the kitchen. Her hand rested on her stomach and just like that, I froze. The truth hit me like a bale of hay to the head. "Oh no."

Raylene didn't seem to hear me, but Madelyn, Mama, and Will all turned to look at me.

"What?" Madelyn mouthed.

"Harlow Jane?" Mama said, lowering her chin.

Will stayed silent, but I could tell he knew the truth.

"Where's Boone?" I asked Raylene, my voice scarcely more than a whisper.

A sound escaped from her throat, but her attention never wavered from the kitchen, where I could see the mess of okra I'd bought at the market spilled over the counter. Josie had poured half a box of cornmeal into a gallon-sized Baggie. I didn't have fried okra, so she was going to make some.

"Raylene," I said again, more forcefully.

As if she'd just registered my voice, she jerked her head toward me, breaking her trance.

"Where's Boone?" I asked again.

She swallowed, staring, and then shook her head. "He's . . . he's g-gone."

I felt three pairs of eyes on me, but didn't break my gaze from Raylene's. "What do you mean, gone?"

Raylene looked up through her moist eyelashes. "Gone. Gone! He was in his crib at home and then he wasn't. He's gone!" Her voice descended to a whisper and her face twisted.

Both Madelyn and I went into question mode, but Raylene didn't seem able to focus. She stared straight ahead for a solid two minutes. Finally, she blinked, breaking out of her trance, and turned to me. "I was in the house. How could . . . could someone sneak in and t-take him? Where is he? Where's Boone?" She grabbed my hand, sobbing. "Where's my baby?"

Chapter 11

Josie stood on the threshold of the kitchen, the knife she'd been using to cut okra hanging loosely by her side. "What in the world is going on?"

I glanced at Will, silently asking him to bring Josie up to speed so I could stay focused on the distraught woman in front of me. It was as if he could read my mind. He was next to her in a flash, his voice nothing more than a low rumble from where I sat as he filled her in.

I tried to pull more information from Raylene. She told me that there was no evidence of breaking and entering, which had raised a whole bunch of red flags for Deputy McClaine. Hattie and Arnie were organizing a search party. And Raylene herself had been frantically driving around Bliss until she couldn't see straight, which had led her here.

"I r-remember you from school," she said through her sobs. "You were n-never like those other g-girls who would stab their best friend in the back if it meant they'd get to d-date one of the football p-players. You were never a mean girl, Harlow. Never a homewrecker."

In a different situation, I'd have smiled at the compliment, but Raylene's baby was missing and my heart was in my throat. "People are out looking for him and I'm sure they'll find him soon," I said, wishing that was a comfort but knowing that it really wasn't.

I left Raylene with Mama and went to the kitchen to fetch her a glass of water. The buttercup retro-style appliances usually filled me with as much comfort as the warm air Meemaw often encircled me with. But not now. Not today. Not with Boone missing.

Will had disappeared through the Dutch door onto the back porch, his cell phone clamped to his ear. A grim expression played on Josie's face, the knife in her hand pointed forward like a weapon, as if she were ready to bolt and join the search party.

In a flash I was by her side, gently taking it from her. "They'll find him."

"Should I—"

I eyed the heap of cut okra on my maple cutting board, the slime of the mucilage looking none too appetizing, but I knew that any true Southerner regarded the odd little vegetable as a delectable bite-sized treat. "Finish the okra," I said.

She sighed, one hand on her belly, and sent a worried glance toward Raylene. "Poor woman. I can't imagine what she's going through. First her husband leaves her, then he dies, then her baby's kidnapped. He's her child, but he's also all she has left of her husband," she said.

"Ex-husband," I corrected.

"Whatever. She loved him once." Her voice dropped to a whisper. "If anyone ever tried to take my baby, they'd be taking a piece of me and"—she picked up the knife again and waved it around in front of her—"I wouldn't stop until I had justice."

She started toward the Dutch door, but I pulled her

back. She blinked and stopped. "We should help, shouldn't we? Maybe we can find him."

I wanted nothing more than to find Boone, but I had no idea where to look. "We can help most by staying with Raylene and keeping her company."

She wiped away the tears that had pooled in her eyes before turning to the counter to finish her chopping, with concentrated force now. "Mark my words, Harlow. There's something not right about this." She stopped and gasped as she whirled around. "Maybe she killed her husband and staged a kidnapping to throw people off the trail!" she rasped.

My suspicions had been more focused on Hattie, but Raylene could have killed Dan Lee, and Josie's theory had merit. "Why would she—?" I began, but I stopped abruptly as ideas started piecing themselves together in my mind.

I stared at Josie, my feet suddenly rooted to the floor. "Say that again."

She put the knife down and started shoveling the gooey okra into the Baggie of cornmeal. "What, that maybe she killed her husband and staged a kidnapping?"

My head pounded—or maybe it was the gate between my property and Nana's goat farm blowing in the wind and smacking against the post over and over again. "No, earlier. About her husband leaving her for another woman."

Her brow furrowed as she thought back. "Um, I said that he'd left her, found a little hottie, and that if anyone did anything to my baby, I'd want justice."

"No." She'd said something else that had stuck in the back of my mind. The gate between the Sundance Kids and my backyard banged again and then it hit me. "You said your baby is part of you."

She looked at me like I was off my rocker. "Yeah—he's growing inside of me."

"But he—or she—is part of you. You said Boone is all Raylene has left of Dan Lee."

Josie slowly zipped up the Baggie and shook it, coating the okra. "Right."

The gate continued to slam outside and my gaze drifted to the door, past Will, who still stood on the porch, and to the goats in the distance. "He's also all Maggie has left," I said.

She stopped shaking the Baggie of okra. "Maggie who works with your grandmother?"

I nodded, another thought whirring into my head. "What if it was Maggie?" I said, my voice scarcely above a whisper to make sure Raylene couldn't overhear our conversation.

I inched toward the archway between the kitchen and the front rooms of the farmhouse. Raylene still sat between Madelyn and Mama.

Josie went back to the stove and started rolling the bag back and forth between her hands. She wrapped a potholder around the handle of the cast-iron skillet she had been heating and lifted it, spreading the oil in the bottom. "Do you really think Maggie could have done that?"

Before I could answer, Will came back inside. "I just got off the phone with Hoss McClaine," he said. "There's no sign of the baby anywhere. They've questioned everyone they can think of—"

I cut him off, my heart racing. "Dan Lee's girlfriend?"

"Maggie Pagonis? Yeah, her too."

"Did Dan Lee have a key to your house?" I called to Raylene.

The three women on the couch turned around. Mama murmured something into Raylene's ear, repeating the question, maybe, and then Raylene nodded.

I whipped back around to face Will and Josie. "Maggie could have gotten ahold of the key. That would explain why there was no forced entry. Maybe she thinks having Boone will let her keep a little bit of Dan Lee."

Josie poured a good helping of the okra into the hot oil. As it sizzled, then settled down to cook, she said, "But where would she hide a baby? How could you keep something like that secret?"

"What if . . ." I trailed off, not wanting to believe that anyone could steal another woman's baby, let alone hide him like I was thinking she might have.

But it made sense. If Maggie did take Boone, she couldn't keep him with her or someone would notice. Bliss was a small town. Some things, like the Cassidy charms, could be kept under wraps, but a stolen baby? Uh-uh.

"What if what?" Will asked, studying me. "You feeling okay, darlin'?"

I waved him away as I edged across the kitchen so I couldn't be overheard. I dropped my voice to a whisper. "I'm fine. I was just thinking that maybe she didn't *plan* to take the baby. Maybe she just did it, and then realized that she'd have to leave Bliss. But someone might have noticed her with a child. So where would she hide the baby in the meantime where no one would think to look?"

Outside, the wind howled and another thought occurred to me. The idea percolated in my head for another second before I managed to voice my thought. "Oh God. Nana said she saw Maggie's car at Sundance Kids earlier."

Chapter 12

The land I inherited from Meemaw, with my little red-brick trimmed farmhouse—bequeathed to me on the very day I was born, although I hadn't learned about it until she had passed—was situated right behind Nana and Granddaddy's five acres. Their land stretched the entire block behind the town square. The city had been wanting to buy it to build a park, but if there was one thing I knew down to my bones, it was that Nana and Granddaddy would never sell.

I hightailed it through the kitchen, out the door, down the back porch, and through the gate separating our properties. The cold air hit me right away, but I braced myself and scurried down the porch steps, racing across the muddy backyard.

Will's voice trailed after me. "Cassidy, what the devil are you doing?"

But I couldn't even slow down to answer. If I was right, then Boone was alone and cold and in danger of being stolen away for good.

I saw Thelma Louise up ahead, standing at the property line as if she were holding sentry. The granddam of my grandmother's herd, her Romanesque nose giving her a haughty air, looked at me with her unblinking eyes as I barreled toward her.

I slowed long enough to skirt through the gate, also long enough for Will to catch up to me. "Are you out of your ever-lovin' mind? What are you doing?"

"The baby," I started to say, but Thelma Louise bleated. She made it sound urgent. Three short, three long, three short. Like the Morse code distress signal, which made the hairs on the back of my neck rise. She bleated again, and I was sure I was right. "What is it, Thelma Louise?" I called.

She turned her glassy eyes to me before taking off across my grandparents' side of the yard. Will and I ran after her, sloshing through puddles, the heels of my boots sinking into patches of mud.

Thelma Louise slowed, turning to look back at me. "He's there, isn't he?" I yelled.

Will was by my side, his hand on my arm, yanking me up every time I stumbled in the mud. "The baby's here?"

"I think so!" We followed Thelma Louise across the open field, past the little stream and the guard dog milling around with the goats, and straight to the outbuilding.

Adrenaline coursed through me. Thelma Louise's bleats were more frantic and sounded like a talk box on a guitar. "Come quick," she seemed to say, but I'd already passed her by and crashed through the barn door, skidding to a stop in the milk parlor. A milking bucket, milking hoses, a bottle of liquid dish soap, another bottle of bleach, and a special hose fitted to the kitchen faucet cluttered the rectangular stainless-steel table up against one wall.

"Where is he?" I asked through my panting.

Will had his cell phone out, his thumb poised over the touch pad, ready to dial the sheriff, I reckoned. "Are you sure?"

"It makes sense," I said, finally catching my breath as I scanned the room. "Grief can send a person reeling. I think she cracked up."

Something hit me from behind, and I lurched forward. I whipped around. "Darla—!" I yelled at the black and white Nubian, but stopped when she bleated at me. She trotted around me and stood next to Thelma Louise, both of them training their enormous eyes with their rectangular pupils on me. I took a few gingerly steps toward them, looking around for any sign of a baby.

"Where is he?" I asked the goats, but, of course, I knew they didn't understand me. Where was the goat whisperer in the family when you needed her?

Right. In Fort Worth getting supplies for her home-made lotions.

Darla trotted over, circling back around me. I dropped my chin, watching her watch me. She lowered her head in response and nudged me forward, past the raised milking contraption, the small cheese room where Nana blended her cheese varieties, and the ladder leading to the roof.

Thelma Louise came around and prodded Will along beside me until we were standing at the threshold of one of the goat's stalls.

"Is the baby in the manger?" I asked with a tense laugh.

They bleated, staring at me with their burning gazes, and I got the feeling that maybe they could understand me.

Darla pushed her nose against my leg, nibbling at the pocket of my sweater. I swatted at her, stepping closer to the hay manger. Nana had put it in the middle of the stall so the goats could spread out around it as they munched.

Thelma Louise turned those shiny eyes to me, her floppy white and black ears swinging as she nodded at me. "What?" I asked, as thunder cracked outside. Another storm brewing.

The two goats stuck their noses into the hay and rooted around the edges. Then, looking up at me again, they took up positions on either side of the manger.

I didn't have to be a goat whisperer to understand where the girls wanted me to look. A sliver of blue peeked over the top of the hay pile. Slowly, I moved closer, my heart in my throat. The sky outside flashed and the lights flickered just as I peered into the manger.

"Lord almighty," I whispered to Will. "Call the sheriff. Call Mama. Get Raylene over here."

Because right there, shivering in the cold, was a tiny baby wrapped in a powder blue swaddling blanket, tucked into the hollow of the manger.

Chapter 13

I'd offered to hold the baby while Raylene talked to a social worker. She stood in the corner, sneaking glances my way, answering questions, so I snuggled the baby against my chest. He seemed no worse for the wear, given his ordeal.

Deputy Gavin McClaine tipped back his dark brown cowboy hat, staring at me like I'd plumb lost my mind, but Nana hurried into the barn at that moment, her arms loaded down with bottles and pumps for her lotions. She dropped them at her feet, her fingers fluttering to the blond streak in her hair. Almost instantaneously, the spot along my hairline where my own blond tuft started tingled. This bit of hair, stripped of almost all color, was another Cassidy trait, but I'd only recently begun to realize that it acted almost like a touchstone between us.

"What in tarnation?" she said as she scanned the barn. Her gaze settled on the baby in my arms. "What are you doin' with a baby, Harlow Jane?"

Where to start? "Nana, it's quite a story." I gave her the abridged version of what had happened.

As soon as I wrapped up, Gavin McClaine cleared his throat, clearly aggravated.

"If you're just about done," he said, and then he continued before I could say anything else. "You're tellin' me that you just happened to figure out that Maggie Pagonis kidnapped Raylene's baby and hid him here?"

Nana huffed, seeming just as aggravated as the deputy. "That's not the important part of the story, young man," she snapped, tapping her cowboy boot on the dirt floor of the stall.

"That's right," I said, gently patting the baby's back. "I just put all the pieces together. Maybe I should be deputized," I added.

Deputy Gavin ignored that comment, instead saying, "Just tell me what you found."

I pointed to the little feeder in the middle of the room, a million questions going through my mind.

He turned to Nana. "And you had no idea this baby was here?"

"He wasn't here this mornin', I'll tell you that," she said. "I reckon Maggie slipped in here after she saw me leave."

Gavin didn't bat an eye, but he was just like his daddy, and I knew that behind that innocent expression was a savvy man who was taking in every detail and processing through every possible scenario. He nosed around the stall, but aside from the manger and a trough of water with a hose slung into it, the small room was empty. Goats didn't need a lot of decor.

He looked at me, holding the baby, before going out to the milking parlor. Chattering voices came from outside, followed by the steady clomp of footsteps.

A minute later, Gavin came back in, Hoss McClaine on his heels.

"Harlow, Harlow, Harlow," Gavin said, "why do you

reckon that whenever something mysterious is goin' on in Bliss, you're right there in the thick of it?"

There was a shift in the air and I felt Will stiffen beside me, but I met Gavin's gaze, my voice terse, but soft so as not to wake the baby. "I reckon I don't know, Sheriff. Just dumb luck, I guess."

"A truckload of dumb luck," the sheriff said. He was a Southern gentleman to the core, but his weathered skin, salty mustache and soul patch, and his unyielding gaze under his bushy eyebrows made it perfectly clear that he didn't think it was dumb luck at all.

Raylene rushed over, her interview with the social worker done. "I'll take him now, Harlow."

I felt suddenly protective of the little baby in my arms, almost as if he were my own. Did Boone need protecting? I still didn't want to believe it, but what if Raylene had had something to do with Dan Lee's death?

But once again, as if he could read my mind, Will laid his hand on my shoulder, silently urging me to respond. I handed Boone over, my body instantly cold with the absence of his warmth. I half expected him to break out in a wail, but the sweet thing just sighed, his little body curling up inside the swaddling blanket as Raylene cradled him against her, covering him with an additional blanket.

She gave me a one-armed hug before the social worker escorted her out of the barn.

"If y'all will excuse us," Sheriff McClaine said to Nana and me, "we'd like to have a look around."

In New York, a detective might have arrived and said they were going to process the crime scene, but this was small-town Texas and the sheriff didn't put on any airs. Gavin stomped on the ground, shooing Thelma Louise and Darla out of the milking parlor and into the yard with the other goats. He started poking around again, emerging from the cheese room a minute later. He held up an inexpensive pastel-colored diaper bag. "Found this," he said.

Nana shook her head, tapping the tip of her cowboy boot again. "This ain't Bethlehem, for pity's sake. Why, that little . . ." She muttered the rest under her breath, but there was no doubt that Nana was steamed. She'd defended Maggie to the women in the Santa dollmaking class, only to find out she was guilty as sin. Maybe not for Dan Lee's murder. But definitely for kidnapping Boone.

Gavin absently snapped the wrist of one of his latex gloves and crouched down in front of his find, searching through it. "Nothing out of the ordinary," he announced a minute later. "Baby formula, bottles, tiny diapers." He held up a diaper the size of his hand, as if to prove they were, indeed, itty-bitty.

The sheriff's cell phone rang from the clip on his rattlesnake skin belt. He answered it with a clipped "Yup?" and then he listened, his lips pursing and his eyes pinching. The air seemed to sizzle.

Nana's boot kept tapping. Gavin peered up. Will rested his hand on my lower back, and I held my breath, sensing something important was being said on the other end of the line.

Finally, Hoss McClaine snapped his phone shut, clipping it back onto his belt. "Well, now, we've just had an interesting development," he said, his Southern accent as thick as good cream gravy.

Gavin stood, holding the diaper bag at arm's length. "What's that?"

"That was Christine," he said, his hand clasping the

phone on his hip. "Deputy Fanchon," he added for Nana's and my benefit, since we didn't know Christine personally. "She arrested Maggie Pagonis on her way back in this direction, but seems she has an airtight alibi on the morning Dan Lee Chrisson died. She was at Beaumont Salon on the square gettin' her hair and nails all done up," the sheriff added.

Which meant Maggie didn't kill Dan Lee Chrisson. And we were no closer to identifying the murderer or eliminating Raylene as a suspect.

Chapter 14

An hour later, Josie, Will, and I were alone at Buttons & Bows. Will had finished replacing the last of the air filters and was sweeping the floors where he had worked. I watched him for a minute, a trifle mesmerized. A down-home Southern man cleaning up after some physical labor. There was something mighty appealing about that.

But even that appeal couldn't take my mind off of discovering Boone, hearing about Maggie's arrest, and my ongoing concern over who had tampered with the railing at the mansion. Maybe sewing would help me figure out who was behind Dan Lee's death.

I'd picked up the scattered trim from the dining room, readying the area for tomorrow's class while Josie finished frying her okra. When she was done, she brought a bowl of it with her to my workroom.

"Here you go," I said, handing her the second blouse I'd made for her. She eyed it doubtfully, but slipped behind the privacy screen to try it on, emerging a minute later. She didn't even bother to look in the mirror, instead heading straight for the cutting table to grab a handful of okra, popping two of them into her mouth and resting her hand on her belly before she spoke again.

"A baby in the goats' stall," she muttered, shaking her head. "That's just crazy."

I batted her hand from the bowl of okra. "Would you quit that? You're gonna get crumbs and oil all over the fabric." And that would never do—even if it was just a polyester blend.

The dark magenta background was made interesting by the embossed floral pattern done in the same magenta, one shade lighter, but looking at Josie in it, I knew it wasn't right. The ruching I planned to do on the extra folds, which would fall just below the breasts, would accent the fullness of Josie's breasts, but now that I saw it on her, I was also pretty sure it would make the fabric flare out a bit too much over her swollen belly.

"Never mind," I said, nixing the blouse. With my hands on her shoulders, I sent her back behind the privacy screen.

"No good?" she asked, snatching another bite of food before she disappeared.

"No good." I sat on the stool, propped my elbows on the cutting table, and dropped my head to my hands. "What would be good?" I muttered. I felt like my creative well was dry as a stretch of South Texas desert.

Will came up next to me and leaned against the table. "You okay, darlin'?"

I didn't look up. I'd been in possession of my Cassidy charm for only a few months, and I was sure that I was already losing it. I should be able to design the perfect garment for Josie—I had never suffered through this many failed attempts—and yet no new designs were coming to me. "Peachy," I mumbled, more to the table than to him.

He laid his hand on my back and leaned down to

whisper in my ear. "Give yourself a break. It's been a tough day. You'll get your mojo back."

A shiver swept up my spine from the combination of his touch and his warm breath against my neck. A quick memory of him kissing me not so long ago flitted in and out of my mind. But the feeling wasn't enough to zap me out of my funk. I wanted to believe Raylene was innocent, but I just wasn't sure, and it weighed on me

"I hope so," I said to Will, but part of me also wondered if I'd been good at fashion design only because of my charm, even if I hadn't known about it until recently, and if I'd now lost it for good.

"Let's go out tonight," he said softly. "Just you and me. No weddings. No debutante balls. No fashion shows. Get your mind off of things."

I turned my head to look up at him and couldn't help but smile. He looked like a rogue outlaw, what with his goatee, his black T-shirt, jeans, and cowboy boots. Either that or the hottest country music star this side of Nashville.

"Deal," I said.

"It's not you, you know," Josie called. "It's me. It's this gargantuan stomach. Nothing could make me look good right now except getting this little babe out of me."

Will straightened up as Josie came out from the changing area. He grabbed his toolbox, but stopped to look at her, giving her a crooked smile. "There's nothing more beautiful than a pregnant woman. I missed it the first time around, but"—he moved his gaze to me, real slow, and I felt a splash of heat spread up my neck to my cheeks—"if I ever get married and get the chance to be a father again, seeing my wife pregnant with my child will be one of the highlights of my life. That's my two cents."

My heart melted a little bit. This was what Meemaw had seen in Will. As if she'd read my thoughts and wanted to confirm that, yes, underneath the splay of whiskers and the mischievous smile, Will Flores was a one heck of a good man, the chimes hanging just outside the workroom window tinkled playfully.

Josie and I both stared at Will, speechless, as he beat a path to the front door, threw up his hand in a quick wave, and left without another word.

Chapter 15

Later that day, I took comfort in my bedroom, mostly because it had been Meemaw's room, and I felt her presence lingering here more than anywhere else in the house. Her old Mission-style rocking chair, with its leather seat and walnut finish, sat in the corner next to an oval mirror. I'd bought a dresser, placing family photos on top, including my favorites of my friend Orphie Cates at Fashion Week, Nana and her goats, and Mama and Meemaw on the front porch.

A few months back I'd realized that Mama's smile hadn't quite reached her eyes in the photograph, but recently Hoss McClaine had put it back there, and I'd be forever grateful to him for that.

It was the picture of Meemaw, her blond streak prominent, her head tilted toward Mama, and her smile as broad and real as I'd ever seen it, that made me smile and made my heart clench in sorrow at the very same time. Family. It was the driving force behind everything Meemaw did.

In the shower, I let the warm water run over me until the bits of sorrow that I hadn't been able to shake, the lingering sadness over Dan Lee's death, Raylene's pain, and baby Boone, washed down the drain. Meemaw had wanted me back in Bliss, and here I was. I was going to make her proud, and if there was any chance I could help Raylene, then I'd do it.

I pushed back the Waverly toile shower curtain, stepping into the cold air. My skin was instantly covered with goose bumps. Not even the fluffy bath sheet or the long terry robe I bundled up in could ward off the chill. So much for relying on the new central air and heat. I slipped my frozen feet into my knockoff Ugg slippers and padded out of the small bathroom, through my bedroom, stepping on the loose floorboard that Will hadn't gotten around to fixing yet, and into the hallway to check the thermostat.

"What in the world?" I muttered. How could the inside temperature have dropped from the toasty seventy degrees I'd had it set at just a little while ago to a bone-chilling sixty-one?

I adjusted it, then hurried back to the bathroom to dry my hair so I wouldn't catch my death, as Mama always said.

I shut the door behind me to keep the warmth from the residual shower steam in the room, turned to plug in the hair dryer, and felt my heart drop to my feet. The oval mirror was still fogged, but right there in the center were crudely printed words. They were already fading away as the steam dissipated, but I knew it was a message from Meemaw. A thrill went through me and my goose bumps vanished. A new way to communicate!

The thick lines ran together and were blurry, but once I put on my glasses, the words were clear.

Help her.

I stood frozen to the spot, staring. "Help who? Raylene?" I asked aloud, my voice sounding tinny in the small room.

The shower curtain rustled. When I turned back, there were more words on the mirror.

She's innocent.

I pulled my robe tighter around my body, trying to ward off the chill. "How do you know? I think she was there, right outside waiting for Hattie. She may have pushed—"

The rest of the sentence caught in my throat as words appeared on the mirror in true ghostlike fashion.

Trust me.

The goose bumps on my skin took on a new sensation, less from the cold, more from the ominousness of those two words. I wanted to trust her. I wanted to believe Raylene and Boone could live happily ever after. But was it the truth? How could Meemaw be so sure?

The shower curtain moved again, but no more words appeared on the mirror. The fog cleared until any trace of the message was gone and I faced only my reflection. My dark hair hung in a stringy, wet mess. I tucked it behind my ear, but stopped short, leaning over the sink to look more closely at the blond streak that started at my hairline. It looked like the stripe on a skunk's back, but was it . . . was it getting blonder?

Somewhere in the distance, I heard bells ringing. I blinked, my mind and my body reconnecting again until I was back in the moment.

Will!

"You up there, Cassidy?" His voice drifted up the stairs.

I forgot about my hair as I hurried back through the bedroom and down the hall, stopping at the top of the stairwell. "Be down in a sec," I called, trying to mask the worry in my voice. *Help her.* Meemaw's words echoed in my head. "Make yourself at home."

Which, of course, he already had. His arrangement with Meemaw had given him free rein of the house to handle her repair needs. Her passing hadn't changed that. He came and went, sometimes before I even registered that he'd been around.

I flew into action, hanging my head down to do a quick blow-dry, putting on just a touch of mascara and bronzer, and throwing on a pair of gray wool pants and a red sweater.

Ten minutes later, I was in the passenger seat of Will's truck making small talk and pushing all thoughts of Raylene, Dan Lee, and Meemaw as far to the back of my mind as I could.

The cold weather, kidnapping, and murder hadn't stopped Bliss's historic downtown from brimming with holiday cheer. We ate dinner at Fuzzy's Taco Shop just off the square, an eclectic little place full of character. Casual, inexpensive, and delicious. Fuzzy's was a Bliss institution.

As we stepped outside after our dinner, the wind hit us full force. Will had changed into khaki Dockers, a navy sweater with an argyle pattern down the center, and a gray wool jacket for our date, but without a hat, the tops of his ears had turned red.

The cold front from the north had dropped the temperature to a teeth-chattering thirty-seven degrees. "It's supposed to get colder tonight," he said, pulling on a pair of black leather gloves.

"Thank God that little baby is safe." I wrapped my scarf around my neck, buttoning my jacket under my chin and pulling my knit hat down over my ears. We walked across the grassy lawn of the courthouse square, then under the pergola, the twinkling lights around us making for a perfect romantic atmosphere. I tilted my head back and took in the details of the structure I knew he'd designed, right down to the location of the grassy lawn and the rectangular slabs of stamped cement forming the walkway underneath. "It's beautiful," I said.

We walked along the bare Texas ash and American elm trees that twinkled with tiny white lights, passed Bliss Donuts on the Square, ambled by a podiatrist's office, and just as we passed An Open Book, the bookstore Josie's sister-in-law, Miriam Kincaid, had just opened, Will took my hand.

And I felt a flutter in the pit of my stomach.

He was right. My mojo was coming back. All I'd needed was some good food, some fresh air, and Will Flores holding my hand. I felt like a fifteen-year-old girl out on her first date.

We walked around the square, passing Villa Farina, Josie's bead shop, a home decor shop, and the red and white awnings of the old-fashioned ice cream parlor.

A minute later, we waited to cross the street at the corner. He pointed at the Victorian-era house across the street. "I hate to ask, but mind if I run into the Historical Society office for a second? I have to grab some paperwork."

"Sure."

The light turned green and we crossed Dallas Street, turning right and ambling up the walkway to the porch. "It'll just take a minute," he said, letting go of my hand as he pulled his keys from his pocket and unlocked the door.

He shut the door behind me, turned the dead bolt, and flipped on the light switch. The old house maintained its historic charm but managed to hold a business office ambience at the same time. The parlor to the right looked like it was used as a waiting room and maybe as a conference area. To the left I caught a glimpse of the small kitchen. Will stopped at the base of the stairs and gestured to the photographs hanging on the walls, and to a display case. "Feel free to look around. I'll be right back."

He took the stairs two at a time, glancing back at me with a slight smile playing on his lips.

That schoolgirl feeling hit me again, but I swallowed the flutters and focused on the historic artifacts. I'd been in the old courthouse at the center of the square and had walked through the museum. My favorite section of the museum's collections was the textiles. Handmade lace, quilts, and homespun fabrics filled one entire room of the courthouse.

The only similar display here was a folded-up quilt sitting on the lowest shelf of the freestanding case. I passed photographs of Bliss's founding fathers, Justin Kincaid and Charles Denison, standing in front of the Denison mansion, one of Bliss's first post office, a little one-horse building that had long ago burned down, and a picture of a stately looking building with a stone facade and a wide cement stairway leading to the double front doors. A hundred years ago, it had been Mission College. When the college moved to a nearby town, the building was purchased by the school district and it became Bliss's first high school. The district had grown, a new high school was built, and now the original Mission College was Mcafferty Middle School.

Farther down were pictures of famous outlaws who'd

passed through the Lone Star State. My own kin, Butch Cassidy, the Sundance Kid, and the Hole-in-the-Wall Gang had a place of honor. Next to it was a photo of a young Jesse James before his death and burial in Missouri, and an older man who went by the name of J. Frank Dalton and who claimed to be the real Jesse James. Finally, a photo of Bonnie and Clyde and the Barrow Gang, who, according to legend, hid out in the backyard of 2112 Mockingbird Lane when my great-great-grandma Cressida Cassidy was a girl.

"Cassidy."

I jumped, startled by Will suddenly standing beside me, the look on his face making me think he'd said my name more than once. "Got lost in the past," I said.

He took my hand and pulled me away from the pictures. "Did you see this? Josie registered it with the Texas Quilt Project before she donated it."

He pointed to the lowest shelf of a curio case and the folded quilt that lay there, showing a worn and frayed fabric faded from age. I couldn't see the whole pattern, but I knew it was a colorful mosaic, or honeycomb, pattern, the hexagon design made from gray and pastel calico prints. The quilter's stitches were short and uniform—a true testament to her skill. A quilter's stitch was like her signature—distinct and identifiable. The pads of my fingers dusted the top of the old cloth, snagging on a small section of broken stitches. "What's the Texas Quilt Project?" I asked.

He riffled through the file he'd brought down as he said, "It's a statewide documentation effort. People bring old quilts in to be photographed. The documenters record information about the quilt maker, fabric, style. Stuff like that. It's recorded on inventory forms."

"So it's the oral history of the quilts?" I had several Cassidy quilts in a closet at the old farmhouse. Meemaw had made one of them, and I thought Cressida Cassidy had made one as well. The other two I suspected were made by Texana, but I'd never been sure.

"This one belonged to Etta Place," he said, "although I don't think they know if she actually made it since it's signed E.B."

I brushed my fingers over the worn fabric, but turned to Will. "Did you get what you needed?"

One side of his mouth quirked up in a sort of half smile. "All set," he said, his smoky gaze traveling to my lips, and I got the distinct impression that he wasn't thinking about the file.

But he held his thoughts and opened the door for me and we braved the cold night again.

"There's a band at Bliss Donuts on the Square," he said.

I laughed. I didn't go out much, and the nightlife in Bliss was a far cry from that in Fort Worth or Dallas. "That's not something you hear every day. Don't bands usually play at the park or down at Buddy's?"

He stopped to stare at me. "Don't tell me you've never been to Bliss Donuts on the Square."

"Okay," I said, smiling up at him. "I won't tell you."

"Let me guess. You're a traditionalist."

"You say that as if it's a bad thing." The quirky donut shop had opened long after I'd moved to Manhattan, and since I'd been back in Bliss, I hadn't ventured away from Villa Farina and the abundance of treats there that I was slowly working my way through.

We started walking again. Will had his file folder in one gloved hand and my hand in his other. "Don't get me wrong. I love Villa Farina—"

This time I pulled him to a stop. "As well you should. What's not to love?" The Italian bakery was almost my home away from home. Bobby Farina made melt-in-your-mouth mini Italian pastries just like his family's original bake shop in New York. "Have you had Bobby's tiramisu?"

He yanked my hand until I was walking again. "I have, and it's amazing, but Bliss Donuts on the Square is a different bird. It's tough for any business to make a go of it these days—"

"Mmm-hmm." I had recurring nightmares that all Meemaw's otherworldly interventions weren't going to be enough to keep Buttons & Bows in the black and that I'd end up losing the shop and the house, all in one fell swoop.

"—so they have bands play and have a bar—"

"With their donuts."

"Which are baked."

"Healthy donuts." That sounded like it would be sacrilegious to a donut connoisseur, akin to an evening gown made out of polyester and plastic beads.

"Maybe not healthy," he said. "But tasty. Amazing variety. Cherry pie. Granola. Lemon. Brie and apricot."

"I'm game," I said as we passed Villa Farina again, hung a right, then a left at the next block.

He pulled me close, letting go of my hand and slipping his arm around my shoulder. I moved closer, my body fitting snugly against his. He was better than the little space heater I kept in my workroom. The cold left me and I felt safe and warm and comfortable.

We stopped at the orange and blue logo of Bliss Donuts on the Square. The band tonight was really a one-woman show. The poster board sitting on an easel in the corner billed the tall, auburn-haired singer as Giselle. No last name, like Cher, Madonna, and Adele. She had a folksy bent to her voice—easy to listen to as you indulged.

"They're square," I said, eyeing the flaky pastry.

"Donuts on the Square. Get it?"

I did. And apparently I wasn't alone. The place was doing a steady business. "Is that Gracie and Libby?" I asked a few minutes later as we waited for a table, sipping our coffee and nibbling our pretzchocamels, the shop's salty-and-sweet concoction.

Will turned, waggled his eyebrows at his daughter and Libby Allen—the two had become fast friends during the Margaret Moffette Lea Pageant and Ball a few months back—but stayed away from their table.

"Good dad," I said.

He kept one eye on the girls as two teenage boys ambled past their table. They kept walking, and Will turned back to me only after the boys had gone. "Hmm?"

"You're a good dad, giving the girls their space."

"That's me, dad of the year," he said with a grimace. I knew he was still beaten and battered after the blowup with Gracie over the truth about her mother and learning that her grandparents, the Mcaffertys, lived right here in Bliss and still knew nothing about her. He'd tried to take Gracie to meet them, but she'd chickened out each time.

"You're doing a pretty great job, Will. Gracie's a terrific girl."

"She is. The Mcaffertys, they're just . . . so different from us."

"She still doesn't want to meet them?"

He shook his head. "Not yet."

He glanced at his daughter one last time before we spotted an empty table in the back corner. From the looks of it, Bliss Donuts on the Square was the place to be. Besides Gracie and Libby, I saw quite a few familiar faces. Jude, the nurse from the hospital, sat at the counter. She waved at me, giving me a quick look up and down to gauge how I was faring with my injuries. I gave her a thumbs-up and a smile, wishing I could hide the slight limp I still had from the fall.

She frowned, as if she could see right through my tough-girl facade, but then the friend she was with said something to her and she turned her attention back to her donuts, the singer, and her companion.

I spotted Hattie and Arnie Barnett at a table in the corner, a stack of magazines between them. Hattie closed her issue of *Country Decor* as we came up. My pulse quickened. I should steer clear of playing detective, but maybe Hattie would say something to alleviate my worry over her and Raylene.

Arnie wore a North Texas ball cap, a quilted plaid flannel jacket, jeans, and work boots, and I got the feeling this was dressed up for him. I liked Will's version of dressed up much better.

He scraped his chair back and stood, rolling up a worn copy of *Numismatic News* and setting it on the chair. He captured Will's hand in a forceful handshake. "Good to see you, man. Out on the town, eh?" He looked from me to Hattie. "Us too."

Hattie gave a strained smile, her jacket wrapped tightly around herself. She looked pale and drawn.

"Are you feeling okay?" I asked her.

A visible shiver passed over her. "Still a little shell-shocked over Boone."

Arnie waved his hand at her. "He's back home with Raylene and everything's fine." He looked back to us and added, "We barely had time to get folks organized and start looking for him when you found him."

Will put his hand on my shoulder, giving me a little squeeze.

"I'm so relieved he's okay," I said.

Hattie nodded, but her color didn't return and all I could think was that maybe it wasn't so much Raylene and Boone that had her spooked as it was guilt. If she'd pushed Dan Lee Chrisson off the widow's walk, maybe her guilt was catching up to her.

She looked up at Arnie. "Let's go check on them."

He heaved a sigh, but nodded and skirted us to help her up.

"Arnie's right. Everything's going to be just fine," I said as I gave her a hug. Her body trembled. Images flickered in my mind, flashes of a Victorian dress, jeans and leather jacket, and a skirt with hidden tucks attached to a lining to create soft flounces, rotating, but I couldn't settle on one and a moment later everything went gray. Why couldn't I picture her in one specific outfit? "You sure you're okay?" I asked, pulling away. Was she sick, or was she guilty of something?

She nodded. "I still can't believe it. What Raylene's going through, it's awful."

We talked for another minute before Hattie took Arnie's arm. "Let's go," she said, slinging her bag over her shoulder.

As they left, Meemaw's message on the mirror came back to me. *Help her. She's innocent.* "Do you think she could have loosened the screws and pushed Dan Lee?" I asked Will after we refilled our coffee. Will wiped the table the Barnetts had just vacated. Hattie and Arnie had both left behind the magazines they'd been looking at. I tucked them in my purse to return them later and slid into the chair. Will sat opposite me, our plate of baked square confections between us. The singer was on a break and low background music became white noise.

"To avenge her sister's divorce?" Will asked as he added cream, but no sugar, to his coffee.

"Exactly. She had the opportunity. She admits she was at the Denison mansion all the time. She was there when he died."

"So were Helen Abernathy and Zinnia James. So was Arnie. So were you."

"But none of us have motives. Hattie does. And I'm pretty sure Raylene was right outside. Hattie called down for her to wait in the car, but what if she didn't? What if it was Raylene, and she snuck in and pushed him off the widow's walk? No more custody battle. No more ex-husband."

Will cradled the heavy white coffee mug. "I don't know, Cassidy. I can't picture either of them as murderers."

Which was, of course, the problem. I couldn't picture Hattie or Raylene as a murderer either, which meant . . . "Not even Helen Abernathy? I can see that," I said with a little laugh, but only half kidding.

"Maybe," he admitted, "but what's the motive there?"

As I thought about this, the most logical, if awful, explanation popped into my head instantly. "They were having an affair, of course."

One side of his mouth crept up in a wry grin. "Of course. I wouldn't have pegged Helen Abernathy as a cougar."

"I know." I sighed, frustrated. "Neither can I." Everything led back to Hattie and Raylene. "I wonder . . ."

One eyebrow arched up as Will eyed me. "Wonder what?"

"The sheriff must have searched Dan Lee's apartment, right?"

"I'm sure they did."

"And it's probably not off-limits, or anything, anymore."

His eyes narrowed. "Probably not."

"And I was just wondering if we, oh, happened by there if, just maybe, the door would be unlocked and we could, mmm . . ." I trailed off, not quite sure what we could actually do.

"You think you'd discover something Hoss and Gavin haven't?" he finished for me.

I shrugged, smiling innocently. "We might."

He leaned back, stretching his legs out and folding his arms over his chest. "That, darlin', would be breaking and entering."

My smile slipped. "Yeah, I guess it would be."

Giselle's break finally ended and she did another set. We listened for a while, our conversation shifting from felonies to Gracie, my shop, the fashion show, and the Santa suit. "I worked on it some more this afternoon after you left," I said, wondering if my charm was working and if I'd stitched any magic into the seams of Will's costume. "You should come back and try it on."

Fifteen minutes later, we were back at 2112 Mockingbird Lane. Meemaw's old farmhouse was a hop, skip, and jump from the square, but it felt like miles with Will driving, me in the passenger seat, and him not knowing a thing about the Cassidy charms. What would he think if he knew? Would he walk out, like my daddy, Tristan Walker, had? Or would he stick around like my grand-daddy had?

I was afraid to learn the answer to that particular question.

I hung up my coat while Will picked up the red velvet trousers. "They're kinda big, don't you think?"

I pointed to the fake belly hanging on one of the dress forms. "That'll fill the suit out."

He peered at what could have passed for a pregnant tummy. "I'm wearing that?"

I unhooked it from the dress form and held it out to him. "It's a sight better than stuffing a pillow under your shirt, right? This won't move or get mashed up. It's . . . authentic—"

"For Santa Claus—"

"Which you are going to be. Try it on."

When he still hesitated, I added, "It's for the kids."

He blew out a breath, finally taking the garments from me and moving with heavy feet behind the privacy screen.

I grinned as he bent over, his head ducking down behind the screen, then popping up again as he pulled the trousers on. I didn't often create designs for men and it showed in the way I'd arranged my dressing area.

The clothes hanging from the wooden slats fluttered and I heard a noise that sounded an awful lot like laughter.

Will's voice rose from behind the screen. "Laughing already? You haven't even seen me yet."

"Meemaw," I said with a low hiss. "Shush."

Will appeared by my side, slipping the half-finished Santa jacket over his jolly belly. The whole thing looked incomplete without the white fur trim, but he definitely appeared to have increased his girth tenfold. Which, surprisingly, didn't diminish his sex-appeal at all.

"It looks good," I said, swallowing the lump in my throat. He looked good.

As I pulled the sides of the jacket together, checking the fit, he put his hands on my arms and pulled me toward him. "There's something about you, Cassidy," he said, his voice low and rumbling.

"Something good?" I quipped.

He lowered his head, his lips brushing mine. "Oh yeah, very good," he said, backing me up against the couch. "This . . ." He gestured to the room. "You. Everything. I didn't know I wanted them, but God help me, I do."

A shiver wound through me at his confession. He hadn't known, but he wanted everything I had to offer. As he kissed me, my hands buried in the soft velvet of his Santa jacket, I realized that my Cassidy charm was working just fine.

Chapter 16

It had been an hour since Will left, but I still felt like Audrey Hepburn in *My Fair Lady*, a silly grin on my face, the kiss between us lingering on my lips and filling me with a sensation that felt like champagne bubbles. My mind drifted back to the phone call Will had gotten from Gracie, the tilt of his head as he'd listened, the way he'd raked his hand through his hair.

"Sorry to cut this off, Cassidy," he'd said after hanging up. "Gracie's locked out of the house."

He'd unbuttoned the Santa jacket, slipped it off and handed it to me. He flipped the suspenders holding up the pants off his shoulders and slid the faux belly off. Suddenly my arms were piled high with half of his St. Nick suit while he strode to the workroom.

Before I'd had time to hang the pieces back on the dress form, he'd disappeared behind the privacy screen and stepped back out, fully dressed. "I'll see you tomorrow," he'd said with a slight grin and another light kiss, this time on my cheek.

"Are you ready?"

Madelyn's voice snapped me out of the memory. Standing next to her in the cold shadows in front of

Parkside Apartments in the north side of town, each of us dressed in black jeans, a black turtleneck, and my curls flowing out from beneath a black knit beanie, I felt my smile slip.

Madelyn peered through the darkness toward the tricolored building. "What are we doing here, Harlow?" she asked. The whites of her eyes were bright under the streetlight and her hands twisted nervously.

"We can't sit by and not try to help Raylene and Boone," I said. "That baby needs his mama. And knowing Gavin McClaine, I'm afraid she's going to wind up in trouble for Dan Lee's death, even if she's not guilty."

She grabbed my arm. "But what if she did it?"

I shook my head. "She couldn't have," I said.

"Harlow, you want to believe that, but who else would have wanted him dead?"

I hugged my coat tighter. "He was the father of her baby. She loved him. She wouldn't have killed him."

Madelyn didn't look convinced, but she stuck by my side as we sidled into the building trying to look nonchalant in our cat burglar outfits. She dropped her voice to a whisper. "And you really think we'll find something the sheriff didn't find?"

My conscience pricked. It was one thing digging into a man's death on my own to help an old friend, but dragging Madelyn into it? "What did you tell Billy, Madelyn?"

"He's in Austin at a conference," she said. "No explaining necessary. But if we get caught—"

As a wave of second thoughts crept into my mind, Will's warning stood out front and center. *Breaking and entering.* Which meant that if we were caught, we could go to the Bliss County Jail.

"You've been mixed up in murder before, Harlow, but now?" Madelyn dragged her toe along the floor like she was in ballet class and was moving from first to third to fifth position. "There's a murderer in Bliss. Whether it's Raylene or Hattie or someone else, we should stay out of it."

"I can't," I said, fighting against the sliver of guilt churning my stomach. "Boone is innocent in all of this. And that baby needs his mama," I said again as we stopped in front of Dan Lee's apartment. Madelyn plastered her back against the wall as I tried the knob.

It turned.

Madelyn grabbed my hand before I could push the door open.

"You don't have to come in," I said.

She moved past me, throwing a glance over her shoulder. "The jailhouse looks pretty nice."

I stifled a laugh, right along with the nerves creeping up my throat, ducked in behind her, and closed the door.

I pushed Will's sensible warning out of my mind and looked around. What would we be able to find that Hoss and Gavin hadn't?

The beams from our flashlights cut through the darkness enough for me to see that the apartment was small, uncluttered, and had entirely masculine decor. If Maggie had spent much time here, she hadn't left her mark. Madelyn opened and closed the cupboards in the kitchen with her gloved hands. "You never know," she said, but the shelves held only plates, bowls, and a few jar glasses.

She checked the last cupboard, slamming it shut a second later. "Three mismatched coffee mugs," she muttered. "He was a sad sack."

I lifted my gaze from the accordion file folder sitting

on the computer desk. "Shh! Someone's going to hear us!" I hissed.

She buttoned her lips, tugging her beanie down, wiry strands of hair poking out from underneath it. "Sorry," she whispered. She angled her flashlight at me, the light shining in my eyes for a split second before she trained it on the file. "What's that?"

"Looks like the divorce agreement. Employment contract. Specs to a house. Newspaper articles. More newspaper articles." I held one up. "This one has his name on the byline. He did a little writing."

"What's the article on?"

I went back to the stack of clippings. "Hobbyists in North Texas." Not very exciting. I kept leafing through the papers, more and more discouraged. We weren't going to find anything, just like Gavin and Hoss didn't find anything. I took out a stack of papers to sort through, starting with a chunk of brittle, aged newspaper clippings. Madelyn slid the accordion file in front of her and dug through it.

A few seconds later, she gasped, tugging at the vertical slats of the folder.

My glasses slipped. I pushed them up, staring at her. "What are you doing?"

"There's a paper stuck at the bottom," she said. "It won't budge."

I took it from her and, without thinking, I tipped it upside down. Pages fell in clumps onto the table. A pencil dropped, bouncing against the cheap pine. I angled the file folder sideways. "Shine the light in here," I said. She did, and as I peered in the folder, the beam landed on the corner of a light-colored piece of paper.

I gripped it between my thumb and finger, pulling as hard as I dared.

Madelyn drew in a sharp breath. "Don't rip it!"

"Whatever it is," I said. It was probably nothing. Just a receipt or something. I inched the paper out until I was able to withdraw it completely. "Got it!"

"It looks like ... Is it a birth certificate?" she asked, directing her light onto the sheet and reading aloud. "'Charles Denison.' Why would Dan Lee have had Charles Denison's birth certificate?"

That was a good question. "It's not the same Charles Denison," I said under my breath. He'd been born around the time of my great-great-grandparents, but this birth certificate was dated thirty-five years ago.

Madelyn looked from the paper in my hand to my face. "So does that mean ..."

I remembered Dan Lee's comment to me that he knew what it was like to not know your parents. Maybe he hadn't meant it literally. The story around Bliss had always been that the Denisons left town after Charles had lost his house to Justin Kincaid. What if they'd changed their names and kept their identities secret to hide their humiliation? "That Dan Lee Chrisson was not who he said he was?" I finished.

My mind raced, trying to piece together what this could possibly mean. If Dan Lee's real name was Charles Denison, that meant that he'd died at the house that had once belonged to his own family.

It felt horribly wrong in my mind. Had he and his family been hiding their real identities all these years? Another question occurred to me. Did Raylene know the truth?

Or Hattie?

Or did someone else discover his secret?

Madelyn sank down on the slouchy brown couch, frowning. "What about this? Your school chum, Raylene, found out her ex-husband was really the great-great-however-many-greats-grandson of Charles Denison and killed him for the family money."

I perched on the chipped coffee table, facing her. "I don't think there is any family money. Charles Denison—the original, I mean—lost the house to Justin Kincaid. The Denison family eventually moved out of Bliss, from what I remember." And apparently came back as the Chrissons.

We both fell silent, thinking, until Madelyn piped up with, "What if she didn't know that? What if he told her, or she found out, and she thought he had money he was keeping from her? What if she thought they were an oil family like the Kincaids?"

I sighed. "Or what if Raylene was just a batty old bessie bug?"

Madelyn stared at me, lips parted. "Sorry, love. I've no bloody idea what a bessie bug is."

"It's a beetle," I started to explain, but then waved my own words away as another thought catapulted into my head. "Never mind. She's got to be perfectly sane. I'm trying to prove Raylene, and Hattie, too, didn't have anything to do with all of this."

"You may not be able to do that," she said.

She was right about that, but I was still going to try. I still wanted to believe in their innocence. Which meant that maybe I was the one crazy as a bessie bug. "What if Dan Lee Chrisson . . . or Charles Denison . . . was mixed up in something else? Otherwise why would he continue to hide who he really was? Drugs? Or maybe gambling, like his namesake?"

Madelyn scratched her head through her beanie. "So why was he even at the mansion?"

A low howl suddenly came from outside as the wind picked up. My hand tightened on the clippings I'd taken from the file and I pointed the flashlight at them. My thoughts raced. Will had said Dan Lee was a history buff, and always at the old house doing renovations. Why? Was he trying to reconnect to his past? "These are old," I said after I'd skimmed the papers. "Historical articles about Jesse James. Bonnie and Clyde." I kept reading, and then filled Madelyn in. "They all came through these parts. Says they robbed a jewelry store on the square, then a stagecoach."

"They hid out in your yard, didn't they, Harlow?" Madelyn asked.

I nodded. "That's one way Meemaw got the farmhouse listed in the historical registry," I said, recalling the story I'd heard too many times to count. Bonnie's mother had been a garment sewer in Cement City, just outside of Dallas. It was tenuous, at best, but I felt a thread of a connection to Bonnie Parker by her presence in my house, as well as through her mother being a seamstress.

"Clyde played poker with Charles Denison before he lost the family home to the Kincaids. Or so the story goes," I told her. "Bonnie and Clyde spent three days and two nights in Bliss before the law caught up with them again."

An image of a young woman in a silk dressing gown suddenly flashed before my eyes, a shimmer of gold on her finger.

Who had that dressing gown belonged to? And what did any of it have to do with Dan Lee Chrisson?

"Anything else?" Madelyn asked.

I finished looking through the articles and my stomach flip-flopped. Oh boy. I nodded grimly. "There's one here about Butch Cassidy."

Chapter 17

Twenty minutes later Madelyn and I had dropped the accordion file at the Sheriff's Department, leaving it at the back entrance where I knew Hoss McClaine would find it. Not entirely ethical, perhaps, but the best I could do. A few minutes later we were back at Buttons & Bows.

"Why was he so interested in all that old history?" I mused.

"And why was he working on the Denison house, pretending he was somebody else?"

"Searching for gold," I spouted, completely blank on any real reasons.

"Or frankincense and myrrh," Madelyn said with a wry grin. "It is Christmastime, after all."

I bit my lip to stop from laughing. If we hadn't been talking about a dead man, after having just illegally entered a residence, both dressed like bad cat burglars, the whole scene would have been funny. We'd found a baby in a manger yesterday, for heaven's sake. "At least the baby's named Boone and not Jesus," I said, feeling more than a little punch-drunk.

Madelyn stretched out on the red velvet settee and

closed her eyes. She'd kept her beanie on her head. Within seconds her breathing slowed and grew steady.

I, on the other hand, knew I wouldn't sleep. I'd wanted to clear my suspicions about Raylene and Hattie's possible involvement in Dan's death, but all I'd done was to open the door into a big ol' endless dry pasture. Dan Lee had been lying to his wife for who knew how long. Sounded like another motive for murder to me.

I doodled in my sketchbook, writing down DAN LEE CHRISSON. Why did he change his name? A cloud of warm air encircled me and my eyelids grew heavy. I was more tired than I'd thought.

I tried to focus on the letters, but they wavered, some becoming darker, almost lifting off the page with a shadowed background. Were my eyes playing tricks . . . or was Meemaw involved? But how could she make the letters dance before my eyes?

I didn't know how she was doing it, but she was. Slowly, a pattern started to emerge. The letters rearranged themselves, as if my subconscious mind knew where they really belonged. And then suddenly, like a zipper closing the gaping back of a garment, it made perfect sense. "It's an anagram," I said under my breath, and then louder, "Dan Lee Chrisson and Charles Denison. They have the same letters."

Madelyn stirred. "What, love?"

"The letters!" I tossed a fringe-trimmed pillow at her. "Dan Lee Chrisson and Charles Denison have the same letters!"

She propped herself up on her elbows. "Why go to the trouble?"

"Maybe it was his way of staying connected to his real identity."

"But why give up his name in the first place?"

"Maybe he thought that if people knew who he really was and saw him snooping around the house his family had once owned, they'd start asking questions."

"Except no one around here recognized him."

I snapped my fingers. "But maybe someone did!"

She looked skeptical. "Harlow, maybe he just wanted to visit the house that had once belonged to his family. He might have been the sentimental type."

She might be the British voice of reason in my Southern mind, but I was sticking with my new theory. Someone had to know that Dan Lee Chrisson was really Charles Denison.

But the question remained: Why was he murdered?

Chapter 18

I called Raylene Lewis first thing the next morning. I wanted to hear from the horse's mouth where she'd been when Dan Lee had died. Maybe Michele Brown had been wrong and Raylene hadn't been on Mayberry Street at all.

She didn't pick up, though. I left her a message asking her to come by Buttons & Bows later that afternoon, and then ran through my theories. Madelyn and I had done well, but I decided that I needed to talk to someone who hadn't just committed a crime with me and who wasn't a tad high on the chase. I considered calling Mama and Nana over, but decided against involving them. We had enough secrets to keep without worrying them over me digging into the latest suspicious death in town.

Will Flores. After my kin, he was the person who came to mind, maybe even before Mama and Nana. But convincing myself that talking things through with him was sane took some doing.

"Are you sure that's a good idea?" Madelyn said when I called to run the idea by her.

"Pretty sure," I said. Not a hundred percent, but close to eighty-five.

"You're not going to tell him everything, are you, love?"

By "everything," I knew she meant confessing about Butch and his wish in the Argentinean fountain, the Cassidy charms, and Meemaw's ghost. "I've thought about it," I said truthfully. I just didn't know if he could accept it.

"Don't. Don't do it, Harlow. Tell him what we found last night if you want to, but not the rest. What if he doesn't believe you? Or worse, what if he freaks out? Takes Gracie away? Blows the whistle?"

The nerves in my stomach coiled and tightened and I didn't know what to do. I mulled it over while I finished the seams on Mrs. James's outfit for the fashion show. I'd seen the look on Will's face the night before when I'd mentioned Dan Lee's apartment. In my experience with him over the last few months, Will Flores was a by-the-book kind of man. He'd also made it clear that he felt something for me. So how would he take the news that I hadn't heeded his warning?

"He won't like it, that's for certain," I muttered aloud.

Something clanged in the kitchen, the sound of metal hitting metal. "Meemaw!" I could run through my theories with my great-grandmother if she'd make her presence known.

I raced through the dining room, past the dining table with the sewing machines left from the day before still set up for the second Santa dollmaking class, and skidded to a stop at the threshold of the kitchen. The rattling sound had subsided, but my nerves still jangled. I looked around for evidence of Meemaw, but the red and white checkerboard-patterned curtains below the sink were still. The copper pots and pans hanging from an exposed beam above the pine farm table swayed slightly, the left-over motion not strong enough to bang them together anymore.

"Dang it all," I said, jamming my hands on my hips and staring down ... Nothing. "Loretta Mae Cassidy, you're gonna be the death of me." And she would. Sometimes having her around was a comfort and I couldn't ask for anything more. But other times, like now when I was already on edge, it felt more like a haunting.

Something rattled behind me, the distinct sound of tinkling glass raising the hair on my arms. I whirled around and gaped. "No, Meemaw! They'll break!"

A dozen old clear-glass milk bottles, each one capped with its own galvanized top, stood in a circular galvanized metal frame. Lightbulbs clustered in the center of the frame, the diffused light shining through the glass. It was a quirky lighting fixture, one that Meemaw had made special, and I knew that the milk bottles, embossed with a cow and the words "farm fresh milk" were irreplaceable.

The distinct sound of glass hitting glass made the hair on my arms rise. Warm air encircled me, but did nothing to calm my nerves. "Meemaw, so help me—"

The chandelier fell completely still, but before I could draw in a steady breath, the Dutch door in the kitchen swung open and a gust of frigid air blew in. The hinges creaked and I could have sworn it sounded like someone was saying, "Tell him. Tell him."

"Fine," I said defiantly, resisting the temptation to stomp my foot. But was she talking about Madelyn and me sneaking into Dan Lee Chrisson's apartment, or was she talking about everything else?

I waited, expecting another haunted response. The

kitchen door swung closed with a quiet click, but that was it. No more clanking pots. No more shimmying curtains. No more rattling bottles.

Madelyn's warning came back to me. *Don't do it. Don't tell him.* But I listened to Meemaw. I slipped on my burnt red Frye harness boots, slung my purse over my shoulder, and hurried out the front door.

The Winter Wonderland festival was set to begin the next day. The square was already buzzing with holiday celebrations. Over the next few days, carolers would stroll the streets, the stores in town would offer last-minute holiday sales, and a reenactment of the Christmas story with Mary and Joseph's journey to Bethlehem and the birth of baby Jesus would play every night at the Opera House on the corner of Dallas and Magnolia Streets downtown. The reopening of the Denison mansion after being closed up for so many years and the fashion show tomorrow night were the last scheduled events.

I turned away from the square and the festivities, instead heading north up Dallas Street to Bliss's town offices. The Planning Department and Will's office were within spittin' distance from Buttons & Bows, housed in the old Baptist church just a few blocks up. Faded brick siding and a peaked roofline showed the church's age. The building had been around since the late 1800s and it looked it. It had been remodeled, and I could almost hear the whispering prayers as I stepped through the door to the old vestibule.

The Sheriff's Department occupied one side of the building and the city offices were located on the other side. I bypassed the law enforcement side, turning on my heel and passing what used to be the sanctuary. I peeked in. It hadn't changed much. The original pews had been pushed up against one wall, but it still felt like a place of worship.

I continued down the hall until I reached Will's office, knocked on the doorframe and poked my head in. Will was hunched over a long table under the windows on the far wall. The model I'd seen at his house a few months ago sat on the table. Miniature houses and buildings dotted the faux landscape of Bliss's town square and historic district. I could see instantly that the room fit him.

"So this is where the magic happens," I said.

He turned, a slow smile gracing his lips and reaching to his eyes. "Come on in, darlin'."

I came up next to him. "It looks done," I said, gazing at the model. When I'd first seen the time and detail he'd put into it, I'd realized how alike we were. He was passionate about buildings, how they fit in the environment, shape, and light in the same way I was passionate about design, textiles, color, and what it all could do for a person.

I pointed toward the domed roof and limestone exterior of the courthouse on the square. "It's beautiful."

"I move it to the museum this week," he said. "Third floor of the courthouse. Bliss's architectural history."

He'd paid attention to every last detail. I imagined that if one plastic composite piece was missing from any of the buildings, he would have known it as surely as I'd have zeroed in on a missing bead or button on a garment.

"You finished my house," I said, pointing to the replica of the little redbrick and yellow farmhouse a block off the square. The roofline and dormers were perfect and the other details were exquisite—the wooden porch, tiny rocking chairs, and even a miniature Buttons & Bows sign next to the arbor, a flagstone walkway, and flowers in the front yard.

I looked around the office. Spread out on his desk were two sets of blueprints. "What are these?" I asked, pointing to the white and blue pages, stalling. I wasn't quite ready to blurt out my crime and my secret family history.

He tapped one set with his fingertips. "These are the original blueprints of the Denison mansion," he said. "And these"—he flattened out the second set—"are the current blueprints based on the remodeling that's happened over the years. We have to use both when remodeling if there's any structural change. The widow's walk, for example, was added after the Kincaids took ownership, but it's not reflected on the blueprints."

It looked like a mess of lines and numbers and smudges to me, but Will bent over the plans, flipped pages, and read the schematics. As I watched him process the information on the plans, I saw another layer to him—and another connection between us. We were both creative and ardent about our art forms, but we were also bookish. We'd gone to school to hone our crafts, had practical experience to understand the foundations, and from there we'd each developed the paths that would help us marry our knowledge with our creativity.

My practical experience with Maximilian had helped me fine-tune my construction skills and my tailoring, but my Cassidy intuition helped me feel the designs on a subconscious level.

Will's job with Bliss probably helped him keep his practical skills up. He worked on city-owned buildings, from the library to offices to park structures, but from what I'd seen of Will and his interest in the historic district of Bliss, that's where his passion lay.

"I want to show you something," he said. "Look right there."

He touched the historic blueprint and I peered at the white space on the drawing, but couldn't make heads or tails of it.

"This is where the widow's walk was eventually built," he continued. He drew a line down with his finger. "And here's where a side bedroom was added on."

I turned on my cowboy-booted heel, pacing Will's office. On the short walk over, I'd prepared myself to tell Will everything, but seeing him again so soon after our date and our kiss sent my nerves spiraling. We had become good friends—more than friends. I cared about him and I cared about his daughter. Suddenly my crime from the night before, coupled with the weight of the Cassidy secret, felt overwhelming. I didn't know if I could confess any of it to him.

My mind raced, going through the options. I could keep it all tight under my belt, but there would always be a big brick wall between us. He could never really know and trust me if he didn't know the whole truth, but would the truth be too much for him to accept? Maybe he'd think the women in my family were all freaks. Maybe he'd think I was more an aberration than a woman enchanted with the ability to help others realize their deepest desires. I drew in a deep breath.

It was time to come clean—or at least partway clean—with him. If he hung around me long enough, he was sure to notice. I was surprised he hadn't already, what with Meemaw's antics.

"Will, I have something to—"

"Harlow!"

My heart plunged to my feet at Madelyn's screech. She stood in the doorway of Will's office, shooting me a frantic look that said, *Don't you dare tell him.* She practically flew to my side and hovered like a hummingbird at a honeysuckle bloom.

From the depths of my purse, my cell phone rang. I dug past the magazines I still needed to return to Hattie, past my wallet and my travel sewing kit, and finally landed on my phone. I didn't recognize the number. "Hello?"

"Harlow Jane," Mrs. Helen Abernathy said. "Come on over here, would you? We have some things to discuss." With that, she ended the call.

Chapter 19

My position in the town's hierarchy was somewhere between that of a ranch hand out on FM Road 31 and Josie's new role as wife to one of Bliss's favorite sons. And I was happy with that. I felt comfortable flying under the radar. All of the Cassidy women did. Most of the time we succeeded in remaining there, but occasionally, being lower on the totem pole got my dander up.

Being haughtily summoned by Mrs. Helen Abernathy put me in a mood. Having Zinnia James request the pleasure of my company was one thing. After all, she was my unofficial benefactor and the business she sent my way was going a long way toward keeping Buttons & Bows afloat—no small feat in a small town prone to polyester and corduroy.

To ignore Mrs. Abernathy's call would lead to trouble, seeing as how she and Mrs. James were . . . I'd been about to finish that thought with the word "friends," but really, I wasn't so sure "friendship" hit the mark. They were cordial, sure, but there always seemed to be a thread of tension between them.

But more than anything, I was curious. I wasn't sure why she had summoned me, but it had piqued my interest. Telling Will about my charm and my recent criminal activity would have to wait.

I left Will and Madelyn to stare at each other, offering them both a quick wave and an "I'll see you later!" Then I leaned into the icy wind as I hurried back home. Why hadn't I driven to the town offices?

A few minutes later, I sat in the old truck I'd inherited from Meemaw. "Come on, Bessie," I said, holding my breath as I turned the key. It took three tries, but it finally sputtered to life. I blasted the heat first thing. It didn't do much to thaw my frozen fingers and toes, but it was a start.

I rumbled north toward the ritzier part of town the Abernathys called home. The house sat amidst grassy fields and slightly rolling hills. Horses meandered across the large properties, and occasionally, a Longhorn, its horns looking far too heavy to be held up by its head, popped into view.

The truck lurched to a stop in front of the Aberna-thys' sprawling stone house. I didn't dare park in the driveway for fear old Bessie would leak oil and tarnish the pristine cobbled drive.

Instead, I parked along the road, tightened my coat around me, and fought the wind as I walked up the stone path, past a little pond, over a mini bridge to the other side of the pond, and up the front steps. I stopped long enough to tilt my head back and stare up at the turrets and faux balcony just above the entry.

The Royal Abernathys.

I reached the massive, hand-scraped wood door, used the door knocker, then stood back, shivering, while I waited. And waited. Finally, as I raised my hand to knock again, the enormous door swung open and Mrs. Abernathy stood there. I stared, my breath catching in my throat. She was wearing the exact outfit I'd imagined her in the day I'd fallen from the widow's walk at the Denison mansion. The asymmetrical lavender sweater was darker than the one I'd imagined, but it buttoned at the top and hung beautifully. A white tailored blouse with darts and a flared hem peeking out at the bottom of the sweater made it a bit whimsical. The look was finished off with coordinating lavender pants.

"Goodness gracious, Harlow, what is it now? Didn't your mother teach you any manners? Every time I see you, you stare in horror."

Mama taught me plenty of manners, but they flew out the window in the face of a memory. Or maybe it had been a premonition. Was my charm evolving? I clamped my mouth shut, trying to school my expression. "I—I'm sorry, Mrs. Abernathy. I just . . . that outfit . . ." I shook the cotton from my thoughts. "You look lovely," I finally said.

She stepped aside, allowing me to pass into the massive front entry. The floor was a continuation of the stone from outside and the whole place reminded me of a medieval castle.

Beyond the foyer was an enormous gathering room that spilled into the kitchen, divided by a long work surface of glossy granite. In the living area, heavy neutral-hued furniture sat in stark contrast to the distinctive stonework of the house. The only bit of homeyness came from a neatly folded stack of throws and a large dark wood antique ladder leaning against a corner wall, with quilts hanging from each of the ladder's rungs.

I recognized a Colonial-era whole-cloth quilt and a broderie perse, a time-consuming project in which flowers and motifs were cut from expensive pieces of fabric and tiny seams were turned before they were appliquéd to a solid piece of cloth. Hung haphazardly on the bottom rung, like the runt of a goat herd, was a traditional pioneer patchwork.

The pieces of women's history lent a personal touch to the room, but they weren't enough to soften the general atmosphere.

She held out her hand to me. The formality sent me reeling—I was so out of my league here. The Cassidy clan had always hung out in the kitchen, no one thought a thing about padding around with their shoes off, and I was pretty sure no one really knew the definition of the word "formal."

Sure, I could sew for the rich and famous all day long, but mingle with them? Um, no. I was a behind-the-scenes kind of girl—the very reason I created clothing rather than modeling it. Well, that and the fact that I had an innate talent for it, and at five seven and size eight, next to a posse of five-foot-ten-inch, size zero women, I was vertically and weight challenged.

I summoned up my Cassidy pride and gumption. Nana had gone to school with Mrs. Abernathy, and Meemaw had probably seen the woman in diapers. I could hold my own with one of Bliss's elite.

I drew off my red suede gloves and started to shake her hand, but she yanked it back as if she'd been burned by my touch. "Your coat, Harlow."

"Oh." The heat of embarrassment rose up my neck. "Oh, sorry. I thought . . ."

Uh-uh. I wasn't going to let three little words zap my confidence. I slipped out of my coat—and the sweater I had on underneath my jacket—and gave them to her. "Never mind."

After she handed them off to a maid, she turned back to me. Her lips pursed. "Thank you for coming. You're looking none the worse for wear after your fall."

"Still a trifle sore, but I'm fine." There was no point harboring resentment because the woman didn't like me. I reminded myself that whatever she felt stemmed from the falling-out she, Mrs. James, and my grandmother had had years ago. It had nothing to do with me.

"Fashion emergency?" I asked, letting my lips curve up.

She didn't return the smile, nor did she deign to answer the question, making it clear that I wasn't on her speed dial even if she were in fashion crisis. Instead, she gestured to the high-backed gray velvet couch. "Have a seat, Harlow."

Again with the formality. A checkered NASCAR flag went up in my head, but I scooted toward the sofa—by way of the quilts, just to take a closer gander at the fine stitching and intricate details—finally perching on the edge of the sofa and clasping my hands in my lap. "Love the quilts," I said. "Are they family heirlooms?"

"Of course. Why else would I keep them?" she said snootily. "Quilting bees. Underground railroad. Marriage quilts. My family did it all."

"I just saw one at the Historical Society that's part of the Texas Quilt Project—"

She held up her hand, silencing me. So much for idle chitchat and Southern hospitality. I knew why I'd come, but good Lord, why had she called me here? Maybe she wanted to pump me for information about Zinnia James. Or was I about to be chastised for not having the outfits complete for the Winter Wonderland fashion show? What if she wanted to coerce me into helping her convince my grandmother to sell her property to the city? Or . . .

I tried to wrangle my spiraling thoughts, but finally I decided to just let them all go and cut to the chase. "What can I do for you, Mrs. Abernathy?"

Her heels clicked against the wood floor as she walked around the seating area and lowered herself onto a black linen slipper chair. The accent pillow behind her back made her posture perfect and I wondered if the woman ever slouched. Or relaxed. Perhaps she was missing that particular gene. "Harlow," she said, followed by a weighty sigh, "that man plunging to his death has put quite a damper on the fashion show."

It was a big downer for Dan Lee Chrisson, too, I thought grimly.

"Don't get me wrong," she continued. "It was a tragedy. Thank heavens you weren't hurt."

"Thank you," I said, seizing the opening. "Did you know him well?"

"Well enough to know he didn't belong on that widow's walk. What in heaven's name he was doing up there we may never know, but he was, and now he's dead. But, Harlow, we've put too much time and money into the renovations of the house to let this stall the reopening."

"I don't think it will," I said.

"We need to do some PR. The Winter Wonderland starts tomorrow, and we have just days until the fashion show and the grand reopening of the Denison mansion. All the kids think Santa's dead. Or at least the man who was to play Santa."

"But Will Flores is taking over," I said. "The suit's just about done and he'll be ready to hear all the toy wishes of the boys and girls."

Her chin drifted down. "Is he, now?"

"Yes. I told Mrs. James. It's all worked out."

She folded one arm over her chest, angling the other up to cup her chin with her hand. "Splendid. That saves you scads of time. No need to scramble to find someone to fill in. Will Flores," she said, more to herself than to me. "Not robust, but yes, he'll do."

I bristled. Mrs. James had put me in charge of all the events leading up to the fashion show. Mrs. Abernathy's criticisms at this late date rankled me. "He'll more than do, Mrs. Abernathy. He's going to make a great St. Nick."

"Yes, of course," she said, but I wasn't sure she'd actually heard me. "So he'll be ready for pictures this afternoon then?"

I sputtered. "What pictures?"

"PR, Harlow. I just got off the phone with Mrs. Brighton, that amateur photographer who seems to work just about everywhere. She'll take them. She was the best I could do on short notice. We'll meet at the Denison mansion at three o'clock sharp, do the photo op, and make sure that everyone in town knows that Santa is alive and well."

"Will has a job, you know—"

"You say he's agreed to play the part, so he'll have to make the time for this," she said, waving away my objection. "We've invested far too much time and money to let this event collapse because that man was nosing around and fell to his death."

"Mrs. Abernathy!" I exclaimed, but her words sent my thoughts reeling. What made her think Dan Lee had been nosing around, and what did she think he was looking for?

"Oh, come now. I'm not going to mince words with you. I know far too much about the Cassidys and how you all love to be coy."

I stared at her, struggling to stay seated and not simply storm out. "Why do you think he was nosing around?" I asked after my anger passed.

"Oh, for heaven's sake, he was paid to work on the renovations." She leaned forward, just enough to punctuate her words and leave me wondering what else she knew. "It's too bad he fell, but he had no business out there on the widow's walk."

"He fell, Mrs. Abernathy," I said slowly, "but it wasn't an accident."

She didn't bat an eye, but the line of her lips drew thinner. "Is that so," she said, more of a statement than a question. "That is unfortunate."

"He had a baby—"

"And a girlfriend, from what I hear," she snapped. "Don't paint him as some saint, Harlow. He was a coward. He left his wife and child and took up with a pretty young thing who'd stroke his ego."

I couldn't argue with any of that, but there was something about Mrs. Abernathy's intensity that gave me pause. "That doesn't mean he deserved to die."

"Well, of course not, but it's not your business."

She was right, of course, but images of Raylene's tearstained face and her little baby, Boone, were permanently stamped in my mind. I was determined to do what I could to help her, if that was even possible.

"The sheriff says the railing was tampered with. Will looked at it too. The screws were stripped. They couldn't be tightened." I met her gaze. "Someone pushed him, Mrs. Abernathy, and I'm trying to figure out who."

Chapter 20

Design school had taught me that a dart is a short jab into a pristine piece of cloth. Maximilian taught me that garments can be founded on the concept of darts, and with the right fabric and perfect fit, they can make a piece of clothing beautiful.

But Meemaw taught me that a dart is nothing but an incomplete line. "A painter uses color, Harlow. A composer uses notes. A writer creates images with words. We use lines in the same way—to express ideas and thoughts and evoke emotions."

A carefully placed dart gives a designer control. The Santa suit had no darts. No lines to control. And walking into the Denison mansion with the suit draped over my arm, I felt my lack of control spill into the whole Winter Wonderland event.

Yes, the halls of the old Victorian were decked with evergreen boughs, poinsettias, sheer wire-rimmed red ribbon, and shimmery glass ornaments delicately piled in a silver bowl sitting on the occasional table. But a frenzy of angry words came at me, batted back and forth from two voices I recognized all too well.

"This is absurd."

"It's necessary. The man died. We need to—"

"You are a manipulative—"

"No, pragmatic."

"You've turned this into a circus."

"Zinnia Hecker James, so help me," Mrs. Abernathy said, a thread of venom in her voice. "We need to do this damage control, and we need to do it now."

I slung the garment bag over my arm and looked for a way to slip past the parlor where they were arguing, but it was impossible. The kitchen was straight ahead, and the stairs were to the right. They'd see me no matter which way I turned.

I did the only thing I could think of. As quietly as I could, I turned the doorknob and backed outside into the brittle cold.

"Where are we sneaking off to?"

"Lord almighty!" I gasped, spinning around.

Will stood just behind me, a wicked little grin on his face. "Mexico? The Bahamas? Somewhere warm."

"Why, Mr. Flores," I said, doing my best Scarlett O'Hara, "I do believe you're proposing something indecent and immoral." And tempting. "But if we leave," I said, playing along and giving a pointed look at the door, "who'll make sure Mrs. James and Mrs. Abernathy don't kill each other?"

"Let Gavin McClaine earn his keep 'round here."

I had a fashion show to put on and kids who needed to sit on Santa's lap. "I don't think Deputy Gavin has the gumption to handle those two women. They're at each other's throats in there."

"Ah, hence the sneaking out." He took the garment bag from me. "My new duds?"

"All ready for your debut as St. Nick."

"Great," he said, but the enthusiasm in his voice didn't reach his eyes.

He started to open the door, but I put my gloved hand on his, stopping him. "Will?"

I'd escaped a full confession earlier, but the urge to tell him everything kept surfacing inside of me and I couldn't tamp it down. Meemaw always told me that piecing together a quilt was like figuring out how the different parts of your life worked together. Sometimes things clashed, but mostly you ended up with something warm and comforting, even if it wasn't what you'd planned. But there was nothing comforting about the argument going on inside the mansion, or about the death of Dan Lee Chrisson, aka Charles Denison. There was nothing warm and fuzzy about suddenly being wrapped up in another suspicious death. And there was nothing comforting about keeping secrets from Will.

Now was not the time or the place to talk about my charms, but I needed to tell him about what Madelyn and I had discovered.

He paused, his hand on the door handle.

Quickly, and through chattering teeth, I filled him in on what Madelyn and I had done after he'd left the night before, ending with, "So it looks like Dan Lee Chrisson was really Charles Denison."

He lost his smile altogether. "You broke in?"

"The door was unlocked. I figured the Sheriff's Department left it open, or maybe Maggie went back there and left again in a hurry." I'd come up with several possibilities, but really, did it matter?

Will put his hand on the back of his neck, looking down at me with humorless eyes. "That was risky, Harlow."

I'd been around Will enough to know that he used my given name only when he was ultra-serious. Usually it was Cassidy or Darlin'. He'd called me Sugar once or twice, but I could count the number of times he'd called me Harlow on one hand.

Harlow was my great-great-great-grandmother Texana's maiden name, but it didn't sound quite right spilling from Will's mouth.

"I know," I admitted, "but I thought we might find something, and I was right. He wasn't who he said he was. Maybe Raylene figured that out. Or Hattie and Arnie. Or maybe Mrs. Abernathy did. One of them could have been blackmailing him."

"That assumes he had some important reason for keeping it a secret," Will said.

"He must have. Why else change your name?"

He frowned. "You need to tell Hoss," he said.

Relief flowed through me. He didn't look thrilled, but he didn't look horrified either. "Do I?"

"If it'll help their investigation, then hell yes."

He was right, of course. I'd have to tell the sheriff. I'd just leave Madelyn's name out of it.

"There's something else," I said, the cold seeping into my bones. My fingers and toes had turned numb and I was sure my nose had to be as red as Rudolph's.

He waited, not looking the least bit chilled by the thirty-five-degree weather. "Mrs. Abernathy ..." I hadn't really put into words what had been bothering me since the day I fell from the roof, but ...

"What about her?" he prompted.

"Mrs. James and I met her here just after Dan, er, Charles Denison died. The thing is, Mrs. Abernathy and Mrs. James are like clones of each other."

"Don't let them hear you say that," he said with a wry smile.

"Oh, I won't. But they are. Always dressed to the nines. Completely tuned to what others think, say, and do. And punctual. They grew up the same as Loretta Mae and they have her same philosophy."

"You mean about showing respect to whoever you're meeting by being on time?"

I soundlessly snapped my gloved fingers, frozen through the knit. "Exactly. If you're late, then it's a slap in the face to the other person, saying you don't respect their time."

"Don't know if I agree with that," he said. "Sometimes things are out of a person's control."

"Right, but that's just it. Not to them. Mrs. Abernathy was late that day. Granted it had been raining, but she said the traffic light was out on Henrietta."

"What are you getting at?"

"I'd just come over Henrietta and the light was fine—"

"It could have gone out after you were there."

"Maybe, but there wasn't any traffic. Not a soul. So even if it was out, she wouldn't have been late."

"So what are you getting at?" he repeated.

I hesitated. "It's nothing I can put my finger on."

"What? Spill it."

"It's just . . . what if she was the one to have a fight with him? She was late, and I don't think it was because of the light. Something was on her mind."

He dropped his hand from the doorknob. "Did they know each other?"

I didn't know the answer to that. "Just through the project here, I think, but that's another thing. Isn't it strange that Abernathy Home Builders did the renovations for the house? They usually build new homes, not remodel old ones."

"Yeah, we were surprised they bid on it with Barnett," he said. "They came in pretty low. But that has nothing to do with Charles Denison, or whoever he was."

"Mrs. Abernathy told me that Dan Lee was nosing around where he shouldn't have been. What could he have been looking for?"

"It's an old house," he said with a shrug.

"That used to belong to his family. What if . . ." I struggled to put the idea that had been formulating at the back of my mind into words. "What if something's hidden here? What if Mrs. Abernathy knows and that's why they bid on the job? And what if Mrs. Abernathy wanted to stop Dan Lee from finding whatever it is?"

His eyebrows lifted as he followed my train of thought. "And you think she really could have pushed him off the widow's walk?"

"Maybe that's why she was late. Maybe she'd already been at the house, but then had to leave and circle back to meet us outside."

The door flung open and I jumped, ramming into Will. "Harlow," Mrs. Abernathy said. She leveled her gaze at me, her dark eyes narrowing as if she knew exactly what I'd been saying. "I thought I heard you come in a few minutes ago."

I swallowed the lump of nerves that had climbed to my throat. "I was—"

"Never mind." She stepped aside, letting us pass. "You can go upstairs and change," she told Will.

There was no arguing with her. At the top of the stairs, Will shot me a backward glance, but then he disappeared into a room, garment bag in hand. In a few minutes he would emerge as Santa Claus.

Mrs. Abernathy beckoned me with her finger. "You come with me."

I followed her into the parlor. Mrs. James stood at the window in her low-heeled navy pumps, trim navy skirt, and cream-colored blouse.

"Harlow, my dear." Mrs. James strode toward me, her arms outstretched. She clasped my hand in hers. "Once again, you've saved the day."

Mrs. Abernathy hadn't shifted her attention and I felt the heat of her gaze on me. "How did I do that?" I asked nervously. If Mrs. Abernathy was a murderer and if she suspected I knew anything, there was nothing stopping her from doing to me what she'd done to Dan Lee.

"You've given the kids Santa Claus. This whole thing would have been a flop if your Mr. Flores hadn't stepped up."

"He's not my—," I started to say, but stopped as the front door opened and Madelyn bustled in, camera equipment in tow.

"It's a bloody icebox out there," she exclaimed as the strap of her camera bag slid down the puffy sleeve of her down jacket. She shifted her load, grabbing for it and setting it on the floor.

I rushed toward her, taking the tripod from her arms.

"Thanks, love. Put it over by the screen."

I followed the direction of her extended arm.

And stared, slack-jawed.

Right there in the corner between the staircase and the entrance to the kitchen, big as day, was a dark fabric backdrop hanging from a horizontal bar that was attached to two light-stand supports.

A lush Christmas tree, fully trimmed with twinkling white lights and Victorian ornaments, an enormous over-stuffed thronelike chair, and a painted open box filled with red-and-white-striped candy canes sitting on top of an antique side table created the holiday scene. So this was where Will would play his part as Santa Claus.

A dull pounding started in my temples, wending its way around to the back of my head. How had I missed seeing that whole setup? Maybe I had a concussion and the doctors had missed it.

Madelyn's voice floated in my head like gauze in a summer breeze. She angled her head at me. "You okay, Harlow?"

"What? Oh, yeah, I'm fine." I said, trying to swallow my worry. I'd just been distracted by Mrs. James and Mrs. Abernathy, that was all. My powers of observation were fine. They had to be. Fashion design is all about high standards, exact measurements, and precision when cutting patterns. I need to see the details . . . even non-sewing-related things.

Madelyn looked skeptical, but the clomping of footsteps on the stairs pulled her attention away from me. "Well, would you look at that," Madelyn said.

If I hadn't known it was Will, I never would have guessed it. The red suit fit him perfectly, the soft velvet shimmering against the folds of dark shadows that highlighted the sumptuousness of the fabric. The beard he'd affixed to his face completely masked his goatee, and with the fur-trimmed hat, the gleam in his eyes was like a beacon.

"As I live and breathe," I said, placing my hand to my fluttering heart. There was something about a man who'd dress up as a jolly old elf. "It's Santa Claus."

At the bottom of the stairs, he gave me a mischievous smile. "Want to sit on my lap and tell me what you want for Christmas?" he said, the rogue.

Did I? I felt heat creep up my neck, settling on my cheeks in what I was sure was a scorching blush. I did.

Mrs. Abernathy, her attention thankfully off of me, clapped her hands in quick succession. "Let's get started, shall we? Mr. Flores, you sit there."

She directed him to the throne while Madelyn set up her tripod. "The light's a trifle dim in here," she uttered under her breath, but still loud enough for us to hear.

Mrs. Abernathy scowled. "Don't you have a flash?"

"Of course I do," Madelyn said. "But . . ." She put one finger to her cheek, thinking.

Mrs. Abernathy's foot tapped impatiently. "What is it, Mrs. Brighton?"

Madelyn shook away whatever had been on her mind. Mrs. James cleared her throat and glided across the room, scooping up a potted poinsettia and the quilt from the rack. "Helen, Harlow has a long list of tasks to do for the fashion show, and I'm sure everyone else is plenty busy. Let's get started, shall we? Harlow?"

"Ma'am?"

"Bring a few of those gifts over and place them around the tree."

A pile of beautifully wrapped boxes tied with gold and red ribbon sat next to the settee. They were light as air. Faux gifts.

I carried a few over and arranged them on the tree skirt. Mrs. James handed me the quilt and then crouched to put the poinsettia among the gifts. "Drape that over the arm of the chair, would you?"

Adding the homespun element softened the scene.

"It's a nice touch," I said. Will shifted as I arranged the old quilt. A section of stitching had come loose, a few pieces of the patchwork gaping to reveal the batting underneath.

As I refolded it, hiding the torn section, Will's hands snaked around my back. "Oomph!"

I lost my balance, flopping onto his lap, the silky strands of his white beard tickling my cheek, his plump belly soft against my side. "I knew you'd end up here," he said, a definite twinkle in his eyes. "Just where I wanted you." And then more quietly, so only I could hear, he asked, "What do you want for Christmas this year?"

I could hear Meemaw's voice in my head. *True love, Harlow. It's magical, and without it, you don't have anything.* My great-grandmother's charm had always been foolproof. What Meemaw wanted, Meemaw got.

She'd wanted me home in Bliss. Check.

Wanted Gracie Flores in my life. Check.

I was pretty sure she wanted Will and me to settle down together and make a passel of Cassidy-Flores babies.

And I wanted . . . him, too.

Love. Since discovering my Cassidy charm, I'd been afraid that realizing one of my own dreams, namely falling in love, would mess with my gift. It was another reason I was so hesitant about telling Will about my charm. He might balk and leave, but what if he didn't? What if he stuck around, we fell head over heels in love, and my Cassidy blessing flitted away?

I tamped down the fluttering in the pit of my stomach. "I'll have to get back to you on that," I said coyly. I disentangled myself from his oh so warm and cozy lap and ducked my head to hide the heat that had risen to my cheeks.

Madelyn glanced up from the digital screen of her camera. "Ready?" she asked after I'd moved out of the way.

"As I'll ever be," Will said.

I couldn't see his lips through the silk of his snowy beard, but I sensed his smile. Sensed that what he wanted for Christmas was me.

Madelyn snapped away, taking a series of pictures, directing Will on how to sit, which way to look, where to put his arms, and every other nuance of his position she could think of. "Bugger," she said, half under her breath.

"What?" Mrs. Abernathy asked.

"I want to try it without the backdrop. To capture the mood of the house, you know?"

"I thought we agreed—"

Madelyn held up her hand, stopping Mrs. Abernathy's words on her pursed lips. "You said you wanted the backdrop, but it's not working. There's no ..." She paused, as if she were searching for just the right word. "Life," she finally finished. "The pictures are flat."

The wallpaper in the small central room was alive with color. The old-fashioned brown, green, gold, and copper tea rose pattern climbed up an ivory background. No question, it would give the photos character that black backdrop didn't.

But Mrs. Abernathy didn't agree. She shook her head. "The house isn't alive. It doesn't have a mood. We'll work with what you have."

But Madelyn stood firm. Photography to her was like dressmaking to me. It was her passion, even if it wasn't the thing she made a living doing. She had an eye for telling stories through pictures. Every now and then, she placed a picture or an article in *D Magazine* or *Texas*

Monthly. She'd done one recently on women entrepreneurs and had included me in it.

She shrugged her shoulders back, straightening up to meet Mrs. Abernathy's steady gaze. "Every house tells a story," she said matter-of-factly, "just like every outfit Harlow makes for someone becomes part of that person's story."

"That's true." I'd made Madelyn several outfits. Each had enhanced a part of her character that had been buried. She'd blossomed, become more confident, but really I thought she'd become more . . . Madelyn. An enriched version of herself.

Will spoke from his throne. "It's the same for a house. For a building of any kind, but especially for something as old as this place. Hidden nooks and crannies, secret passageways, scars on the wood, handprints in paint on the porch. Every corner has a story to tell."

I snuck a glance at Mrs. Abernathy. Was there something hidden in a nook or cranny here that she and Dan Lee had both known about?

But her gaze remained steady, her foot had stopped tapping, and I chased away my suspicions. The woman was part of Bliss's old guard. She couldn't be involved in anything as sordid as murder.

"Clothes are clothes," she said. "And a house is a house. The people who came before don't stay behind."

Maybe not in her world, but she didn't know about Loretta Mae, or the fact that all the Cassidy women apparently hung around 2112 Mockingbird Lane after they'd crossed to the hereafter.

Madelyn had already started taking down the backdrop. Will maneuvered around his belly to help her. I moved the light stands and before long she was snapping pictures of Will again. She paused to look at the camera's digital screen. "Much better," she said. "Now lift your chin, Will. There you go. And look left, uh-huh . . ." She peered through the viewfinder and snapped away.

Ten minutes later, she suddenly tucked her camera into her bag, straightened up, and announced, "Done."

I heaved a relieved sigh. Now I'd be able to skedaddle back to Buttons & Bows and get back to the fashion show garments—

"Harlow, when will you have the newsletter ready?"

I gaped at Mrs. James. "Wh-what?"

She frowned at me, the faint outline of blue veins visible under her papery skin. "Helen said you'd take the pictures and create a newsletter—"

"She did?"

We both turned to Mrs. Abernathy. Mrs. James was looking for confirmation and I wanted an explanation.

But Mrs. Abernathy wasn't behind us. I peeked into the parlor. She wasn't there. I looked in the kitchen. Not there either.

"Where'd she go? Mrs. Abernathy!"

"I'm right here, Harlow, for heaven's sake."

She glided across the hardwood floor from the other side of the staircase. She'd come from an odd nook, tucked under the incline of the stairs, a tiny powder room with a sloped ceiling.

I hesitated, my polite Southern roots making me want to hem and haw around the question burning in my mouth, namely, had she been searching for something? But of course that didn't make sense. She'd had plenty of opportunity over the last six months to scour the house for hidden treasures. "I'm making a newsletter?"

"Well, of course," she said, as if there were no other

possibility and how thick was I to not understand that? "And some flyers to post in the businesses on and off the square."

"You never—"

"What did you think needed to happen after these PR photos?" She leveled her steely gaze at me, and not for the first time I wondered why she disliked me so. "Are you, or are you not, in charge of this part of the event?"

"Well, yes, but—"

She flicked her hand toward Madelyn and Will. "You do it, or have one of them do it. I don't care. I just need it e-mailed to me as soon as possible so it can go out to our mailing list."

"But the fashion show—"

She stopped me with another wave of her hand. "Without a Santa, the kids won't want to come. And without the kids, parents won't come. And all our effort will have been for naught."

"We've sold a hundred tickets already," I reminded her. We weren't completely dependent on Santa Claus for people to show up.

"A hundred is good, but we were counting on the additional people to support the vendors. Your grandmother is one of those. Goat lotion, or something."

Mrs. James refolded the quilt, taking it back to the parlor. "If we're to make this an annual event, we need it to be a success, Harlow," she said, coming back to the entry room.

"I'd do it, love, but Billy's home from Austin and we have a holiday dinner at the university tonight," Madelyn said. She pulled the memory card from the camera and handed it to me.

I tucked it into my pants pocket. It seemed I was facing an evening at the computer instead of at the sewing machine. Not what I'd had planned.

Time was running out. It was going to be a long night. My eyesight would be strained by the time I was finished trying to design the perfect outfit for Josie, threading needles, getting set up for tomorrow's Santa dollmaking class, and sewing straight seams. At the rate I was wearing out my eyes, come the new year, I'd need to visit the eye doctor, update my exam, and get a new pair of glasses.

And all this just when I felt like I was on the right track with figuring out what had happened to Dan Lee Chrisson.

Chapter 21

I sat in my old yellow truck, dug my sketchbook out of my bag, and started to jot down the thoughts rattling around in my mind, competing for my attention. If I got them on paper, maybe my head would clear and I'd be able to think straight. That had always been Meemaw's philosophy. She called it a trigger list. "Hit the main points, Harlow," she'd told me over and over again, "and the rest will fall into place. It's like piecing together a quilt, one scrap at a time."

I wrote down what I knew, which, as it turned out, wasn't much.

> *Raylene and Dan Lee divorced, but not so amicably*
> *Maggie Pagonis stole Boone*
> *Loose railing on the widow's walk*
> *Hattie protecting her sister?*
> *Mrs. Abernathy: Dan Lee had no business nosing around that house*
> *Why were the bolts loose in the first place and who could have done it?*

This last question stuck out like a prairie dress would at Mercedes-Benz Fashion Week. The same people circled in my mind. The Barnetts, Raylene, and Mrs. Abernathy. They all had keys to the house, and any one of them could have loosened those screws. Plus there was Mrs. James's missing key to consider.

I added one more thing to my list.

Dan Lee Chrisson had been born as Charles Denison. Why had his family hidden who they really were, and was he after something at the Denison mansion?

No matter how I cut the fabric, the pieces of this mystery quilt didn't fit together right. No, something was missing. But as I pulled up to 2112 Mockingbird Lane in my rumbly pickup, a movement from the porch caught my eye and the question left my head. "Thelma Louise, if you're causing trouble again, so help me ..." I muttered under my breath, yanking the steering wheel to the right and angling the truck alongside the curb.

In seconds flat, I was out of the cab, coat pulled tight to ward off the chill, and charging through the arbor and gate leading to the front yard. I hurried up the flagstone pathway, taking inventory of the lush winter growth in the yard—a peculiarity, given how cold it had been. Pansies lined the path, bluebonnets sprouted from the icy ground, and even the wisteria was going through a blooming cycle. Mama had a way with plants, and she spread her charm all around, whether she wanted to or not.

And it all looked just fine. Better than fine. I slowed down. In fact, it looked abnormally perfect, which meant ...

"Harlow, what in heaven's name are you doing standing there like that? Come on up here and let us in the house."

Mama. She stood on the porch, tapping her booted foot, her lips pursed in exasperation. "Meemaw never locked the door, you know," she said. "Here I thought I could help you with some of your sewing for a spell, but—"

"Things around Bliss have changed," I told her. The murder of a bridesmaid in my front yard was evidence of that. A dead Santa was proof. "But I would have left it open if I'd known you were coming by," I added, walking toward the porch steps.

The rocking chair creaked, and from the corner of my eye, I saw it moving back and forth. "Meemaw—" At the top of the steps, I turned, expecting to see the misty ghost of my great-grandmother. But I stopped short. Raylene Lewis sat on the old wooden rocker cradling and cooing to her baby.

Oh! I'd plum forgotten that I'd left her a message and asked her to come over. "I didn't see you!" I said, hurrying to the front door and plunging the key into the lock. The temperature had dropped to thirty-three degrees, a good mite too cold for a mother and her swaddled babe. A good mite too cold for anyone to be out.

I held the door for them, closing it against the biting chill once they were inside. The faint scent of evergreen— as much as a mostly fresh five-foot tree from the hardware store could emit—floated in the air. Buttons & Bows didn't have the ambience of the Denison mansion, but it was home.

Mama whirled around, whipping her Longhorns cap off her head and hanging it on the coat tree next to the front door. No matter how old she was, she would always be a down-home country girl at heart. No pretense, no gussying herself up beyond her Wranglers and UT clothes (which she wore on account of Red and me both graduating from the Austin university), and no lollygagging around the bramble bush. "Where in tarnation have you been?" she demanded.

Mama's temper flare-up didn't faze me. I hadn't inherited that tendency, but she'd been this way since I was a tiny thing, and I imagined she always would be. In ten seconds flat, she'd simmer down and be back to normal. "Doing a photo shoot of Santa Claus," I said, trying my darnedest to ignore the sudden image I had of her in a calf-length, scarf-hemmed lacy white wedding dress, a veil attached to the white cowgirl hat on her head. Oh Lord. It was cheesy—but completely her.

The baby's gurgling drew my attention away from the realization that Mama and Hoss might well get hitched before too long, and that in all likelihood I'd be designing a dress that would have made Annie Oakley proud.

Boone's tiny fingers curled around the flannel blanket he was wrapped up in and the tip of his pink nose peeked out from under the knit hat on his head. "He's adorable, Raylene," I said, tossing my portable sewing bag on the sofa.

I held my finger out and he gripped it with more strength than I'd thought possible. His eyes were cornflower blue. He looked at me with such intensity, I had an inkling that he could see everything about me. "Can I hold him?"

She handed Boone over, making sure I had a good grip on him before she let go. "I still can't believe he's really here," she said as she brushed the back of her finger to the side of his face just like I had. There was something about the pudgy cheeks of an infant that just begged to be touched. "I thought I'd lost him for good. I owe you, Harlow."

Mama's foot stopped tapping and her shoulders relaxed. She moved to Raylene's side and slung her arm around her shoulder. "You won't never have to worry about that happening again," she said.

Raylene sucked in a few deep breaths, gathering up her composure as she blew them out. "No, I guess I won't."

Her voice trembled, just a touch but enough that I took notice. Was it relief that she had her baby boy back safe and sound, or—

My mind zipped back to the thought I'd had when I'd first met Raylene. Had she come to see where Dan Lee had died, or to revisit the scene of her crime?

Boone squirmed. He threw himself backward, catching me off guard.

"Watch him!" Raylene cried.

I slid my hand up to brace his neck and head, holding him in front of me. "What are you doing, little guy?"

His eyes were like saucers as he looked at me and his feet, wrapped in the flannel blanket, pressed against my stomach. I turned my head away, whipping it back around to face him and making an "O" with my mouth.

I'd been hoping for a laugh, but instead his lower lip quivered. "Don't cry," I said quietly. "It's okay. I'm the one who found you in the stable, remember?" I smiled, but Boone didn't blink. Didn't smile. Didn't look like he trusted me. It was as if he knew I was wondering about his mother and if she could have been the one to push his father to his death.

I looked to Mama for a split second, and in that moment, Boone let out an earsplitting cry.

Raylene surged forward, gripping Boone's swaddled body and pulling him away from me. "Come to Mama," she said, turning him around and snuggling him against her chest. "I won't let anythin' happen to you."

A shiver danced up my spine as she stroked his back and cooed, soothing him until he stopped crying. I didn't know what to believe. Was saving Boone from his father on her list of things she'd do to protect the child, even if it meant shoving him off a balcony?

My head felt full of cotton. Raylene sank onto the sofa and Mama scooted into the workroom and took up hemming one of the dresses hanging on a dress form. I grabbed my sewing bag, pulled out my cloth-covered sketchbook, and flipped to the back. "What did you want to talk to me about, Harlow?" Raylene asked as she draped a second receiving blanket over her shoulder, covering Boone's head as she nursed him.

I'd spent the last hour thinking that Helen Abernathy might well be behind Dan Lee's death, but now that Raylene was in front of me, I was back to the most obvious answer. With Mrs. Abernathy, it was all a big blank theory that Dan Lee had been searching for something in the house, but with Raylene and Hattie, the motive was much clearer.

My stomach churned. And if it were true that she'd pushed Dan Lee off the widow's walk, then a murderess was sitting on my sofa, nursing a baby, and that was more twisted than an Oklahoma tornado.

"Raylene," I said, sitting across from her on the love seat. "I was at the Denison mansion when Dan Lee died."

She looked at me, eyes wide. Her lower lip quivered, but she held it together. "I know. I can't believe you're okay after that fall."

That made two of us. "Hattie was there too."

Boone gurgled, pulling away from her. She stroked his head, helping him latch on again. "I was, too," she said. "We came together, but when I saw Dan Lee's truck, I couldn't go in. I started to, but I . . . I just couldn't," she said, her voice beginning to crack with emotion. "So I waited in the car."

I stared at her, my mind a jumble. She hadn't tried to hide the fact that she'd been right outside when her ex-husband had been killed. She didn't lie to give herself an alibi. And I wanted to believe her.

We were silent for a few seconds before Mama scooted out of the workroom, the dress she was hemming for me draped over her arm. "Did you kill him, Raylene? Tell us the truth, now. Did you sneak in, climb those stairs, and push him off the widow's walk?"

I gaped at her, speechless.

Mama just popped her eyebrows up and shrugged at me. "Well? It's what you're beatin' around the bush about, ain't it?"

Boone suddenly lurched, pulling free of Raylene again. His back arched, he sucked in a deep, quiet breath, and then let loose a raucous cry.

Raylene had gone pale, but she cooed, trying to calm Boone down. "Shush now."

"Mama!" I said, finally finding my voice.

But Raylene raised her sad gaze to me before I could chastise my mother any more. "I didn't do it," she said quietly. "I didn't want Dan Lee dead."

Chapter 22

Mama had finished hemming the dress for one of the fashion show models and finally she and Raylene had gone. I spent the next hour directing all my energy to Josie's outfit for the fashion show. It was the one thing I knew would help clear my mind and process all the different scenarios surrounding Dan Lee's death.

I'd exhausted every idea I'd come up with for Josie. I'd designed a sleeveless blouse for her to wear with skinny jeans and flats. I'd used shirring to create a ruffle down the center of the blouse, and a bright magenta gave it a fun, flirty look.

Maybe I was looking at it all wrong. Maybe solving the mystery of Dan Lee's murder was what would clear my mind. Where Josie was concerned, my charm had been failing me. Which made sense. A single blouse couldn't turn around whatever she was feeling about her changing body.

I turned to the front of my sketchbook, poising my pencil over the blank page. Waiting for inspiration to strike.

Nothing.

I closed my eyes and pictured Josie in my mind. Olive

complexion, lush hair, and curves. The swell of her belly had stolen her waist. That shouldn't be throwing me off. But it was.

A stack of sewing and fashion magazines was piled on the end of the cutting table. I sighed and grabbed one off the top. Anything for a thread of inspiration.

I flipped through, trying to imagine Josie in leggings and a tunic or in a jacket buttoned at the neck. Nothing seemed quite right.

I just started drawing, hoping something decent would materialize. Several quick strokes of my pencil later, I considered the line drawings I'd come up with. I drew a collar on one, added bell sleeves to another, and scratched out the third one altogether. "That darn stomach," I uttered under my breath. I needed to just drape it on the dress form.

I went out into the front room of Buttons & Bows and opened the door to Meemaw's antique armoire. Not too long ago it had held the gowns Mrs. James, Mrs. Mcafferty, and Nana had worn to the Margaret Moffette Lea Pageant and Ball when they'd been barely sixteen years old. Mrs. James had taken hers, and Gracie Flores, who'd worn Mrs. Mcafferty's, had taken that one. I'd hung Nana's from a satin-covered hanger that was now on a hook in the far corner of the room.

Now the armoire held carefully folded and organized lengths of fabric I'd collected over the few months I'd been back in Bliss. I'd had to be judicious about acquiring too much stuff while I lived in New York. My thimble-sized apartment, shared with Orphie, barely had room for us and our sewing machines. Extra tubs of fabric weren't manageable.

But now? I ran my fingertips over the folded edges. I

could embrace my addiction. When I saw something I loved at my favorite online designer fabric store, Emma One Sock, I waited twenty-four hours just like Meemaw had taught me. "If you still dream about it a day later, then give in to the impulse without guilt."

And I did.

I pulled out washable silk, letting it fall open. Gorgeous, but not quite right for Josie. She was less high society, more girl next door.

After refolding it and tucking it back into its spot, I let my fingers drift again until they settled on three yards of an artsy sheer zebra print. Maybe . . .

But I hesitated, and then moved on, not convinced.

My hand seemed to move on its own, like fingers lightly touching the planchette on a Ouija board as it spells out words. I didn't have my own Ouija board, but I wondered if it would be a way to communicate with Meemaw.

The idea vanished as my hand stopped on a linen and metal woven stripe. Completely wrong for Josie. Below it was an Italian wool sweater lace. It would require a lining or layering, and bulking Josie up wouldn't benefit her silhouette, so I dismissed it.

But I couldn't tear my attention away from that spot. I worked my fingers between the two fabrics. They dug, almost on their own, as if they were excavating for dinosaur bones at the nearby Fossil Rim dinosaur park.

A second later, I pulled out three yards of a colorful viscose tweed from India. Although it looked like a silk tweed, the fabric was softer and had more drape. Christmas red, a bright evergreen, citrine, yellow the color of the North Star, lilac, and bits of black were woven together with a beautiful hand-loomed look.

I'd snapped up the designer fabric in Dallas, no clue what I'd make with it. But I'd known then that I had to have it. Holding it now, I could see Josie wearing an open, comfortable and fun, yet elegant, jacket made from the nubby tweed. I laid it over the love seat, then turned back to the armoire for a solid fabric for the skirt. It took some digging, but finally I found a complementary warm red poly/viscose/spandex blend, ideal for a pencil skirt. With a stretch panel, it would give her a clean, sleek silhouette, but it would have enough stretch to be comfortable. A black knit shirt underneath would elevate the whole look. It was perfect.

The challenge would be crafting a well-fitting jacket in just a day and a half. For a pregnant woman. Oh boy. I knew I was finally on the right track, but I had to get started, which meant I needed to call Will.

Pronto.

After four rings, he picked up, his voice all cowboy gravelly as he said, "Hello?"

But I had no time to think about how the one word slipped under my skin and made me feel warm all over. "I need your stomach," I blurted.

"I knew it," he said. I could hear the smile through the phone connection, as if he could read my mind.

"What did you know?" I asked as I riffled through the armoire, searching for the black knit, finally finding an entire stack of T-shirt material. It paid to have what amounted to my own personal store; no need to waste time with a trip to a fabric shop.

"That those situps I do when I'm bored would pay off eventually."

I stood up, holding the black fabric to my chest. Heat rushed to my face, but I managed to sound indignant rather than embarrassed. "Not your stomach, Will Flores," I said. "Santa's belly. The insert I made. I need it."

"Cheating on me with another Santa?"

"With a pregnant woman. Josie. I need to drape a jacket, and for that I need to make the dress form pregnant. Which means I need the Santa belly. Can you bring it by?"

"Anything for you, darlin'," he said.

I smiled to myself. The first time he'd called me that, he'd showed up at 2112 Mockingbird Lane, thanks to Meemaw, and I'd ended up chasing down Thelma Louise in the front yard. It had rankled me like no tomorrow then, but it had grown on me. A "darlin'" from Will wasn't like a "darlin'" from some swaggering, tobacco-chewing cowboy down at the honky-tonk. No, it was meant just for me, and there was something sweet about that.

The doors to the armoire gently swung back and forth, the creaking from the hinges sounding like a satisfied laugh.

Meemaw.

I couldn't see her, but I knew she was here. "I admit," I said to the empty room, "you were right."

The squeaking of the hinges changed to "Yep, yep, yep."

I laughed, feeling calmer than I had in days. I hardly felt any aches from my fall, my scrapes were healing, and I was beginning to think that my charm of helping other folks discover their desires might actually work for me, too. "Meemaw, you are incorrigible."

The pages of the magazine I'd left on the workroom table fluttered until the glossy fell open. I knew Meemaw's MO by now, and while a Ouija board might be easier, this was more fun.

I laid the phone on the coffee table and went to the workroom. *Stitch* was open to an article called "Ruffle

Love." Inset boxes featured a little girl dressed in a chocolate mint ruffled shirt, another in a red-and-white candy
cane ruffled skirt, and a third showed a subtle gray scarf
in dark and light gray. The captions talked about the
playful nature of ruffles, about letting go and just having
fun, and about making a statement with color choice.

I scanned the pages again. What was Meemaw trying
to tell me?

My gaze drifted back to the precious candy cane skirt,
then to the scarf, and an idea surfaced. I'd asked Libby
Allen, Gracie Flores, and Holly Kincaid to be Santa's
helpers at the Winter Wonderland festivities. I'd already
made them festive holiday outfits for the fashion show.
Libby's mom had taken them out to find red tights and
Santa hats, but the outfits just didn't feel complete for
elves. But now . . .

I had the ruffling foot for my Baby Lock serger sewing machine. I could whip up three whimsical scarves
like the ones in the picture, using red and white fabrics.

"Great idea, Meemaw," I said, wondering for about
the millionth time just how she knew what I needed
when I didn't even know.

God love her.

I marked the page with a scrap of fabric, closed the
magazine, and went back to my sketchbook. In just a few
minutes, I had the rough drawing of the pencil skirt, the
fitted knit top, and a cascade jacket with wide flap lapels
and a curved hemline.

And best of all, I knew in the very center of my core
that this was the right outfit for Josie. No more guessing.

With the elf scarves, this outfit, and Will's Santa suit,
I'd be up to date and—

"The newsletter!" It had completely slipped my mind.

I whipped around at the sound of the front door closing. I hadn't heard it open, and darn those bells, anyway. They only worked when they wanted to.

Will came in carrying the Santa belly. "You okay, Cassidy?" he asked.

If there was one thing I was not, it was a complainer. Meemaw always said that come hell or high water, the Cassidy women did whatever they said they would. So no matter what, I would get everything done.

She'd also said that only a fool cowboy squats with his spurs on. I hadn't ever been real sure what that meant, but I suddenly had an inkling. If I'd gotten myself in too deep with my commitments, it wasn't nobody's fault but my own.

So. No throwing a hissy fit and stomping on it.

I gestured to the yards of vivid, multihued tweed lying over the back of the love seat. "Just fine," I said. "I finally figured out what I'm going to make for Josie to wear in the fashion show, is all."

"Uh-huh." He angled his head off to one side, considering me. "And I have some primo ranchland in West Texas I'm selling for a cool ten million."

I stared at him. "It'd take ten acres to graze one cow over there—" I stopped when he smirked, and it dawned on me that he'd been poking fun at me. "Okay, maybe I'm not just fine, but I'll be fine just as soon as I get Josie's outfit made." And created the three ruffled scarves I was now determined to do . . . and finished the Santa dolls with my class . . . and got the newsletter done and sent out so we actually had people show up to the Winter Wonderland event . . . and . . .

"Cassidy."

My attention snapped back to the present. Will was

looking at me like he'd said my name a few times. "Thanks for bringing the belly back," I said, closing my sketchbook and moving it next to the stack of magazines. I stopped short. The issue of *Stitch* was open again—to the same article on ruffles. But I'd closed it . . .

Letters seemed to lift off the page like 3-D images. *Let go. Have fun. Love.*

My breath caught in my throat as I pieced together what Meemaw was trying to tell to me. This was her message. It hadn't been about the ruffled scarves, although that was a nice perk—it had been about her playing matchmaker with Will and me. Again.

"It'll happen if it's meant to, Meemaw," I said under my breath.

"What?"

Will's voice brought me back again.

"Just talking to myself," I said, turning to see him watching me, a curious tilt to his head. Gracie stood next to him. I did a double take. "Hey, Gracie. I didn't hear you come in."

She grinned at me. "That's because I opened the door real slow so the bells wouldn't jingle."

"Really," I said, nodding as if she'd pulled off a trick worthy of Houdini. But inside I was pretty sure that Meemaw was the one playing tricks.

"You have a lot on your mind, Cassidy," Will said, handing me the fake belly. "We can help, you know."

One thing about the Cassidy clan was that we relied on each other, but didn't often let other folks into our circle. It was easier to protect our secrets that way. But slowly and surely, our circle was growing. Nana had married Granddaddy, of course, and it had lasted—the one Cassidy woman to stay with a man since forever.

Mama had let Hoss McClaine in and they were as cozy as two coon dogs sleeping on the front porch. Josie and Madelyn had become my closest friends back in Bliss, and Gracie was like a ... a ... well, truth be told, I didn't know what she was like. A sister? A cousin? A daughter? Maybe a little of each. She was someone I liked to be around ... and have around.

And then there was Will. I liked him. I liked him like sweet potatoes like marshmallows. Like corn bread likes honey. Like pecans like pie. I just liked him. There, I admitted it.

My fear that falling for him might zap my charm into smithereens was just that ... a fear. I didn't know if achieving my own happiness would mean I wouldn't be able to help other folks find theirs. Meemaw seemed hell-bent on bringing us together. Maybe I could take a chance.

I strapped the belly onto one of the dress forms in the corner of the workroom. I had plenty of time to think about Will Flores later. Right now, I had to admit that he was right. I had a lot on my mind, and a little help would go a long way to easing my stress.

As I turned back to them, I rattled off the tasks on my To Do list, tapping the pads of my fingers as I went. "Not including solving a murder," I said. He frowned, and I continued. "I have to drape and pattern and make Josie's outfit, ruffle some fabric to make scarves, set up for the Santa doll class I'm teaching, decorate the tent for the Winter Wonderland ..."

Will's eyes glazed. There wasn't a thing on my list that involved a hammer, muscles, or fixing things.

I groaned. "And that darn newsletter Mrs. Abernathy wants ..."

I leaned back against the worktable, grateful that I didn't have any spurs on. How was I going to get it all done?

"I can do that," he said, nodding succinctly.

"Do what?"

"The newsletter."

I stared. "Really?"

"Sure. I can't solve a murder, at least not this instant. I can't sew a straight line. I'm not a dollmaker. And we can't decorate right now, so, yeah, out of your list, I can do a newsletter." He held out his hand. "Where's the flash drive?"

I felt a ray of light shine down on me as I dug it out of my jeans pocket and handed it over. "Are you sure?"

"Cassidy, you go do what you do best. Go sew something."

Chapter 23

I put my sketchbook on the worktable and took stock of how I felt. The worries careening through my mind had settled. "You're right, Meemaw," I said to myself. "Will's a good guy."

The lights overhead flickered in response. I made a mental note to check out a book on Morse code from the library. Maybe that would help us communicate better.

"I know," I whispered quietly to the lightbulb so Gracie wouldn't hear me—it made me feel a little ridiculous. "You're always right."

The light flickered again, faster this time. From the corner of my eye, I caught a glimpse of a filmy white cloud. Cataracts . . . ? No. Meemaw was trying to show herself to me.

"Um, Harlow?" Gracie said behind me, her voice lilting.

"What's wrong?"

She stared at the flickering light, but as I took a step toward her, the whisper in the air vanished and the room went still. The light glowed steadily and not a ghostly form was in sight.

"N-nothing. This house . . ."

I sighed. "I know. Loose wiring," I said, making my voice breezy through the ache in the pit of my stomach.

Most of the time, having Loretta Mae around me was like walking into a room of old friends. That feeling of love and acceptance fills every space. But sometimes, I thought, as I took one last glance over my shoulder, it was more like a favorite jacket that was missing a one-of-a-kind button, or the empty space in your mouth after you'd lost a tooth.

Gracie shrugged away whatever she'd been thinking and sat at the serger in the workroom. She tugged at one of the four large spools of thread. "I've seen these at the fabric store," she said, a hint of awe in her voice. She drew her hand away. "Are you sure . . . ?"

"Every seamstress has to learn how to use one eventually."

She grinned up at me, her sixteen-year-old enthusiasm reminding me of how I'd felt sitting next to Meemaw while she sewed. I'd watched every stitch she made, absorbing her love of fabrics, buttons, and trims, not knowing that my unique ancestry would someday give me a magical sewing talent and that one day it would become my whole world.

I showed Gracie how to work the machine and set her on her way, ruffling the red strips of fabrics that she would attach to the white ruffles she'd do next. She pressed her foot against the pedal and the machine zipped along, slicing off the excess fabric, creating a tidy edge.

She tilted her head back and looked up at me. "So cool!"

It was serger love. I knew it well. I'd bought a used Baby Lock when I was in high school and had made sweatshirts and fleece throw blankets and pillowcases until they were bursting out the windows of my bedroom.

I watched her to make sure she had it figured out, smiling as she murmured happily to herself. She was a natural. Next I peeked out the French doors of the workroom. Will sat at the little computer table in the dining room, tapping away on the keyboard. His lips moved as he worked. And he'd laughed at me for talking to myself.

A blanket of warmth washed over me, and honestly, I couldn't say if it was Meemaw, back again—or the fact that Gracie and Will were here with me, each of us working on our own projects, but like we belonged together.

From the coffee table, the pages of the *Victoria* magazine I'd picked up in Fort Worth fluttered. Another message from Meemaw.

I snuck a glance at Will to see if he'd noticed, but he was intent on the computer screen. As casually as I could, I moved to the seating area, perching on the edge of the love seat. The magazine was open to an article on Victorian decorations. Blown glass, balls of mistletoe, and handmade gift embellishments were featured.

The packages I'd wrapped for Mama, Nana, and Granddaddy and placed under my small Christmas tree were wrapped in plain brown paper. I'd drawn delicate white Japanese cherry blossoms and dark branches on the packages and tied the gifts up with black iridescent ribbon. "What?" I said under my breath as I flipped the magazine closed. "You don't like my gift-wrap style?"

In one quick motion, as if someone had grabbed the pages and flipped them open, the glossy was opened to the very same page.

"I'll look later," I said quietly.

"You okay?"

I jumped at Will's booming voice. "Yeah, great!" I said, hopping up and scurrying into the workroom. I got to work on Josie's outfit, the sound of the serger and the tapping of Will's fingers on the keyboard fading to the background. With each passing second, I was sucked deeper and deeper into the draping and pattern creation of the jacket, like Alice tumbling down the rabbit hole, emerging in a different world. It came together effortlessly—now that I had a clear vision of what I was doing.

Time seemed to slow as I marked the muslin with fabric chalk to create a mockup of the piece, measuring, tracing, cutting, and pinning until I was satisfied with the result.

After a while, Gracie's voice drifted into my consciousness. "So I totally want to get that for the baby."

I blinked, realizing that the serger had stopped, and slowly came back to the here and now.

"Is this enough?"

I turned to face Gracie—and a mountain of red ruffles that was as tall as the sewing table. Maybe taller. "Good Lord, that's a whole lotta ruffles."

"Yeah, I got a little bit carried away." She frowned, patting the top of the pile like she wanted to push it down. "Too much?"

"We do need three scarves," I said. "I bet it's just enough."

As she scooped the pile aside, I sat at the table and started the tedious process of changing the serger thread from red to white. For two solid years, I'd had to use the manual to remember exactly how to do it. Now it was old hat, but it took a while.

Gracie pulled up a stool and watched me as I worked,

absorbing every detail. She was so intent, I wondered if she was holding her breath. Finally, as I started on the last spool of thread, she snapped out of her fascinated daze. "You know everything, don't you?" she said, not really asking me if I did, but more in awe.

I laughed. "Not hardly. I don't think you can ever know everything about sewing and design. You just keep educating your taste, experimenting with patterns, and developing your style."

She nodded, and I could almost see her filing away my words to recall and think about later on.

"So what do you think about the quilt for Josie and Nate's baby?"

I threaded the last needle, tested the tension by ruffling a scrap, and then moved aside so she could start on the white fabric. "What quilt?"

"I saw it at Vintage Baby on the square. It's got zippers and buttons and all these cloth compartments."

"On a baby quilt?"

"Well . . ." She hesitated. "Maybe for when he . . . or she . . . is a toddler?"

"I'm sure Josie will love it," I said, "and babies need interactive toys. It sounds great."

She perked up. "Oh, it is! It's got all these toys tucked into hidden spots and it's so colorful. Not really vintage at all, so I don't know why they carry it, but it's really cute. And it's on sale because of the festival." She turned and started on the white ruffles.

"Done," Will announced. He came into the workroom carrying two sheets of paper.

I looked at his handiwork while he went over to check out Gracie's project. "Think you have enough ruffles?" he asked.

She looked up at him, wrinkling her nose. "Got a little serger crazy. I'm going to make scarves for everyone!"

He gathered up a handful of the red ruffles and held them under his chin. "I'll wear it everywhere," he deadpanned.

"For my friends," she said, batting him away.

They stayed another hour, Gracie finishing her white ruffles and Will tinkering with the loose board on the stairs. I continued to work on Josie's jacket, my mind still processing everything that had happened in the past few days.

My thoughts drifted to the holiday decorations from the magazine on the coffee table and I realized Meemaw thought I should make some. In all my spare time, I thought. I'd already strung garlands on the front porch and the banister. Surely that was enough.

Then again, a few mistletoe balls scattered through the rooms would be an easy final touch, and it would give me another opportunity to take a look around the mansion. I'd been lucky, discovering something potentially important at Dan Lee Chrisson's apartment. With any luck, lightning would strike twice.

Chapter 24

The next morning came quicker than a Texas thunderstorm. Day one of the Winter Wonderland festival was in full swing, but for now the women in the Santa doll class were toasty warm inside Buttons & Bows, sipping steaming cups of coffee, grazing on sugared pecans, and rubbing the pomegranate goat's milk lotion Nana had brought over onto the backs of their hands.

"You're gonna sell this at the festival later, right?" Olive asked.

Nana shook her head. "Only at the fashion show."

Michele dipped two fingers into the container and took another dollop. "What's in it? My skin feels like silk," she proclaimed.

Nana beamed. "That there is like my own secret potion. It took a whole year before I perfected it, but now it's ready."

The five women—Diane, Michele, Olive, Madelyn, and Eleanor—sat at the dining table with stacks of trimming materials in front of them. Mama hadn't made it back yet. I gave Nana a finished Santa body and slid into the chair next to Mrs. Mcafferty.

"Now do we get to decorate?" Olive asked.

"Yes. And that's the fun part!" I pointed at the bins I'd lined up on the other side of the railing that divided the raised dining room from the main room of Buttons & Bows. Faux and real fur, beaded trims, lace, yarn, ornate buttons, and more filled the plastic boxes. "I've put out even more materials for you to choose from. Use whatever you like."

Diane and Michele whispered to each other with the closeness shared between sisters.

Madelyn held up her lopsided figure, frowning. "This is why I take pictures."

Mrs. Mcafferty turned to look at Madelyn's Santa. She'd been sitting quietly, but now she spoke up. "He's actually quite adorable. He has character."

Madelyn spun the doll around and studied him. She placed him on the table, let go, and he toppled over. Over and over she tried, but he was just too top-heavy to stay upright.

"Give him a few good squeezes," Nana said, snatching him up and digging her fingers into the form. Her hands were strong from all the goat milking she'd done over the years, but it didn't make a difference. Madelyn's Santa wasn't going to stand upright.

"We need to unstuff him and try again."

Madelyn arched one thin black eyebrow at me. "Unstuff him? You can't be serious."

I put my hands on my hips and tried to look stern, not an easy task with my hair in braids, the bruises from my fall off the roof turning a mottled yellow, worn jeans, and a plaid snap-front blouse that would have made Meemaw proud. "He won't stand upright if we don't."

"I'll just lean him up against a candle. Or something."

"But, Madelyn, we have to fix him."

"Uh-uh." She scooted her chair to the right. "I like Mrs. Mcafferty's take on him. He's got character. A bloody lot of character," she added.

A wallop of giggles went around the table.

"Y'all are loopy." I laughed, then said, "And we only just started." But I had to admit, Madelyn's Santa did look whimsical. He'd be the one giving out whoopee cushions to all the kids on his list.

The town gossip started as each of the women rustled through the bins. "I got a newsletter in my inbox last night about the Winter Wonderland," Olive said.

Diane and Michele both raised their gazes from their dolls. "Me, too," Diane said, and Michele nodded, adding, "We both did."

"It was done quite well," Mrs. Mcafferty said, throwing a wink in Nana's direction. "I didn't know Helen had those skills."

"Will Flores did the newsletter," I said.

Mrs. Mcafferty's cheeks paled. "Naomi told me some time ago that she was sweet on him for a while."

Oh boy. Will didn't think the Mcaffertys knew that he'd dated their daughter. Wrong.

"He's here all the time," Nana said. "Of course, Gracie, his daughter, works here now. Eleanor, do you know her?"

I waggled my eyebrows at Nana, trying—in vain—to get her attention. I didn't want her talking about Gracie.

Mrs. Mcafferty sputtered before answering. "I don't . . . know her, but I . . . I've seen her around town."

"She's quite a seamstress," Nana continued, completely oblivious to my silent pleas.

"She's quite . . . lovely," Mrs. Mcafferty said, and darn it if she didn't sound wistful.

This time I froze. And if she knew about them dating, was it possible . . . ? Oh no. Could she know that Gracie was her granddaughter? Why, oh why, hadn't Will simply insisted on introducing Gracie to her grandparents instead of letting her decide when she was ready?

I stared at Mrs. Mcafferty, wishing that my gift included reading minds. It didn't, so I was left trying to read her expression instead. She'd managed to hide whatever it was she'd thought when she'd heard Will's name, but she couldn't hide the sadness in her voice. I'd heard it.

She knew.

And I didn't want to let on that I knew she knew.

"Eleanor," I heard Nana say, "we're collecting a few things for Raylene Lewis and her baby. They've been through the wringer."

"That's an understatement," Diane said.

"I heard that Hoss McClaine questioned her," Mrs. Mcafferty said. "In fact, I heard that he and his deputy son think she might have pushed Dan Lee."

The gossip mill was in full swing. I gave a deep sigh. Or at least I thought about giving a really deep sigh, but I kept it in. I just wanted to listen, so I tried to take a step back and be quiet.

Michele tied off her knot. "Let me tell you, I've been praying for that mother and child both night and day. And that poor man. Even if he was . . ." She leaned in, dropping her voice. "Even if he left Raylene, and even if his girlfriend stole that baby, he didn't deserve to die."

I couldn't agree more. "Dan Lee kept to himself, didn't he?"

"How he ended up with a sweet girl like Raylene is beyond me," Diane said.

Ah, but was she sweet, or was she a murderer?

Nana cleared her throat, getting back to the original subject. "I'm fixin' to make the rounds and pick up donations from folks."

Mrs. Mcafferty's brow furrowed in thought. "Naomi left behind a closet full of clothes, and I have a stack of quilts I picked up a long time ago from Ethel Bishop." She paused, tapping one finger on the table. "No, I guess I can't pass along the quilts. Rudy is sure the name Bishop on them means they're worth a fortune, but . . . ah, never mind. All that's old history. Everyone likes the shiny version of those old stories, anyway—"

She broke off, heaving a sigh. She turned to Nana and then to me. "I've always wondered something."

"You've never been a shy one, Eleanor," Nana said. "Spit it out."

"It's no secret that you come from Butch Cassidy's line, but that wasn't even his real name." She tilted her head to one side. "Why do you all keep Cassidy as your name?

That was something we'd been asked over the years by discerning historians. Butch Cassidy had been born Robert Parker. Harry Longabaugh was the real name of the Sundance Kid. Even Etta Place was thought to have been born under a different name.

"Let me tell you," Nana said. She loved the old stories. "Texana Harlow fell in love with Butch. She never knew him as anything else, and when Cressida was born, they agreed that she would be a Cassidy and not a Parker. It's been that way ever since."

Having descended from Butch Cassidy gave each of us our own sense of family and history, above and beyond being a Massie or a Walker. We didn't know who

Butch was before he was part of the Hole-in-the-Wall Gang, so calling ourselves anything other than Cassidy felt like being connected to a cloud.

Mrs. Mcafferty had gone still. Nana patted her hand. "What is it, Eleanor?" she asked.

Like any small town worth its salt, Bliss was full of secrets. Mrs. Mcafferty had supposedly had a fling with Jeb James just before he and Zinnia began dating. Zinnia James knew that Naomi and Will had produced Gracie. Did Nana know it, too? Had she kept quiet all these years about Eleanor Mcafferty's granddaughter living right under her nose? And from what Mrs. James had told me, they all three knew about the Cassidy charms.

"I have an old blanket or two," Mrs. Mcafferty said, laughing stiffly. She pulled her hand from Nana's, clasping her fingers together. She hesitated a second, and then added, "You can come on by for some of Naomi's old things. She told us . . . that is, we had a row. I don't reckon she wants them—" She swallowed and I imagined the lump of pain going down her throat. "She's not . . . not coming back."

I slipped into the kitchen and pulled a plate out of the cupboard and stacked it with lemon bars that Mama had sent over with Nana. My head was swimming from the possibility that Naomi had told her parents about Gracie. Was that why they'd fought? And was that why Eleanor Mcafferty was here now?

Oh Lord, would the secrets never stop?

Chapter 25

The women spent nearly four hours around the dining room table, laughing, gossiping, and concentrating as they decorated their dolls.

Yarn was unraveled and attached, instantly giving the dolls beards. Collars were made of strips of fur or decorative trim. The dolls were adorned with bits and pieces until they looked lush and fanciful.

"Gorgeous," Olive proclaimed, holding her Santa doll out so Madelyn could snap a picture of it.

Diane and Michele compared their creations. "We could leave them out all year long," Diane said. "They're just so adorable."

"Yours is the best, Madelyn," Mrs. Mcafferty said. "He's got himself a quirky personality."

"He's a keeper," Nana agreed. She fingered the metallic strands in the beard on her own doll. "Who would've ever thought you could unwind the pieces like this?"

She patted me on the shoulder before padding to the kitchen, slipping on her Crocs, and opening the Dutch door to the backyard. "See y'all later," she said, her doll tucked under her arm.

One by one, the women cleaned up their areas, gingerly cradling their Santa dolls as they trickled out. Finally only Madelyn was left. "Do you like it?" I asked her as I gathered up what was left of the trim, reorganized it in the correct bins, and did a quick sweep of the floor.

She set the Santa doll on the coffee table by the settee. He toppled over, landing on his back. "We could probably glue a half circle base on the bottom to lift his front," I said after she set him up again and he fell right back down.

"Phft!" She waved away the suggestion. "That, my dear Harlow, was enough crafting to hold me for a good long time. Like I said, I'll prop him up."

She leaned him against the hand-carved wooden box I kept in the center of the table, slowly let go, and backed away.

He stayed put. She clapped, and then held her camera up and snapped a picture of him. "He is awfully nice," she said, grinning. She might be done with crafts for a while, but she was proud of what she'd made.

She'd put her camera back in her Epiphanie bag and had her Santa tucked in the crook of her arm.

"Madelyn?"

She stopped at the door. "Hmm?"

Ever since that moment with Mrs. Mcafferty, I felt like a fissure had slowly been opening up inside me. Will and Gracie weren't my family, but they were beginning to feel like they were. Did I tell them what I suspected? Did I go find Mrs. Mcafferty and try to speak to her? Or did I zip my lips and join the secret keepers of Bliss—which included Nana and Mrs. James? I wanted to ask Madelyn what she thought.

"Did you tell him about your charm?"

"Not yet." I hadn't seen him again, but it was still weighing on me.

"A few secrets aren't a bad thing. I'm not going to tell Billy about our adventure the other night. No need to worry him," she said.

"I told Will about that."

"Did you, now? And he didn't mind?"

"I don't reckon he liked it," I said. "I have to talk to him about Gracie." I decided to tell her.

"You sure you want to get involved?"

"No." But I gathered up my coat and followed her onto the porch, locking the door and hanging the hand-made wooden sign telling potential customers that I'd be back in an hour. The truth of the matter was that I didn't think I could see Will and Gracie much longer without giving away that I had a secret burning inside me. Nana and her cronies had had a pact that they'd honored for decades. If this was about the Cassidy charm, I might feel differently, but this was about a divided family.

Gracie's divided family. And that I could do something about.

Madelyn gave me a hug. "Chin up, Harlow."

She headed off in her compact car and I headed the opposite direction in Meemaw's old truck.

Will wasn't in his office. The receptionist for the town offices arched a thin eyebrow at me, giving me a once-over. One drawback to being an up-and-coming fashion designer in a small town was that people expected me to always look the part. Faded jeans, even when they were paired with a stylish blouse, expensive boots, and a custom-tailored jacket, were still just jeans.

I didn't get the feeling that the woman would be paying any visits to Buttons & Bows. And that was too bad, because I could picture her in a flowing ankle-length dress made of silk-screened teal rayon. Her loss.

"When will he be back?" I asked.

"He's probably gone for the day. He's at the museum in the courthouse on the square finishing some things up before the grand reopening tomorrow," she said. Her eyebrow arched a bit higher. "Guess he didn't tell you that, huh?"

Her snide tone triggered a new thought. Maybe the dirty looks she was giving me were less about my jeans and more about the fact that I was here to see Will. I knew I was beginning to feel something pretty strong for him, but the fact that—I glanced at her nameplate—Millicent Price seemed to feel something for him too caused a band of jealousy to coil in my gut.

Looked like the same jealousy was rearing up inside her.

I uttered a quick thank-you to Millicent before scurrying out the door.

The holiday shoppers were out in force. It took three trips around the square before I found a parking space. With my coat zippered tight against the cold, I hurried across the street to the courthouse. Up the walkway, up the steps, and into the limestone building that had once been the county seat.

I wound in and out of the small rooms, stopping every few minutes to look more closely at some of Bliss's historic artifacts. There were sections with old furniture set up to represent a typical room in the late 1800s. Free-standing glass cases held photographs and bios of some of the earliest residents. I stopped in front of a display about the Kincaid family, with photos of Justin and

Vanetta, their first house—a modest ranch-style house just off of what was now the square, a sampling of lace made by Vanetta herself, and newspaper articles about historic events in the town.

I glanced at the clippings. Bliss had a storied past replete with bank robberies, a jewelry store holdup, and a brothel, all of the samples on display dated from the same year. I leaned closer, reading the headlines:

Bonnie and Clyde Leave Their Mark on Bliss after Bold Robbery in Broad Daylight

The Randolph House, Madame Annabel's Brothel, Burns to the Ground

Pincher's Jewelers in Possession of Retired Coin from U.S. Mint

Charles Denison Loses House on Mayberry Street to Justin Kincaid

I paused as I read the final headline, delving into the article itself. The details Will had told me were exactly what was in the paper. A poker game gone bad.

But in the end, it didn't actually reveal anything about what Dan Lee Chrisson might have been searching for in the house formerly owned by his family, if he'd been searching for anything.

I went back to the first article, about Bonnie and Clyde. They were as infamous as Butch Cassidy was around these parts. Over the years, they'd been glamorized, but the original articles about them had been harsh and truthful. They'd practically taken the town of Bliss hostage, robbing every business on the square and absconding with everything they could get their hands on.

I moved on to the next display case. It held the same quilt that had been in the Historical Society's office the night I'd gone there with Will. It had been refolded, probably to show the signature of the quilter. I didn't know much about quilting, but I did know that a signature helped authenticate it. The writing was faded, and so close to a ripped seam that it was almost impossible to read. I leaned closer to get a better look, but the letters were faded. I made out an *E* and two *N*s, but nothing else. This quilt had been used, and probably loved, which is just the way it should be. Just as cloth and garments tell stories, quilts did, too.

Another newspaper article was framed and displayed. I gave it a quick glance, ready to move on, but I recognized the woman photographed in the picture and stopped cold. My great-grandmother, Loretta Mae Cassidy.

I read the headline and, instantly, an ominous feeling passed through me.

Search for Missing Husband Over

Oh Lord. I scanned the article, pulling out the highlights. The husband in question was Bobby Whittaker. He'd simply vanished one day, leaving behind his wife, Loretta Mae, and their daughter, Coleta.

My lungs tightened, the air inside them suddenly thick and toxic.

The story of Loretta Mae's marriage was something that was never talked about. From bits and pieces I'd heard over the years, I'd assumed it had been a lot like

Mama's, with my father packing his bags and hitting the road. Just like that. Magic wasn't something he had any inclination to deal with.

Mama had raised Red and me on her own, just like Loretta Mae had raised her daughter, my grandmother, on her own. I'd grown up thinking that was how it was supposed to be. The Cassidy women just didn't get hitched.

But maybe the truth was that they got hitched just fine, but the men never stuck around.

I kept reading, finally getting to the part about Meemaw. Suspicion fell on Loretta Mae Cassidy Whittaker when she refused to talk to the sheriff. While Mr. Whittaker's whereabouts are still unknown, Mrs. Whittaker is no longer a suspect.

No longer a suspect. My blood ran cold as I wondered how Loretta Mae had been cleared. Her Cassidy charm was that whatever she wanted came true. Had she wanted her husband gone? She'd been young then, and maybe not as able to control her gift. Every action has a consequence. Meemaw had drilled that truth into my head. Mama grew flowers, but she also grew an abundance of weeds. Nana whispered to the goats, but the goats whispered back. Endlessly. What I created helped people realize their hopes and desires. The catch? Sometimes those hopes and desires weren't good. Or ethical. And I had no control over that.

But what about Meemaw? Had she started out making wishes willy-nilly, with no concern for the fallout? If she'd wanted Bobby Whittaker gone from her life, had he just walked out, or could there have been a more permanent consequence?

My head spun and I had a sudden feeling that the secrets would never end.

"I thought that was you," a voice said when I turned to the next display case.

I gasped, startled, and spun around. Will. "Just the person I came to see," I said, channeling some levity and making my voice sound light. More light than I felt.

"Lots of cool history in here," he said, gesturing to the article.

"Yeah," I said, forcing a smile. I didn't want him to know that the article about my family referenced a big secret skeleton in our closet, one I hadn't even known about. "Lots of history."

Mentally I tucked the saga of Bobby Whittaker and Loretta Mae away and focused on why I'd come to see Will. He'd had Gracie all to himself since Naomi had left her in his arms when she'd been an infant. He'd been waiting for Gracie to be ready to meet her grandparents, but now he might not have a choice.

One corner of his lips curved up and he leaned in to give me a quick kiss. I hated knowing that as soon as I told him what I'd come to say, that smile would morph into a worried frown.

"You moved the quilt," I said, deciding to ease into the blow.

"Made sense. More people come to the museum than to the Historical Society's office."

"Hmm." I glanced around, noticing the careful attention to detail in the displays. Everything was neatly labeled and looked ready for the grand opening.

"The display of the city is in here." He led me into another room, where the model of Bliss was the centerpiece. It sat under a Plexiglas cover, looking magnificent and unbelievably detailed.

"It's amazing." I walked around the table, starting to

notice things I hadn't seen before: miniature lights on the tiny trees dotting the town square, the shop signs, including Two Scoops, Seed-n-Bead, and Villa Farina, and a cascade of flowers covering the archway in the courtyard.

"Took more than a year to finish," he said.

The longest it had ever taken me to complete a project was forty-seven days, and that had been my very first gown—when I was seventeen. I'd made my own prom dress, creating the pattern, a muslin mock-up, and hand-embroidering the bodice. I'd also had to go to school and work at Sundance Kids with Nana, helping her tend to the goats. I'd finished the creation barely in time to go to the dance with my date. Creating garments gave more immediate satisfaction than architecture did. I admired him for being able to stick with his creation for so long. It was his art. His passion.

He pointed to Meemaw's redbrick house, tracing his finger past the yellow siding and toward the backyard and the edge of Nana and Granddaddy's goat farm. "There's Thelma Louise."

I looked closer, noticing the tiny goat reared up on its hind legs at the gate between Nana's and my properties.

"You have her figured out," I said with a laugh.

"Firsthand experience." He picked up a bottle of glass cleaner from the corner, sprayed the top of the case, and wiped it clean with a wad of paper towels. "Finished with Josie's outfit?"

"Almost," I said truthfully. "I got a little sidetracked by the Santa doll class and . . ."

"And . . ." he prompted.

"And one of the students. Mrs. Mcafferty."

He grew still, his blue eyes graying. "She was in your class?"

"Mmm-hmm."

He set the cleaner and paper towels on the case and turned to face me. "Spit it out, Cassidy."

Either I was terrible at masking my emotions, or he was starting to know me pretty well. Maybe both. "I think . . ." I trailed off, not knowing the right words to say.

"What? What do you think?" He knew something was up. His smile was already gone.

I swallowed, mustering up my gumption. "She mentioned the Winter Wonderland newsletter. I said you'd made it and she . . . she turned pale and . . ."

"Harlow," he said, his tone urging me to just come out and say what was on my mind.

"I'm pretty sure she knows about you and Naomi and . . . Gracie."

I wasn't sure what I expected, but it hadn't been utter and complete silence. His whole body grew tense, like he was on high alert during a military action. Very gently, I put my hand on his shoulder. "Will?"

My voice seemed to shake him out of his daze. "What did she say?"

"It's more what she didn't say, or how she said it. She mentioned that Naomi dated you, and then my grandmother told her that Gracie worked at Buttons & Bows, and Mrs. Mcafferty got really quiet and really pale and . . ." I replayed the conversation in my head in case I'd missed something. "They were talking about the newsletter you made, then about collecting blankets and things for Raylene Lewis. Mrs. Mcafferty said something about some quilts, but then . . . then Gracie was mentioned and her whole manner changed. She knows," I said, completely sure.

He paced the length of the room, his hands in his pockets and his arms pressed close to his body. "I should have taken her months ago. I guess I hoped we wouldn't have to face it. The Mcaffertys may have figured out about Gracie, but that doesn't mean they'll want her." He faced me, the gray of his eyes boring into mine, his jaw pulsing. "I don't want her hurt."

I read between the lines. What he was most afraid of was losing her to the Mcaffertys. "She's a strong girl, Will," I said. "And she loves you. Nothing's going to change that."

He gathered up the spray bottle and the paper towels, and putting his hand on the small of my back, he led me through the rooms to the stairs. We passed a group of men gathering up their tools and planks of wood. "All the renovations are done," one of them said. "Finally."

I recognized Arnie Barnett and stopped. "Hey, Arnie. Tell Hattie I said hey. Is she coming to the fashion show?"

Arnie grabbed hold of a circular saw and gripped a two-by-four under his arm. "We're plannin' on it. Been workin' on that house forever, and what with Dan Lee passin', well, I figure we gotta be there for the big day."

"See you then," I said.

He waved and then handed off the boards to the guy next to him.

Will ushered me back outside into the biting cold. Despite the nearly freezing weather, we hadn't had any black ice. So far Mrs. James's plan of buying up all the salt possible had worked. I just hoped her superstition held.

"What are you going to do?" I asked Will, wishing for all the world that I hadn't been the one to take his smile away.

"I'm not sure, Cassidy. I have to think about it." He

walked me to my truck, holding the door open for me, then shutting it after I slid into the driver's seat. I cranked the handle, rolling down the window. "Thanks for the heads-up," he said.

All I could do was nod. Being thanked for warning him about a big upset in his family felt wrong.

But Will wasn't about to shoot the messenger. No, instead he leaned in, his lips lightly brushing mine, heating the air between us.

"Anytime," I said, feeling my cheeks blush.

"I'll talk to you later," he said.

"I'll be around." The engine rumbled and I backed out, turning the truck toward the Denison mansion. I couldn't do anything to smooth the coming bumps between Will, Gracie, and the Mcaffertys. I couldn't find out the truth about Loretta Mae and my great-grandfather—at least not this second. But I could make sure that everything was set at the old Victorian, that the fashion show went off without a hitch, and that I did everything I could to save Raylene from any more heartache. I amended that last goal. I wanted to save her from heartache . . . if she was innocent. At the very least, I aimed to get to the truth about whatever had happened to Dan Lee.

Chapter 26

When I arrived at the Denison mansion, the door was unlocked. I was sure Mrs. James was here somewhere. There were too many last-minute tasks for her not to be in and out.

I looked around, making mental notes of what needed to be done, but pulled up short in the kitchen. Raylene Lewis stood at the island busily chopping celery and red onions on a cutting board, her eyes dry, but red-rimmed.

Nana had been right. Raylene had been through the wringer—but was any of it her own fault?

When I looked at her, a multitude of images flashed in my mind. Not one of them rose to the surface. I saw her in different outfits, but there wasn't an orange prison jumpsuit in the mix.

I peered into one of the bowls set on the counter. "Chicken salad?"

"Mmm-hmm. I offered to help Mrs. James with the appetizers. I need to do something to keep busy. Hattie's got Boone for a little while."

Another bowl held egg salad dotted with red pimientos, and a third had thinly sliced cucumbers. "Tea sandwiches?"

"My specialty," she replied.

She spooned a dollop of chicken salad onto a pumpernickel round and handed it to me. I popped the whole thing into my mouth, groaning as I swallowed. "Delicious," I said, remembering that she'd said she wanted to open a bed-and-breakfast and serve high tea.

"Can I ask you something?" I spooned another bit of chicken salad onto a bit of crust.

"About Dan Lee?"

I nodded. "I'm pretty sure his name was actually Charles Denison."

She stopped in mid-chop, the knife trembling in her hand. Her voice dropped to a whisper. "How'd you find out?"

"It doesn't matter," I said, hoping she'd drop the question. "Did you know?"

She set down the knife and leaned against the counter. She brushed back a strand of hair that had fallen over her forehead. "I knew his family was from these parts," she finally answered. "After we were married, I found out his father had changed the family name. Not that he told me, mind you. I found his birth certificate."

At last, some bit of truth. Probably the same one I'd found. "Why'd he change his name? Do you know?"

But she shrugged. "All he ever said was that his father thought it would be easier on them not to have to live up to any expectations about being Denisons, or falling from grace. It's hard enough just being a normal person, forget about trying to live up to the Kincaids. That's what he always told me."

"Because Charles Denison lost the house to Justin Kincaid?" I asked. I could understand it, in a way, but I didn't think anyone would care nowadays.

"Dan Lee told me the family never forgave Charles Denison for gambling away their home. I reckon they're the ones who didn't want to be reminded about what had happened."

I could understand that, though I would never deny who I was or the blood that pumped through my veins.

Raylene's eyes glazed and she slipped into a memory. "I remember I told Hattie when I found out his real name. I didn't know what to do. Arnie was headin' out to Fort Worth for a collectors show, but my sister, bless her heart, she knew I was beside myself. I couldn't see straight. I just couldn't forgive him, you understand? He lied to me. We have a child who's a Denison, and I didn't know nothing about that family except from the stories the old-timers around here tell. You know that Miranda Lambert song 'Baggage Claim'?" she asked, blinking away her daze.

"Of course." Miranda was a fellow Texan—a hometown girl who'd made good.

"That line in the song, about her dragging around some guy's sensitive ego? Well, it made me realize that Dan Lee maybe had a whole lotta baggage that I sure as hell didn't know about. If he lied about that, what else was he keeping from me?"

She definitely had *that* right. I came back to my other theory, the one that explained why he was so interested in the old family house. Maybe something was hidden there.

It would explain why he kept on living as Dan Lee instead of Charles Denison, and it would also explain why he spent so much time on the renovation.

My ideas expanded, sprouting and developing. If someone, like Helen Abernathy, for instance, knew he was related to the Denison family, and he was seen poking around at the mansion, would they put together that he was searching for something? And if someone like Mrs. Abernathy, who had had kin around the time the original Charles Denison had lost the house to the Kincaids, noticed his actions, would she *know* what he was looking for?

Raylene knowing about Dan Lee's real identity was not really the answer I'd been hoping for. If she hadn't known the truth about him, her motive wasn't as strong. But she did know. Could she or Hattie have planned how to get revenge? One of them could have arranged to meet him here, lured him up to the widow's walk, and shoved him off.

Good Lord, I hoped not.

I left her to arrange her tea sandwiches, another idea tickling the edge of my brain. I hadn't been able to figure out what Dan Lee might have been looking for, but then a possibility hit me like a bolt of lightning. The article at the museum! Bonnie and Clyde had robbed Bliss blind. The stories those old-timers talked about had the outlaws staying right here in this house. What if they'd stashed something here and Dan Lee had known about it?

The front door swung open, with an accompanying burst of north wind swirling in. I was startled, but my rush of nerves simmered down as Gracie dashed in, grabbing hold of the door, positioning her body behind it, and walking backward until she'd pushed it shut. "Harlow! Where are you? Harlo—"

"Here," I said, coming out of the parlor.

She yelped, jumping and slapping her hand to her chest. "Oh!" Then, as if the fright was just a minor blip, she scurried toward me. "Look! I bought it. My dad said it could be from both of us and he gave me the money and I went and bought it."

"Bought what?" I asked, eyeing the hand-sewn shopping bag she'd made swinging by her side.

She plunked down on the step below us and pulled her treasure out of the bag. "The baby quilt for Josie's baby."

It was about three by three and was just like Gracie had described it. Each patch had a different activity—zippers and buttons and pouches—all made to keep a baby entertained. "She'll love it, Gracie," I said, pulling down one of the jumbo plastic zippers to see the hidden teething ring tucked away inside.

"I know the baby'll have to be older, but Josie's gonna get tons of those onesies and you'll probably make the baby a whole wardrobe, so she'll need something for later on, right? My dad said it was a good idea."

"You and your dad are absolutely right," I said. "It's a great idea and Josie'll love it."

She heaved a relieved sigh and ran her fingers through her hair. Raylene popped her head out of the kitchen and Gracie yelped. "Oh!" Her cheeks stained red. "I'm so sorry! I didn't know you were here."

"It's okay," Raylene said after I introduced them. "My baby's not old enough for that yet"—she pointed to the activity quilt, which Gracie had refolded and was sliding back into her shopping bag—"but when he's a little older, he'll love it."

Realization dawned on Gracie's face. Her eyes grew round and her mouth followed. "Your baby was the one found at the goat farm, wasn't it? Boone, right? That's a really great name. I might, like, name my own baby that one day. Would you mind?"

Raylene brushed her wool skirt down over her legs, trying to keep her smile light. "What is it people say? Imitation is the best form of flattery, or something like that, right?"

Gracie clapped, nearly bouncing up and down. "Good!" She looked around, like she'd lost something. "Is he here?"

"He's with his aunt for a little while," she said.

Gracie, with typical teenage exaggeration, scrunched her lips to one side and dipped her chin in disappointment. "Darn."

"You'll get another chance to meet him, I'm sure," I said, hoping I was right and that Boone wasn't about to be whisked off to foster care while his mom went to the pokey.

Raylene went back to her cooking while Gracie and I headed outside to the covered tent to check on the setup for the fashion show and the tables for the craft fair. I didn't dare turn on the outdoor patio heaters with their bronze bases and heated glass tubes. I had no idea if Mrs. James had lined up extra propane tanks along with her bags of salt, but the biting cold meant we'd need the heaters nonstop during the festival, and I didn't want to risk running low on propane by using up the heat now.

Gracie and I managed to make sure everyone on the master list, as well as those stragglers—like Nana—who'd signed on late, had a space to showcase their wares. Our fingers were numb and our lips blue by the time we were done. Which was just when Mrs. James poked her head in to see how we were doing.

"Would you look at that," she said, nodding with approval. "It looks perfect."

I chuckled to myself, thinking Mrs. James had impeccable timing, just like my granddaddy's sister, the one we called Aunt Babe. Whenever it came time to wash up the dishes, she mysteriously disappeared, returning again just when the task was about finished. "I was just gettin' ready to come help you!" she always proclaimed, as if we worked too darn fast.

"Harlow," Mrs. James said after Gracie and I moved the last table into place and were finishing stringing the twinkling white lights and running a strand of holly-dotted garland down the center of it. "About my outfit for the fashion show—"

I froze. She hadn't even finished her sentence, but it felt as if the air had been sucked out of the room. She'd stopped by to pick it up the day before. Had something happened to it? Had she ripped the hem?

The feeling that there was a problem with one of my creations was akin to telling a baker that her cake was lopsided. And tasteless. "What's wrong?"

She seemed to sense my concern. "Relax, Harlow. Goodness. Nothing's wrong. I just took the wrong bag, that's all."

I blew out the breath I'd been holding, slapping my hand to my chest. "Oh, Mrs. James, you scared me!"

She pulled her scarf around her neck to ward off the chill, but her cheeks were already pink from just a minute in the tent. "Good heavens. I just brought it back for you, is all. If you'll bring mine to the event, I'd be forever grateful." She beckoned us toward the house. "Tomorrow the heaters will make this place nice and toasty, but for now, come on out of the cold."

As we followed her inside, I handed Gracie two enormous woven bags filled with mistletoe and Styrofoam balls. "Wanna tackle this quick little project?"

She pulled out the sample—a round ball of the green plant, topped with a glittering gold ribbon.

"It's beautiful!" she exclaimed, looking up at me in awe.

I hated to burst her bubble, but I couldn't take the credit. "It's a Victorian kissing ball," I said. "I saw it in a magazine." Thanks to Meemaw. I knew it was the perfect addition to the holiday decorations, and being a glutton for punishment, I had to include them even if I didn't actually have time to make them.

Her expression turned soft and romantic. "Victorian kissing ball," she said dreamily, as if she could feel the words floating away from her.

I'd gotten the traditional plants from Mama. It didn't matter the time of the year, how much rain we got, or if it froze every night. She could grow anything, and with a simple glance, she could make a plant double or triple in size. I couldn't do anything at a glance, except read a person's color palette based on how dark or light their hair, skin, and eyes are, and whether or not the underlying tone is warm or cool.

But Mama? She could start with seeds and before long, she'd have a garden full of luscious plants.

Gracie reached into the second bag and took out clusters of rosemary, sage, lavender, lemon geranium, boxwood, anise hyssop, and oregano. These would fill out each of the balls, but the mistletoe, which my granddaddy had cut from the cedar elm and hackberry trees Mama had concentrated on, would be the centerpiece of each one.

Libby, Stephen, and Sandy Allen had already hung greenery throughout the house for me, draping it around the outside of the front door and over the archways and banisters inside, and wrapping long evergreen boughs around the fence and porch railing out front. I'd made an enormous wreath for the front door and a full evergreen swag dotted with red berries adorned the fireplace in the parlor.

The kissing balls were the final touch.

"So do they work just like regular mistletoe?" Gracie asked after she'd sorted through the different types of greenery and had organized the materials. She'd left all but one of the six-inch floral foam balls in the bag, but she'd taken out the twenty-four-gauge florist's wire, a pile of pretty little bells to hang from the bottom of the ornaments, and yards and yards of shimmering gold ribbon.

"They sure do. The article said that during Victorian times, a gentleman would try to waltz under the kissing ball so he could steal a kiss from his lady."

"But we don't waltz," she said, frowning.

"We don't need that pretense anymore. People aren't quite so uptight as they were in the 1800s."

"Thank God," she said, more to herself than to me. I watched her for a second, trying to decide if the comment meant she had a boy she'd like to meet under the kissing ball. But I couldn't tell.

"Just stick the mistletoe in? Is that it?" she asked, jamming a sprig of lavender into the ball.

"That's pretty much it, yup. Simple."

She plopped down, diving into the task. She poked the sprigs of mistletoe into the foam ball, filling it in until it was a jumbled mess. "It doesn't look like the sample," she complained after a few minutes.

Boy, oh boy, was that the truth. Fronds sprang this way and that, with no rhyme or reason. Gracie had a gift with fabric and sewing. She was just discovering it, true, but it was evident. Not so much with floral design, I thought.

She huffed, jabbing another sprig of rosemary into the ball.

"You have to work with the stems, not against them," Raylene said.

She'd finished the food preparation—at least for the time being—and sidled over to the table, sinking down in the chair next to Gracie. She picked up the sample, holding it by the sparkly gold ribbon. "It's like a garden. You can't force the sprigs in. You have to feel where they go, piece by piece." She paused and cracked a smile. "And then you trim it."

"I put shears in one of the bags," I said.

Gracie picked through the pile she'd dumped out onto the table, but came up empty-handed. She pulled the other bag between her legs, bending over and rummaging through it, finally straightening up, holding the garden shears up like a trophy. "Got 'em."

As she offered them to Raylene, I had a flash of protectiveness. If Raylene had shoved Charles Denison off the widow's walk, then Gracie was in the company of a murderer. I didn't want to believe it, but hell's bells, we all were. My doubt turned to straight-up anxiety, as pure and harsh as a batch of freshly brewed Texas moonshine.

My mind raced through my options. (1) Gather up Gracie and the mistletoe and hightail it out of the Denison mansion; (2) pretend that everything was grand and that Raylene wasn't a suspect in a murder (not really a feasible option given that I was a Cassidy and Cassidys faced everything head-on); or (3) go fishing.

I opted for number three. In my heart of hearts, I didn't believe Raylene could have done anything to

Charles Denison, so I truly believed she was innocent. But as Meemaw always said, an ordinary person—meaning anyone but her—couldn't wish something into being. And even with her sheer force of will, she couldn't make people do something they weren't inclined to do. I hadn't come back to Bliss only because Loretta Mae had wanted me to. I'd come back to Bliss because it was my home, and somewhere deep inside, I'd wanted to return to my roots and my family.

It was the same for my charm. When I sewed for someone, their desires rose inside them and were realized. But the consequences of those desires sometimes had a sharp edge; things didn't always work out the way I expected them to.

If Raylene did, in fact, have a hand in Charles Denison's death, it had been personal. She wouldn't turn on us, would she?

I chastised myself for even questioning it. Of course she would. Anyone would do anything to protect a secret like murder. So maybe number three, going fishing for more answers, trying to gather information from Raylene to clear her, at least in my mind, wasn't the smartest thing to do. And I could almost guarantee that Will didn't want Gracie in the proximity of a potential murderer.

But how did I get Gracie out of here without upsetting Raylene, in case she was innocent, or—if she was guilty—because an agitated murderess didn't seem like a good idea.

"I'm hell on heels, say what you will . . ." The Pistol Annies' song broke into my scattered thoughts.

Gracie's cell phone. She answered. "Okay. Mmm-hmm. Sure, Daddy." She hung up, stuffing the phone back into her pants pocket and looking up at me. "Can I take these home to work on them, Harlow? My dad's on his way to pick me up."

Problem solved. Gracie would go home and be safe in her own house with her daddy.

"Sure—"

"Just close your eyes and feel the plants," Raylene said. She took the mistletoe-laden foam ball and trimmed as if she'd made a thousand of the decorations and the process was old hat.

Gracie watched her in awe, uttering an amazed "Wow" when Raylene was finished. The mistletoe ball looked more perfect than the sample. Lush and festive, but not so perfect that it looked fake.

Raylene had a definite gift.

"Thanks," she said. "I worked in a florist shop when I was in high school. If I ever open my shop or bed-and-breakfast, I'll be doing this type of thing all the time."

A pang of regret for Raylene filled me. I knew just what it was like to have something you wanted so badly you could taste it.

Mrs. James came back into the kitchen, her shoulders sagging slightly. I had a vague recollection of a Bible verse about each of us carrying our own burdens. What was Mrs. James lugging around that bore down on her?

And then it hit me. Mrs. Mcafferty had sat right in my dining room during the Santa doll class and said that she had a quilt that had belonged to Ethel Bishop. The name had rung a bell, but I hadn't thought much about it. But now it resurfaced. I'd researched Butch Cassidy plenty over the years. Nobody was really sure what Etta Place's real name was, but there were plenty of folks who speculated that it was Ethel Bishop. How could I have forgotten that?

My lungs clenched, as if the air had suddenly been sucked out of them. The room started to spin. Jebediah had had an affair with Eleanor Mcafferty before he'd married Zinnia. What if . . . oh God . . . what if Eleanor had gotten pregnant and . . .

I followed Mrs. James's gaze, and suddenly I knew where her thoughts were. Everything fell into place.

Gracie. She'd known all along who Gracie Flores's grandparents were, but she'd kept it a secret. I hadn't thought too deeply about why she hadn't told, but a collision of ideas suddenly converged in my mind.

One of them careened to the forefront. The three pageant dresses in my great-grandmother's wardrobe. Gracie had worn a green gown—the very one that Eleanor Mcafferty had worn when she'd been a Margaret in the annual ball. And the only one Mrs. James had told me was authentic. It had belonged to Etta Place.

Another recollection crystallized in my mind. Gracie was a gifted seamstress, on par with where I'd been at the same age, and when she'd touched that gown, she'd been lost in a daze, as if she could see the history that dress held within its seams.

"Oh Lord," I whispered. "The dressing gown." The same thing had happened right here, upstairs, when she'd touched the silk robe worn by Pearl Denison.

Words Mrs. James had spoken a few months ago came back to me when we'd talked about Eleanor Mcafferty wearing the green Margaret gown. "Your great-grandmother took one look at her," she'd told me, "and said things were as they should be; it belonged to her."

What Loretta Mae wanted, Loretta Mae got. Most often, she wanted the truth even if it took years and years for that truth to come to light.

That Margaret dress had belonged to Eleanor back then because she'd already been pregnant with Naomi. Loretta Mae had to have known she'd been carrying a child with Cassidy blood running through her veins. Meemaw wanted that dress, one day, to belong to Etta Place's other great-great-great-granddaughter.

Gracie.

Chapter 27

While I'd gone off on a rabbit trail in my mind, decoding Gracie's family heritage, she and Raylene had whipped up two more kissing balls. Mrs. James had sidled over to me and now she rested her hand on my forearm. "I can see by the look on your face that you've figured something out," she said to me so only I could hear.

Before I could even fathom an answer, a robust "Ho! Ho! Ho!" came from the foyer. Will's gravelly baritone bounced off the ornate wallpaper and into the kitchen.

"In here!" Gracie called.

We heard the door close and the *clomp clomp clomp* of his boots crossing the hardwood floor. They paused—probably checking out the holiday decorations, I thought—then resumed.

"It was never my story to tell," she continued softly. "Eli and Jeb . . ." She paused, swallowing heavily, as if it was difficult to think about her husband and Mrs. Mcafferty, even after all these years. "I always wondered, you know. She married Rudy so quickly. But I wasn't sure until Naomi was about five years old. We ran into them on the square one Sunday. I remember it, clear as day.

Jeb bent down and ruffled her hair. Seeing them side by side like that . . . well, I just knew."

But she'd never said a word. Don't ask, don't tell. Bliss was full of those kinds of secrets.

"Knew what?" Will asked. I'd been so transfixed by Mrs. James that I hadn't heard him come up beside me.

"Nothin'," I said, inadvertently dropping the "g." "Just idle gossip." That affected his daughter.

He looked at me funny, as if he could tell I was holding back, but Gracie popped out of her chair before he could question me any further. "Daddy, look!" She held up the kissing ball she'd just finished, with Raylene's help.

If it upset him to see his daughter sitting with a woman some people thought capable of murder, he didn't show it. Or maybe he was just really good at hiding his feelings. Either way, he ambled over to Gracie and bent down, planting a kiss on the top of her head. "Where do these go?" he asked, but he turned and winked at me. I got the feeling he knew *exactly* where he'd like one to go. Right over my head. It was mistletoe, after all.

I smiled, pushing my glasses up the bridge of my nose to distract myself. Gracie's lineage had thrown me for a loop, one that was going to be more tricky to unravel than a strand of yarn for the Santa dolls' beards. My head swam with all the secrets swirling around town. I needed my sketches and my workroom and the sanity that fabric and threads and buttons and bows offered me. Buttons & Bows was my safe place. My thinking space. And right now all I wanted to do was get back to my little farmhouse, work on Josie's outfit, and in the process sort through the web of mysteries I found myself tangled in.

Chapter 28

Mama dropped by soon after I got home, her sheriff beau in tow. Now Hoss McClaine sat back on my sofa, his left leg bent, his ankle resting on his right knee, looking more content than I'd ever seen him. Mama crouched in front of my little Christmas tree, one arm casually draped over his brown leather boot. She gazed at each of the wrapped gifts resting on the pale green satin skirt—an heirloom from Cressida Cassidy, Butch and Texana's daughter and my great-great-grandmother. I didn't have many things that had belonged to her, but this tree skirt, hand-embroidered with snowflakes, was something I'd found in Meemaw's attic and I knew I'd use it every year. A note, in Loretta Mae's shaky cursive, had been pinned to it.

Made and embroidered by Cressida Harlow (Parker) Cassidy, circa 1930.

"Harlow Jane," Mama said, "my goodness, but these packages have to be prettier than whatever it is you've wrapped up." She looked at Hoss. "Aren't they plain gorgeous, honey?" she asked him, the "honey" more of a

Southern endearment than a pet name. Mama called nearly everyone honey.

"Yes, ma'am. Plain gorgeous," the sheriff said. A funny little smile danced on his lips, but with his iron gray mustache, soul patch, and the black cowboy hat on his head, he still looked intimidating. Or maybe it was my recollecting all the times I'd spent in his office, being read the riot act.

I peered at the colorful lights decorating the tree and the ornaments Mama had given me—a new one each year to represent what I'd accomplished or what I was passionate about. Most of them were sewing machines, spools of thread, dress forms, or some other trinket that had to do with dressmaking.

I chased away the memories, focusing on the moment. Christmas in Bliss. Mama had always done her best to make the holiday magical for Red and me. It didn't matter that our daddy had walked out on us. It didn't matter that she'd never had money to buy us all the fancy duds and big-ticket items the well-to-do folks in Bliss were giving their children. We had fresh-baked cinnamon rolls, roasted turkey and corn bread stuffing, and handmade gifts for each other.

Nothing much had changed. The treasures inside the wrapped packages Mama was admiring—necklaces strung from handmade felted beads for Mama, Nana, Josie, my sister-in-law, Darcie, and Mrs. James—had been made with love. And I thought they were just as pretty as the wrappings themselves.

For the color-blocked scarf for my newly discovered cousin Sandra and red cabled mittens with black and white cuffs for Libby, I'd recycled several different sweaters that had been more than fifty percent wool fiber, one of them a cashmere set I'd found in a Hoboken thrift shop. I'd used the technique of fulling, or washing the disassembled sweaters in extra-hot water. That, and the agitation, made the fibers interlock. The result was a thick felt perfect for scarves, mittens, bags, decorative flowers, bags, and anything else I could imagine.

I had planned to give Gracie a special one-on-one lesson on dyeing fabric for her Christmas gift, but if my thinking was right and she was a cousin, she needed her own pair of mittens, too.

"Mama," I said, not able to keep my wonderings to myself any longer. "Etta Place had a child by Butch Cassidy."

"Mmm-hmm. Old news, honey."

Old news that had resulted in a second Cassidy bloodline. And maybe a third offshoot.

"I also heard that Jebediah James had a little"—I glanced at Hoss McClaine, wondering how to phrase the thought—"something-something with Eleanor Mcafferty."

She looked up at me, here eyes narrowing just enough for me to see that she was curious. "I reckon I've heard something about that."

"That's old news, too. Happened before she married Rudy," Hoss said.

"Is that right?" I said, playing innocent.

He nodded, a satisfied smile tickling his lips. He looked pleased at having something to contribute to the conversation. "That's right. Funny," he mused, running the pad of his thumb over the soul patch on his chin. "Naomi Mcafferty don't look much like her daddy, does she?"

Mama and I both whipped our heads around to stare at him. Gossip? From the sheriff?

"She favors her mother, is all," Mama said, but from the way she looked at me, her head angled to one side and her eyebrows pulled together in alarm, I knew that she'd got my meaning.

She picked up another gift, this one a pretty throw I'd made for Josie and Nate. It was their first Christmas as a married couple, and the blanket was meant to commemorate it. "You even wrap things with flair. You have a gift, Harlow Jane," she said, turning to me as she spoke.

The corners of my mouth lifted, but I knew the smile didn't spread all the way to my eyes. With Hoss sitting there and not looking inclined to move anytime soon, Mama and I had two choices: (1) Drop the conversation until later, or (2) be cryptic.

An invisible thread of understanding passed between us. We were going for number two. "I reckon we all have gifts of one kind or another."

"I guess I do have a way with plants."

"You guess?" Hoss let out a belly laugh. "How many sprouts and flowers and weeds d'ya have growin' at your place, Tessa? Good grief, it's practically a jungle over there." He spoke slowly and with a thick drawl that stretched out his words until "there" became "thar."

"And what about your mama and those goats?" he went on. "I've never seen nothin' like that. If I didn't know better, I'd say they actually understand each other."

Oh boy. People didn't often speak of the Cassidy charms in the open, and we preferred it that way. We did our thing, folks considered us eccentric—in a good way—and that was that.

I held my breath, waiting to see if he'd say anything else, but he seemed to be done with his observations.

Cryptic meant we had to tread lightly and lead up to the real point of the conversation slowly and without raising a bit of suspicion. I turned back to Mama, wondering how to get from point A in our conversation to point D, given that Hoss wasn't budging from his spot on my sofa.

"What's your gift, Sheriff?" I asked.

"Ferreting out bad guys, I reckon," he said after a few seconds' pause.

Mama patted the sheriff's knee. "You are mighty good at that." She placed Josie and Nate's present back under the tree and then turned to me. "Gracie's been working with you for a while," she said. "What's her gift?"

Mama knew exactly what I'd been getting at with the question about Eleanor Mcafferty and Jebediah James. The Cassidy blood would have carried through their child, Naomi, and straight into Gracie. It was the perfect opening. "She's a talented girl. Took to sewing like fuzz on a peach," I said, stifling the cringe that surfaced. I'd been away from Bliss for so long that I'd lost a fair amount of colorful Southern speech, but it was coming back to me full force.

"And not a lick of formal training or lessons," Mama said thoughtfully.

"Nope. Just picked it up on her own. When I tell her something or show her a technique, she gets it"—I snapped my fingers—"just like that. And do you know, she's got some special connection to fabric."

Hoss arched a bushy brow at me, shifting his gaze until it zeroed in on the stacks of fabric against the wall in the workroom.

"Yes, I know," I said. "Fabric-aholic. It's a prerequisite for every seamstress."

Mama wasn't about to be sidetracked. "Does she, now?" she asked.

Once again, I mulled over how to phrase it so she'd get my meaning but Hoss wouldn't. "I've seen her touch a garment and be swept away by the history in it."

"Like she can see the past," Mama said quietly, musing.

"Exactly."

Mama nodded thoughtfully, but her eyes had opened wider than normal and her nostrils flared slightly. I could almost see the thoughts darting in and out of her head because I imagined that they were the very same thoughts making their way around mine. Did anyone else know about Naomi Mcafferty being Jeb James's daughter? Did Naomi have any magical charms? Did she know the truth about her lineage?

"Mama," I said, changing the direction of my thoughts. "All this talk about family has me wondering—"

"Were we talkin' about family?" She darted a glance at the sheriff, who, I admit, I'd momentarily forgotten was there.

"I've been thinking about family, I mean, what with Red and Darcie coming in for the holidays, and such."

Hoss McClaine's expression was blank and he seemed awfully intent on studying the colorful Christmas tree lights, but I knew that while we might think he wasn't paying attention, he was likely catching every word, nuance, and look Mama and I had shared.

"I was just wondering," I said, thinking he might actually have a little insight to the story of Loretta Mae and Bobby Whittaker. "I was at the courthouse on the square yesterday."

"Old John and Arnie did some fine work there, from what I saw," the sheriff said, nodding with approval.

"Renovation ain't easy, 'specially when the Historic Society gets involved in things. Old John knows everythin' there is to know about them old houses."

"They were just wrapping things up when I was there. Will Flores made a model of the square and the historic district. This house is on it, Mama."

"Is that so?" Mama asked, but she was back to perusing the gifts under the tree.

"Yes, ma'am, that's so." I picked up my lookbook, absently flipping through the pages, trying to be nonchalant. "They have some old quilts. A few old newspaper articles. Oh, and an iron and sewing machine from the turn of the century."

"I guess we'll have to go give it a gander," she said, looking at the name on a gift tag dangling from another package.

"There was one about—"

The Christmas tree suddenly jerked, sending a shower of pine needles cascading through the branches and right on top of Mama's head. They pooled on the tree skirt below her.

Which was strange. The tree was still fresh. I didn't have a cat. No small critters had climbed the trunk. Which meant only one thing.

Meemaw.

"About what, Harlow?"

I considered defying Meemaw, but there was really no reason to at the moment. She'd gotten her point across. She wanted me to hush up about whatever her past was with my great-grandfather, Bobby Whittaker, and I could oblige, for the moment. But not forever. It was my own family history, after all. "About Butch Cassidy and the other old outlaws from around here," I said. "Probably nothing you don't already know."

For now I would focus on Gracie's part in the Cassidy family tree. It had been shaken, once again. Which meant more people to keep secret . . . and more people who had secrets to keep.

Chapter 29

Christmas Eve morning, the day of the fashion show, I sat bolt upright in bed, panting. Beads of sweat dotted my forehead. I wasn't sure what I'd been dreaming about, but a panicky feeling stayed with me.

I'd gone to bed thinking about the newspaper articles I'd seen in the courthouse museum. Meemaw and her missing husband were on my mind, but there was something else, something about Dan Lee Chrisson and his murder, that was preoccupying me.

Finally, I got up, pulling on a fleece jacket and slippers, and padded downstairs. I made a mug of herbal tea, dribbled in a touch of honey, and sat down at the computer. I started Googling, starting with Meemaw's name. I got a few hits, but nothing that dated back to when she was a young married woman. Bobby Whittaker didn't come up at all.

I sat back, sipping my tea, the warmth of the cup spreading to the chilled tips of my fingers. Eventually it also spread to my brain, making me more alert. Meemaw's message in the mirror came back to me again. *Help her.* She thought Raylene was innocent.

Which meant Hattie rose to the top of the list, and

Helen Abernathy a distant second, if only I could fathom a motive.

I came back to the idea that Dan Lee wanted something in the Denison house, something that, perhaps, Bonnie and Clyde had hidden there. But wouldn't anything hidden have been found by now?

The door on that thought process slammed shut. Absently, I typed in Charles Denison's name, sitting back to see what magic Google could come up with.

Plenty on Charles Denison, the first, as it turned out, but nothing on my Charles Denison. I scanned the articles, but nothing struck a chord. It was the same information I already knew.

But he'd lived for who knew how long as Dan Lee Chrisson, and Madelyn and I had found at least one newspaper clipping of an article he'd written. I Googled his pseudonym, scrolling through the listings that popped up. No Facebook page. No LinkedIn profile. But several links to articles he'd written.

I cleaned the lenses of my glasses on my jacket and zeroed in on the results. He'd written for different regional magazines and newspapers. One, for the *Dallas Morning News*, was about hobbyists, just like the article we'd seen in the accordion file in his apartment. Another, for a coin collectors magazine, talked about coins President Roosevelt had the U.S. Mint produce and then melt down. Finally, there was one opinion piece that had been run in several different regional magazines. I clicked on each one, ending on the editorial "Take Back Your Family History."

And suddenly I knew what I had to do.

It was still too early for the courthouse square to be swarming with people, but Villa Farina, Bliss Square Donuts, and the mom-and-pop coffee shop just down from the Sheriff's Department were plenty busy. "Excuse me. Pardon me. Ow!" I made my way slowly through each one, checking for either Hoss or Gavin McClaine. They hadn't been at the town offices, and they didn't seem to be on the square.

I didn't know Gavin well enough to guess at where he might be, but I did have an inkling about Hoss. I pulled my cell phone out of my bag and dialed Mama. She answered before the first ring had finished, but her voice was groggy. "Harlow Jane, what in tarnation?"

"Sorry, Mama. I need to talk to your boyfriend."

"Usually you call him the sheriff, but today he's my boyfriend? What do you need, sugar?"

"Mama, is he there?"

A loud rustling sounded in my ear followed by muffled voices. "Mama?" I waited. More low talking. "Mama!"

The rustling stopped and a gruff voice sounded in my ear. "Simmer down, Harlow. What is it?"

"Hoss! Thank goodness. I was wondering if, well, if maybe I could take a look at something that's probably in your office?"

"My office," he repeated, but not as a question.

"Right. In your office. Or somewhere at the Sheriff's Department."

"And just what would we have over there that you'd be interested in?"

I opened my mouth to speak, but got tongue-tied. "Let me guess," he said, and I realized that that the question was more rhetorical, anyway. "Might it be a brown accordion file belonging to one Dan Lee Chrisson, born as one Charles Denison, that you're interested in?"

I swallowed the lump in my throat. "Could be."

"Uh-huh. And do I want to know how you know about this folder?"

"Mmm, probably not."

"You're probably right. I'll be there in ten minutes," he said.

"Okay," I said.

"And, Harlow?"

"Yes, Sheriff?"

"Just so we're clear, my Christmas present to you is your freedom. Can't wrap a shiny red ribbon around that and stick it under your tree, but it's my gift just the same."

I got the message loud and clear. He wasn't going to throw me in the hoosegow for my crime. "Thank you, Sheriff," I said, breathing a sigh of relief, but I wasn't sure he'd heard me. The line was already dead.

I'd given up trying to figure out what happened to Dan Lee purely to keep Raylene and Boone, mother and son, together. Now, more than anything, I just wanted to know the truth. I'd fallen from the very same balcony as Dan Lee had. If not for dumb luck—and the fashion show tent breaking my fall—I'd be dead too.

Someone was responsible for that.

I felt a smidgen closer to the truth after meeting with Hoss, but the pieces still didn't all fit together.

I milled around the house, getting dressed in gray wool pants I'd designed and made and a red cashmere V-neck sweater that Orphie Cates had bought for me at a clothing shop in SoHo one year. As I pulled my hair into a loose bun, I stared at the blond streak sprouting from my temple. It fairly glowed. Or at least seemed five shades lighter than it had the night before.

I gasped, remembering flashes of Libby and Gracie from my dream. It was just like theirs. Or theirs was just like mine.

I fluttered my fingertips over the thick lock, wondering what in the world it could mean.

Just as I was leaving, my cell phone pinged. A text message from Mama.

Meet me at Villa Farina before the fashion show.

I'd finished the garments for the fashion show, but even so, could I spare the time? I'd have to do final tweaks once the women were in their outfits, and I wanted to make sure Will hung up the Victorian kissing balls. Not to mention that the temperature had finally dropped to well below freezing. Mrs. James's theory that buying the salt would prevent the freeze hadn't worked, but thank God she'd stocked up. It would help avoid any spills if the sidewalk grew treacherous.

And, truth be told, I wanted to take another gander at the widow's walk now that I had an inkling about what Dan Lee had been looking for. Walls couldn't normally talk, but maybe, just maybe, these ones would.

But a hot pumpkin spice latte and a giant gingerbread cookie sounded mighty tasty as a pick-me-up treat. Maybe I could spare a few minutes . . .

My thumbs went to work, texting back to Mama.

Meet you there at 1:30.

That gave me an hour and a half to get everything together. Josie would be here before too long. Her fitting felt like a monumental litmus test for my designing ability. If she liked the two outfits I'd made for her, not only would whatever her big dream of the moment was come true—as long as it wasn't an unlimited supply of Chubby

Hubby—but I'd have made a pregnant woman very happy.

I unzipped the garment bag and stood back to give Mrs. James's ensemble one final look. A few wrinkles interfered with the presentation. It needed pressing, I decided.

I plugged in my upright steam iron, then took the outfit out of the bag, hanging it on the iron's attached garment hook.

"It's perfect," I said aloud. And really, it was.

I'd debated sleeveless or not for the senator's wife, but had gone with the former, topping it with a complementary tailored jacket that fit together with the dress like two pieces of a jigsaw puzzle. The nipped-in waist and straight-cut skirt with a zippered back would give an hourglass shape to Mrs. James, all the while maintaining her classic style.

I preened, just a tad. The dress, in cranberry red, was really a design feat. I'd created origami pleats along the neckline and topped the dress with the collarless jacket fitted underneath the edge of the neckline.

I didn't know what the garment for Mrs. James might help her accomplish—I'd already created several pieces for her over the last few months, and each had served a purpose in her life, but I wondered, would my charm ever wear out and no longer work for a given person? Was there a limited amount of magic to go around? Or maybe it would help her come to peace with the fact that before long her husband would know he'd sired a child with Eleanor Mcafferty and that he had another granddaughter . . . Gracie Flores.

A minute later, the steam iron was heated and ready

to go. I ran the brush along the fabric, letting the steam do its job. Once the wrinkles were gone, I bagged the garment again, hanging it on a long, sturdy hook just inside the French doors of the workroom.

One down, one to go.

I scooted around the boutique portion of my shop, straightening pillows, organizing the samples on the rolling wardrobe cart I kept in the back corner, tucking the rest of the gifts I'd wrapped under my Noble pine tree, and generally tidying.

I dusted Meemaw's old Singer and swept up the cuttings in the workroom. Nervous energy. Will had agreed to take the mistletoe decorations Gracie had finished up to the Denison mansion, but I needed to be there to make sure everything else was in order, that the kissing balls were hung in the right places, and to check the final fittings for the fashion show.

I was regretting my decision to postpone Josie's visit until the last possible moment. She'd be here any minute to try on the outfit I'd made for her, an eleventh-hour fitting since I couldn't stand the idea that she might nix it out of the gate as she had the others. She was going to be stuck with this outfit whether she liked it or not. Working with a temperamental and emotional pregnant woman was less than typical—and even less enjoyable—for me from a dressmaking standpoint. The outfit had to fit now, but I also wanted it to fit her in three months when she was ready to pop, and it would be extra good if she could transition the outfit to wear after baby Kincaid was born.

I picked up a throw quilt, folding it in half, then in half again. A frayed seam caught my attention and I headed into the workroom with it instead of laying it over the back of the sofa. Letting things sit around and pile up wasn't my style. If I could squeeze in a quick repair while I waited for Josie, that's what I would do.

The perfect color of thread sat on the cutting table in the center of the room—a brand-new spool of crimson red. "Thank you, Meemaw," I said to the air, because I knew she was being helpful.

I pulled a needle from the special section of my pincushion, threaded it, and set to work, folding the smallest bit of fabric over to create a finished edge, then using an invisible stitch to close up the pocket the tear had created.

A second later, the front door was flung open. Josie's voice boomed, "Harlow!" before she actually set foot in Buttons & Bows, but then she scooted in, as fast as a five-months-pregnant woman can scoot. She slammed the door behind her, sending the bells hanging from the knob into a jingling frenzy.

The tip of her nose was pink and the olive skin of her cheeks flushed from the cold chill outside. "I'm starving," she announced, stopping at the steps leading to the dining room and kitchen.

"Uh-uh. I'm fresh out of okra," I said. Not to mention it was way too early in the morning for fried vegetables.

She fluttered her hand, shooing away the very idea of the vegetable. "I'm over okra."

What? Had Texas gone back to being a republic? Was the earth off its axis? "Now you're just talking crazy," I said, staring at her. A Southern woman couldn't ever truly be over okra. It was cornmeal-covered candy. It was better than popcorn. It was a delicacy, maybe not on par with, say, escargot, but still tasty fare for Texas.

She sighed, looking momentarily dreamy. "Well, maybe not entirely over it, but I've moved on."

I was afraid to ask what was currently tickling her culinary fancy, but I posed the question anyway.

"Brussels sprouts cut in half, cooked in olive oil, and salted," she answered. She licked her lips, and I could almost see the miniature cabbages dancing like sugar plums in her head.

"Sorry, Josie. I'm fresh out of brussels sprouts, too." I'd dropped the quilt and thread, and now I hightailed it over to her, cutting her off before she could detour to the kitchen and start rummaging through the refrigerator for some other tasty morsel.

She frowned. "You have nothing for a pregnant woman?"

I steered her toward the workroom. "Nothing."

"Harlow Cassidy, you're a coldhearted woman," she said, but her eyes sparkled and she laughed.

"You'll thank me after you see the outfits I have for you."

Before I even finished speaking, her laugh turned to a growl. She looked down at her protruding belly, drawing her eyebrows together in a sharp V. "I'm sure the outfit is great. It's this body that could use some help—Wait. Did you say outfits? As in more than one?"

I pushed up my glasses before putting my hands on her shoulders and looking her square in the eyes. "Yes, plural." Finally coming up with the pencil skirt and the jacket concept had been a huge boon to my maternity clothing confidence, so I'd taken another idea that had been rattling around in my head, stayed up well past midnight every single night, and managed to produce a second outfit for Josie to try on. If it didn't work, all I'd lost was sleep. But if she liked it . . .

Making a pregnant woman happy was worth the red-rimmed eyes and the yawns that escaped from me every now and then.

I took the first outfit—a maxi dress in a flowing floral chiffon, flutter sleeves, cut on the bias with a décolleté neckline, and a coordinating maxi coat—down from the hook just inside the French doors. And then I held my breath. Designing maternity clothing, I'd decided, was more difficult than menswear, and menswear presented a lot of challenges.

I needn't have worried. The second Josie laid eyes on the maxi dress, her jaw dropped and she clapped her hand to her mouth. Her face lit up, her rosy cheeks as bright as strawberries on her olive skin. "That's a maternity dress?"

I nodded, handing it to her to try on. She took it and slipped behind the privacy screen. A minute later she was flinging her T-shirt and stretch-paneled pants over the top of the wood-slatted partition, and then she floated out from behind the screen, the skirt of the maxi hanging beautifully, flowing around her like cascading silk. I held my breath, watching her walk across the workroom. I'd cut the front to hang longer, compensating for how Josie's round stomach would pull the fabric up, especially as it continued to grow.

She stopped in front of the oval mirror and gazed at her reflection.

The bells on the front door jingled, followed by a low whistle and a "Wow."

We both turned as Nate came into the shop.

From the growing rouge on Josie's cheeks, and the pointed way their eyes met, I got that Nate liked the maxi dress. Or rather Josie in the dress.

"She's a miracle worker," Josie said, after the spell between them broke.

"You're the miracle," he said. Ah, Mr. Romance. I never would have pegged him as that, but Nate loved Josie, I had no doubt about that.

"I have another outfit," I said, taking the other ensemble from the hook.

She slapped her hand over her open mouth. "Is that tweed? I love tweed!"

Nate looked to the ceiling. "You know," he said, a pillar of patience, "I offered to take you shopping in Dallas for maternity clothes, but—"

Her choked squeak stopped his words on his lips. "Nate Kincaid, why on God's green earth would I go shopping in Dallas when Harlow is right here? If she can't design something that makes a person look good, then no one can." She gestured to the maxi dress she still wore. "I haven't felt this good in ... in ... I don't know how long. I don't even want any Chubby Hubby."

I smiled to myself. My design had won out over Ben & Jerry's. That was a monumental success.

He gave her a kiss before she moved back behind the privacy screen to try on the second outfit. Five minutes later, she emerged no longer looking like a stunning pregnant bohemian woman. Now she looked like she could hold her own with the muckity-mucks in their super-posh suites at Cowboys Stadium. The wide flap lapels of the jacket and the curved hemline were fresh and stunning.

Josie floated across the floor, her head held high, her belly front and center, and an air of contentment I hadn't seen on her face since her morning sickness had started. I felt flushed and satisfied, as if a ribbon of warm air were circling the room, leaving swirls of comfort in its wake.

The phone rang, so I left them alone and went to answer it in the kitchen.

Michele Brown's Southern drawl came from the other end of the line. "Harlow, I'm real sorry for callin' so early, but I thought you'd wanna know."

"Would want to know what?"

"I was reading through the *Texas Monthly*."

The hairs on the back of my neck stood up. I leaned against the kitchen counter. "Mmm-hmm?" I prompted when she hesitated.

"It's just that, well . . ."

"Michele, you can tell me. What do I need to know?"

"I was flipping through a back issue and, well, there's an article and do you know, it's by the man who died. Dan Lee Chrisson."

"Yeah, I discovered a few of his articles online."

Michele hemmed and hawed for another few seconds before saying, "I'm just wonderin' if this story might be . . ."

"If it might be what, Michele?"

"About you," she finally spit out. "It's dated a few months back. If you want, I can e-mail you the link."

"Yes, please," I said, giving her my e-mail address. I sat down at the computer in the corner of the dining room, hearing the tap, tap, tapping as she typed. By the time I opened my e-mail, a message was there.

"Got it," I said. I thanked her and we hung up.

I clicked on the link and was taken to the permalink page with another article written by Dan Lee Chrisson. I hadn't seen this one when I'd Googled him the day before. I read the title: "Spreading the Magic: How One Man's Wish Can Impact Multiple Families."

A lump formed in my throat.

I read the first line and the lump grew to the size of Houston when I saw the name Robert Parker, aka Butch Cassidy. Oh Lord.

I hunched forward, my head swimming as I read. Inexplicably, the melody to Roberta Flack's "Killing Me Softly" strummed in my head. He was singing my life with his words. That's exactly what I felt like. The article was about my family. The Cassidys. All of us.

He'd changed our names, thankfully, but he'd obviously done his research. He talked about Parker's transformation into Butch Cassidy, his romantic dalliances with the Sundance Kid's future girlfriend, Etta Place, and other women from Fanny Porter's brothel in San Antonio's redlight district, Hell's Half Acre.

I took comfort in knowing that he hadn't blown the whistle on us. Maybe we were just innocent bystanders in his research on Bliss, the outlaws here, and the town's history.

I prayed that the Cassidys wouldn't ever be held up for public scrutiny and vilified, but I also knew I had to tell Will the truth before he found out in some other way. I could only hope that he could understand and accept the truth—and me, once he knew.

I printed the article and tucked it into my sewing bag, then scurried back into my workroom. Josie was behind the privacy screen, and Nate waited with the garment bag, ready to add Josie's second outfit to it.

"I gotta go," I called to Josie. "Meet me at the Denison mansion in an hour, okay?"

She emerged from behind the screen in the clothes she'd arrived in, her hand on her belly.

"Do you ever sleep, Harlow?" she asked me, handing Nate the clothes. "You're going to wear yourself down."

"When Winter Wonderland is over I'll sleep," I said. And after I learned the truth about who'd tampered with that railing and why Dan Lee Chrisson died. And after I told Gracie and Will about Gracie's relation to Butch Cassidy—and what it meant. I grimaced, wondering just how all of this would play out. "Eventually."

Chapter 30

Ten minutes later I had my sewing bag, the garment bags with the outfits for the fashion show, and extras of everything I could think of, just in case something went wrong, all loaded up in the truck.

I tooled up Mockingbird Lane and drove around the square until I was in front of Villa Farina. I could have walked, but I planned to head straight to Mayberry Street afterward with all the garments I still had. They hung from a makeshift hook in the passenger seat, blocking my view out the right window but staying wrinkle free. A portable hand steamer poked out of my sewing bag. I had everything I needed to make sure the fashion show went off without a hitch.

I parked the truck across from the bakery. A teenage boy darted from parked car to parked car, sticking goldenrod flyers under windshields. The square was abuzz with activity. Carolers strolled, singing in harmony. The lights on the trees around the courthouse twinkled.

The boy headed my way, thrusting a half sheet of paper toward me as I lowered my head to the wind and pulled my coat closed. He wished me a Merry Christmas and then hurried on. Poor kid. He was risking frostbite to give folks flyers that would freeze to their cars and then would get thrown away.

I tossed the paper onto the seat of the truck, wound my scarf around my neck to ward off the chill, and darted across the street. Arnie Barnett sat in his truck in front of the bakery, reading. I waved to him. He waved back, but when I didn't stop to talk, he went back to his magazine.

Normally the pale green scallop-edged awning, small tables and chairs, and scent of pastries and coffee filled me with comfort and joy, but this afternoon, the cold was too strong even for freshly brewed java.

I waved to Gina behind the counter. Hattie came toward me, two holiday-themed to-go cups topped with plastic lids in her hands.

I doubled back and held the door open for her. "Thanks, Harlow."

"See you at the fashion show?"

"We have to leave a touch early to go down to Fort Worth, but we wouldn't miss it. Are you ready?"

"As I'll ever be. I might could end up behind the scenes biting my nails, but I'm ready." I grinned, but I was only half kidding. I had lovely, strong nails, but if the ball of nerves coiling in my gut kept tightening, I'd start chewing and wouldn't stop until I had nothing left but nubs.

She lifted one coffee cup in a mock wave, then braced herself against the cold and hurried to her truck. Arnie jumped out of the cab and met her at the curb. He took one cup of coffee from her hands, snatched the flyer from his windshield, then held the door for her so she could get out of the cold.

The pewter overcoat she had on was well cut and looked nice, but I couldn't stifle the image I had of her in an Irene jacket straight out of the 1860s, nipped in at the waistline and flaring slightly beneath, braiding running around the neckline, sleeves, and in the back. If Raylene ever did open up her own bed-and-breakfast, Hattie could work there and wear the Irene jacket I imagined.

Inside Villa Farina, I found Mama at a table near the front counter, her hands cradling a heavy white mug. A plate of pastries sat in the middle of the table, a magazine next to it, and a steaming cup was waiting for me. "I got you a pumpkin spice latte," she said as I sat down.

"Mmmm." I put the article I'd printed on the magazine, stripped off my gloves, and wrapped my hands around the warm ceramic mug. "Perfect."

"Sugar," she said after taking a bite of a flaky chocolate croissant, "I've given this a lot of thought, and I think you need to tell Will."

I choked on the sip of creamy coffee I'd just taken. "Tell him what?"

"Everythin'," she said, though it sounded like "everythan." "About Butch Cassidy. About our charms. About Gracie and what you reckon her gift might be. The whole kit 'n' caboodle."

My blood ran cold and my warmed fingers turned to ice again. It's what I planned to do. What I knew I needed to do. But suddenly an image of my father—or what I imagined my father looked like—walking away from my mother flashed in my mind. If I told Will about the Cassidy charms, he might well do an about-face and walk away just like Tristan Walker had done to Mama.

I looked up as her hand covered mine. "I don't know if he'll understand," I said.

"Hoss does."

I stared at her. Mama never had been one to mince

words. Her bluntness was one of her gifts, at least in my mind, but at this moment, a little buildup would have been nice. "What?"

She tapped her fingers against my hand and I looked down. And noticed the ring the sheriff had given to Mama a few months back. She normally wore it on her right hand, but now it was on her left, and on her—

"We're gettin' hitched, Harlow Jane."

I sat up straight, my mouth fighting between smiling and frowning. "Hitched?"

"Tyin' the knot. Bitin' the bullet. The old ball and chain."

"Married." I started grinning and then I couldn't stop. "Mama, that's wonderful!"

"I think so, too. We'll do it in the spring, I think. Maybe early summer. And I want you to make my weddin' dress."

"Well, of course. I wouldn't let you get hitched wearing anybody else's creation."

She nodded, smiling, but her hand squeezed mine and her smile faded. "Sugar, I want you to know—"

She sounded so serious, like the lead-in to some ominous bomb she was going to drop, that I had to fight the hammer suddenly pounding in my temples. "I had to tell him everythan."

I leaned forward. "What do you mean, everything?"

"Everythan'. The wish Butch made in Argentina. Our charms. Meemaw's ghost."

I felt the blood drain from my face. "Everything?" I asked again.

She nodded sagely. "Everythan'. No secrets. You have to start a relationship with a clean slate. I kept secrets from your daddy, and you know how that turned out."

I frowned. Yes, I did. It had left her husbandless and Red and me fatherless. "What did he say?" She was still wearing the ring, so he hadn't walked out on her.

"He's a man of few words."

"You told him you had a magical gift and that Loretta Mae hangs around as a ghost and that we're all charmed and he didn't say much?"

"Because he pretty much knew it already," she added. "All except the part about Meemaw."

My heart hammered in my chest at the implication of that. "How could he pretty much know already?"

"Honey," she said with a shake of her head, "people think we're an odd lot. They come around when they want some special plant that they think'll help 'em with their arthritis or somethin', or like Will, goin' to Nana when those dang goats were givin' him grief. No one talks about it, is all. They don't put words to it."

I ran through the list of who all knew about our charms and who else seemed sort of clued in. Mrs. James knew, of course. Her daughter, Sandra, and her granddaughter, Libby, were our relations and were charmed. She'd also had a pact with Nana and Mrs. Mcafferty back when they were kids, which meant Mrs. Mcafferty knew.

I also wondered if Mrs. Abernathy knew something. Or if she at least suspected. Michele Brown had told me about the articles by Dan Lee Chrisson, so she pretty much knew, even if I hadn't confirmed it.

Madelyn Brighton knew.

Aside from Madelyn, though, none of them knew about Meemaw's ghostly presence. She and Hoss were in a club by themselves with that bit of knowledge.

"We'll talk about the weddin' later, honey, but I really do think you should fess up to your man. If Gracie is

Cassidy kin, no matter how far back, or how thin the line—well, then, he has to know."

She was right, of course.

She released my hand and picked up the Dan Lee Chrisson article I'd printed. Her eyes flashed as she gave it a quick perusal. I caught movement in my peripheral vision. The vibrant red blooms on the poinsettias scattered around the bakery, I realized. The leaves swayed, ever so slightly, as if a tiny breeze had disturbed the quiet air. But I knew they were reacting to Mama's energy. "He seemed to have known," she said.

I picked up the magazine, thumbing through it to distract myself from Mama's charm potentially going haywire. If I was calm, maybe she'd stay calm and the poinsettias wouldn't grow like Jack's fairy-tale beanstalk.

I flipped through page after page of the home renovation glossy, a few of the images implanting themselves into my brain for future reference. My calmness seemed to work. The holiday flowers settled down again. "Well, I'll be," she said when she was done. "He really tried to stir the pot, didn't he?"

"I guess," I said, but I wasn't so sure. He could have been a lot more blatant than he'd been, naming names and our gifts and fully outing us. But he hadn't.

We ate our croissants, running through the possibilities. I told her about Meemaw's message to me in the steamed mirror.

"I saw the article in the courthouse," Mama said. "It's true, your great-grandfather walked out, just like your father did. But Hoss isn't goin' anywhere, and I'd bet a truckload of turnips that Will Flores wouldn't either."

"What wouldn't I do?"

I whipped around to see Will coming up behind me.

"Well, would you look at that?" Mama said. "Speak of the devil." She scraped her chair back, and before I could say things in Bliss had gone all catawompus, she was up out of her chair, one foot inching toward the door. "I was just fixin' to leave, Will. Take my seat and have yourself a flaky pastry."

He came around and sat in her vacated chair, and then quicker than a spotted ape, she was gone.

"Another Cassidy matchmaker?" he asked, not bothering to smother his crooked grin.

"Guess they're a-comin' outta the woodwork," I said, exaggerating my Southern accent. "Subtlety isn't Mama's strong suit."

"No, I guess it isn't." He flagged down Gina and ordered a cup of coffee, then took a bite of the croissant Mama hadn't touched. "So what wouldn't I do?" he asked again after a beat.

I swallowed, mustering up my gumption. It was now or never. Well, I reasoned, not really, but now was as good a time as any. "You know how I told you that I thought Mrs. Mcafferty might know about Gracie being her granddaughter?"

His smile vanished, the midnight blue of his eyes turning to slate. "I went to see her," he said.

I sucked in a deep breath, but shook my head. "No you did not."

"I sure did."

My eyes burned and as I looked at him, I just wanted to tell him that it would all be okay. But of course I had another bomb to drop and I didn't know if anything would be okay. "Did she confirm that she got pregnant before she married her husband? Did she admit that Naomi is Jeb James's daughter?"

He nodded grimly, running the pad of his thumb across the whiskers on his chin.

Oh Lord. "Do you think Sandra knows?" I asked after Gina delivered his coffee. I'd been so focused on the fact that Gracie was probably my second cousin, I hadn't really registered that that meant Naomi was a cousin, too. We were, all three of us, cousins.

"No idea."

I held my breath, waiting for him to tell me how it had gone with Mrs. Mcafferty. She knew about the family lineage and the charm passed from Etta Place on down to Jebediah James straight into Naomi and now Gracie. But had she told him all of this?

"She was sad that she's missed out on Gracie's childhood. Or at least she seemed sad. I'm going to introduce them at the fashion show."

I exhaled. "What if Gracie doesn't want that?"

"It's time," he said. "It's past time."

"That's good, Will."

He shrugged, then moved his chair closer to me, lowering his voice. "I'm a little worried about her. She's been obsessed with the consignment and vintage shops on the square. She goes in and'll spend a couple hours looking at all the clothes, touching everything . . ."

He kept talking, but his words blended together. She wasn't going to stores that had new clothes because they didn't carry history in them. They had no energy or soul. Oh boy.

"Will," I said, swallowing the lump of trepidation that had lodged in my throat. My mother's words bolstered me up. No secrets. You have to start a relationship with a clean slate.

"Hmm?" he said, taking another drink of his coffee.

Which was a good idea. I stalled, lifting my pumpkin spice latte to my lips.

"Cassidy," he said, prompting me, "you look more scared than a long-tail cat in a room full of rocking chairs."

I choked on my coffee. "Wh-what?"

He shrugged. "I heard Loretta Mae tell a person that a time or two. Seems appropriate. Now come on, just spit it out."

Tell him everythin', Mama had said. My gut was telling me she was right. If Will and I had any chance of developing something real, I couldn't hold back.

Gina packaged up the rest of the pastries, poured our coffees into to-go cups, and I dragged Will to my truck. I turned it on, cranked the heat, and launched into my story.

I started with the love triangle between Butch Cassidy, the Sundance Kid, and Etta Place, moved on to Butch and Texana falling in love, his escape to Argentina with the Sundance Kid, her unexpected pregnancy, and finally his wish on the Argentinean fountain, which bestowed magic on all of his female descendants.

He sat quietly, his face growing more and more tense with each passing sentence. "Let me get this straight," he said when I was finished. "You're saying that, one, you—and all the Cassidy women—are, what, witches? Magical? And two, that Gracie is a descendant of Robert Parker, aka Butch Cassidy, is charmed, and is some sort of distant cousin? Or something like that."

"Pretty far removed, but, yeah, in a nutshell," I said with a grimace. I wished he didn't look quite so uneasy.

"Unbelievable." He shook his head, his brows knitted together, then leveled his gaze at me.

"So Naomi has some magical power, too? Is that what you're telling me?"

My grimace didn't budge. "I reckon she does. Sandra and Libby Allen are both gifted in the kitchen. Sandra especially. Her cooking taps into a person's emotions and makes them stronger or gives them what they need. Libby's is still developing."

His thoughts seemed to stray for a few seconds, and then his face cleared. "You were so calm after you were released from the hospital. It was her food?"

"I imagine so," I said, wrapping my hands around my coffee mug, but it was long cold. What I wouldn't have given for something homemade from Sandra right then. Or for Meemaw to cocoon me in a comforting, warm hug.

Will's lips thinned under his goatee. "And Gracie . . . ?"

"I'm not entirely sure how it works, but I think she gets flashes of the past when she touches old fabric."

He angled his head, looking at me with disbelief. I didn't blame him. Magic was a hard pill to swallow, especially when you were being told your daughter possessed it. "What, like reverse clairvoyance?"

"Yeah, that's a pretty good way of describing it."

"What makes you think she sees the past?" he said tightly.

"Remember back in July when we found the Margaret dresses in the wardrobe?" He nodded, and I went on. "It was like she'd had an electric jolt. It happened again the night Madelyn came over to take her picture for the Margaret Festival. She put on the dress—Etta's dress." I emphasized that it was her great-great-grandmother's gown. "And she went into a sort of daze." ·

I could see his mind working to remember the moments I was talking about.

I hesitated to give him more examples, but finally said, "There have been a few times where I think she's sensed Meemaw around. She's heard something, or felt her presence —"

"Hold on." He closed his eyes for a beat, rubbing his hand against the back of his neck. "The creaky pipes and the drafts ... Are you telling me that all that is Loretta Mae?"

I nodded sheepishly. "Yes."

"And Gracie senses that it's more than old plumbing or a poorly fitted window." It was a statement, not a question, so I sat silently while he worked his way through it. He muttered to himself, assigning a different meaning to some of the things he'd noticed. "So her ability to sew like she does, with hardly any lessons ... that's because of Butch Cassidy and his wish?"

"I don't know, Will. Maybe. Loretta Mae taught me to sew when I was a little girl. Some people just have that talent. I did. I do. Maybe Gracie does too. That might be separate from having Cassidy blood run through her."

"Seeing flashes of the past isn't much of a gift," he said, grumbling almost as if Gracie had gotten gypped.

"Neither is goat whispering," I said.

He snapped his head up. "That's Coleta's charm? Talking to the goats?" He grew quiet for a minute, thinking, then slowly nodded. "Makes sense. I knew she had some special connection with 'em when I saw her coax Maggie Sue away from my horses and out of the yard."

Everyone in Bliss knew Nana had a way with goats, and I knew Will had gone to her for help when his neighbor's goat got through the fence of his property and harassed his horses.

Lots of so-called cowboys in Texas were all hat and no

cattle. Not Will Flores. He was the real deal. Yes, he was an architect, but he also kept a Longhorn and horses and knew his way around a stable.

"Let me guess. Tessa's got a magical green thumb."

"Right."

"And Loretta Mae?"

One by one, he was working through the Cassidy clan. "Whatever she wanted, she got."

"But you're saying she's not really gone."

"Not in the traditional sense," I said after a weighty pause. "But her charm doesn't seem to work the same as it did when she was here. A little less direct, I guess."

I filled him in on a few more details. "The charms can be passed on through the men in the family line, but they're only bestowed on the girls for some reason. No one knows why."

"Your brother?"

I shook my head. "Nope. He always wished he had some magical gift, but neither he nor his boys have it. He used to beg Meemaw for one, like she could wave an enchanted wand and make him magical."

He took a deep breath, his coffee long forgotten. "And you, Cassidy?"

That had been the million-dollar question since I'd been a child. For a long time I was the Cassidy without a gift. "Meemaw used to always say that my gift was my dressmaking." I smiled, remembering. "I would get so mad at her because dressmaking isn't a charm. It's just what I do. What I've always done."

"So you're a talented designer—that's your Cassidy charm?"

"No. It's more than that," I said, remembering how it had finally surfaced as I'd worked on Josie's bridal gown and the bridesmaids' dresses for her wedding. I closed my eyes and let my mind wander.

One by one, images of each of them, perfectly turned out in the garments I'd created, had come to me and I'd realized that my gift was to be able to imagine and design the perfect garment for someone, helping them realize their deepest desires in the process.

"I'm listening."

He was, with full, undivided attention, but he still didn't look happy about it. A hard edge had materialized and he looked big and tough enough to hunt down a bear with a switch. "When I design something for someone, it helps them . . ."

I trailed off, not quite sure how to put it into words. Having a sense of what happened when I designed an outfit was one thing. Expressing it so it didn't sound all woo-woo was something else entirely.

"Get what they want or need."

I snapped my gaze up. Something in the tone of his voice struck me, as if he were speaking from experience. "How did you know?"

"Putting two and two together," he said. "You made Josie's wedding gown and she got her happily-ever-after. At least so far. You made Karen's bridesmaid dress and now I actually see her around town with Tom. Mrs. James got out of the jailhouse." He tapped his fingers on the table, lost in thought for a moment. "But what about—"

"Nell's killer?" I asked, finishing his sentence.

"Exactly. Surely being arrested for murder isn't a person's deepest desire."

"There seems to be a checks and balances system." I'd given a lot of thought to just how my charm worked, and I hadn't come up with any definitive answers. All I had was speculation, so I went with it. "Sometimes people want things, but what we want comes with a price. I don't think Butch realized that making that wish for his descendants would mean we'd have to stay on the down low and protect our secret against people who'd just as soon string us up if they knew the truth. And I also don't think he realized that people wouldn't always stick around once they found out. Like my father," I added quietly.

He contemplated that for a second, pushing his cowboy hat back on his head. Most Texans had two hanging in their closet, but so far I'd seen Will in at least three different ones: a cream-colored straw hat, another in black, and a black felt one just like Tim McGraw and Toby Keith wore. Today he had on the black felt. His eyes softened. "He left after he found out?"

"Yup." I spit out a bitter laugh. "Name's Tristan Walker. Guess it suits him. Mama told him and that was that. He walked right on out and never looked back."

I studied my fingers splayed on the steering wheel, preferring that to the wariness I might see in his eyes.

But then he spoke, clear and reassuring. "My last name's Flores. Which has nothing to do with walking."

I lifted my gaze as he put his hand over mine, and suddenly I didn't long for Meemaw's cocoon of warmth, or a refill on my coffee.

Mama had been right. No secrets. I'd told Will everything, and he wasn't running away.

Chapter 31

"Red!"

Mama's voice boomed. Anywhere else, people might have looked at her like they were wondering if she was identifying the color of Santa's sleigh or declaring her favorite color.

But this was Texas and nicknames were a way of life. Red had been born ginger-haired. Our father, who'd still been around at that point, had nicknamed him Red and it had stuck.

Mama hurried down the long arm of the runway toward Red and his wife, Darcie. "Take a look at you younguns," she cooed, crouching to love on her grand-babies. "You look five years old," she said to Cullen. "And aren't you the cutest little guy around?" she added, wrapping Clay into a bear hug.

"Cullen's holding himself a little taller since his birthday last month," Darcie said, laying her hand on the top of her son's ginger head. "And Clay, well, he's about as rowdy as a boy can be."

Red gave me a good once-over as I approached. "You don't look any worse for wear," he said. "I was expecting more scrapes and bruises."

I was still a little sore, but not noticeably to anyone looking. "The fall was a few days ago. You shoulda seen me just after."

Will was inside the mansion hanging up the Victorian kissing balls, focused on his task and, I'm sure, lost in thought. I'd left him to come out and see what more needed to be done in the tent. Telling him about the Cassidy charms had lifted a weight from my shoulders, and I felt lighter and freer.

I spent the next hour making sure that the evergreen garlands adorned every crafter's table around the perimeter of the tent, that the poinsettia plants lined the steps to the house, and that the mistletoe balls were all hung with care. Cheery Christmas music played in the background, the heaters blazed, and everything was coming together.

Nana had her goat milk lotion packaged in pretty tubs, her dancing goat logo and the name of her farm stamped on classy circular labels and stuck to the top of each container. She'd brought brochures about her award-winning cheeses, as well as a cooler filled with samples and a Crock-Pot filled with her special Dr Pepper, apple, and cinnamon-stick mulled cider. "I'll put them out whenever the shindig starts," she'd said, and then she'd gone off in search of Granddaddy.

I'd managed to scoot upstairs for a quick peek at the widow's walk. It was locked up tight and no revelations came to me. Eventually I went back down to the tent.

Holly Kincaid, Nate's niece, flagged me down from the Seed-n-Bead table Josie had set up. "Harlow!" She waved me over. "What did you do to Josie?!"

My conversation with Will about my charm and making people's dreams come true came crashing back to me. Checks and balances and knowing that people often wanted things that weren't good for them rose to the top. "What's wrong?" My voice rose in a panic. "Is she okay?"

Her jaw dropped open and she stared at me. "Nothing's wrong! I've never seen her so happy. She's ratted out her hair and put on lipstick. Lipstick! Uncle Nate asked her if she wanted to stop by the market for another pint of Chubby Hubby and do you know what she said?"

I shook my head, smothering my relieved smile. "What?"

"She said no thank you. No thank you! She hasn't said no to Chubby Hubby since she found out she was pregnant."

"Wow." Another Cassidy Designs success story. "That's what a good outfit can do for a person," I said.

I thought about adding a testimonial page to the Web site I was going to develop. I could title it "Lives Cassidy Designs Has Changed." I filed the idea away to think about later just as I caught a glimpse of Raylene Lewis. She stood at the door to the kitchen, Boone in her arms, her feet rooted to the spot as she stared out the plastic window of the tent toward the very place Charles Denison had lain just a few days ago.

Hattie sidled up and put a protective arm around her shoulders. Hattie had known the truth about Dan Lee Chrisson's identity. Arnie probably had, too. But who had known what he'd been looking for? She, Hattie, and Boone moved into the tent and wandered through the booths.

A hand came down on my shoulder and I jumped. I whirled around to face Hoss McClaine. Sheriff Hoss McClaine. Fiancé to Mama. My future stepdaddy.

"Howdy," he said.

"Howdy yourself." I smiled up at his weathered Clint Eastwood face, not sure if I was ready to hug the man. "Mama told me the news. Congratulations."

"Thank you kindly." He looked more contemplative than I'd ever seen him. "I'd say you had somethin' to do with her finally giving me the thumbs-up."

"I doubt it. She doesn't need me to help her make up her mind about anything."

"Maybe not," he said, "but she's content now, what with you being back in Bliss. Way I see it, I reckon she feels like she can let herself be happy now that she sees you nearly every day and knows you're doin' just fine."

I narrowed my eyes, furrowing my brow and giving him a mock stern look. "Hoss McClaine, you better treat her right, is all I have to say."

He glared right back down at me, but a twinkle lit up his eyes. "You got an 'or else' to add to that sentence?"

"Nope. Mama'll give you the or else."

He cracked a grin and nodded at me as if to confirm that he wasn't going anywhere and that I didn't need to worry a lick about him and Mama.

Will sauntered up beside me in full Santa regalia. "Trouble over here?"

"No trouble," Hoss said. "Harlow here was just doing some woolgathering is all."

"No, I was not!" I said.

Hoss raised his bushy eyebrows. "Oh yeah, little lady, you most definitely were."

"I was just thinking. That's not the same thing as woolgathering." At least I didn't think it was. "Woolgathering" was one of those Southern expressions that didn't make a whole lot of sense to me.

"Thinking about what?" Will asked.

"Raylene. Charles Denison. Their baby."

Hoss leveled his gaze at me, the playfulness gone. "Gavin's convinced that Raylene Lewis isn't as innocent as she looks, Harlow," he said, his voice low enough so that only Will and I could hear. "You keep out of it, you hear?"

"But what about the articles?" I said. "I know he was after something hidden here."

"She was his wife, so she probably knew. All the more reason why she's the prime suspect."

"But what about Mrs. Abernathy?" Not that I wanted her to be a murderer, but I didn't want Boone ripped from Raylene's arms.

"Right now, Harlow, we don't have enough to piss on," Hoss said, "no matter who's guilty. Just stay out of it."

"Yes, sir," I grumbled, only moderately relieved that Raylene wasn't actually on the verge of being arrested.

I checked my watch and nearly lost my balance. "The fashion show starts in thirty minutes!" Good Lord, I *had* been woolgathering, and for far too long.

I left Hoss and Will and hurried up the center aisle, cutting left to the backstage area. The time flew by as I checked each woman's outfit, made last-minute adjustments, and did a quick microphone test.

Libby and Gracie, dressed in their whimsical elf costumes, complete with ruffled candy cane scarves, came to lead Will inside. His Santa session was starting.

A few minutes later, I stood at the beginning of the catwalk, mike in hand, quaking in my boots. I loved fashion but would never have been a model. Behind the scenes was a better place for me, not in front of the audience.

I mustered up an even voice, cleared my throat, and began. "Good afternoon," I said once the models were lined up.

Mrs. James wriggled her fingers at me from the front row. She was an old pro at this, but she'd wanted me to take the reins this time.

I practiced good public speaking technique by focusing first on someone to my right, then on someone to my left, and finally someone in the back center. "My name is Harlow Jane Cassidy, owner of Buttons and Bows and Cassidy Designs. Welcome to our first annual Winter Wonderland fashion show!"

Applause filled the tent, dying down after a few seconds. I went on to thank Mrs. Zinnia James, the Bliss Historical Society, and the city of Bliss for letting us use the Denison mansion, and all the local businesses that had sponsored the event.

"The fashion show you're about to see was inspired by winter. We started with the idea of a winter wonderland and the magic of the season. Enjoy!"

The first strains of "Winter Wonderland" sounded, the spotlights trained on the catwalk shone, and the first model glided down the runway. I introduced each woman, giving a brief description of the outfit—a female version of a Prussian collar coat inspired by the narrow standing collars of nineteenth-century garments, a trumpet dress with a flared flounce hemline paired with a tailored top, lightweight wool cuffed trousers with a ruffled top—as the models strutted up and down the catwalk.

Every now and then I glanced at the audience to gauge the reception. The women were enthralled. Husbands of the models were watching their wives in awe. And a few of the men were completely tuned out. Hoss

McClaine sat next to Mama, but had his phone out and seemed to be texting. Arnie Barnett flipped through a newspaper, going back and forth to a bookmarked page. And Senator Jeb James looked like he'd rather be anywhere than where he was, sitting next to his wife, Zinnia. Politics didn't take a break for the holidays.

I caught a couple glimpses of Santa poking his head out through the kitchen door. I knew Will had Gracie and the bomb I'd dropped on his mind, but he was doing an award-winning job of keeping it to himself.

Josie made the first trip down in her multihued tweed, then disappeared to change into her bohemian maxi dress. She glided out the second time looking more lovely than ever. I glanced at Nate. His attention never wavered as he watched her every step.

Newlyweds.

Madelyn Brighton snapped picture after picture of each model until, finally, the last one sashayed down the aisle, pivoted at the end, and then sashayed back up, pivoted once again, and headed back down. Each of the models fell into step behind her until the runway was lined with the complete design collection.

The audience stood, clapping and hollering. I grinned, totally satisfied with how it had turned out. Mama was right. I was doing just fine.

But my good mood was dampened when, from the corner of my eye, I saw Raylene dash up the steps and slip into the kitchen. Something was going on, and she wasn't just fine—not by a long shot.

Chapter 32

My curiosity got the better of me. As I hurried through the audience, I stopped short when I came upon Hattie and Arnie arguing in hushed voices, back and forth, back and forth, until he finally threw down his paper and stormed away.

"Are you okay?" I asked Hattie. I bent to pick up what he'd been reading. *Numismatic News*. It was really more of a periodical, I realized. Sort of a cross between a newspaper and a glossy magazine with a newspaper-like headline across the front page and articles about coin collecting.

"Oh yeah, I'm fine," she said. "He wants to go to the Cowtown Coin and Gun Show, and I want to stay here. I don't wanna leave Raylene. Is that wrong?"

"Of course not," I reassured her. "She's your sister and she's been through a lot."

I handed her Arnie's paper before I excused myself and headed inside. The holiday tunes came through speakers Abernathy Home Builders had installed for the event, and the festive mood spilled into every room. Trays of Raylene's tea sandwiches lined the island, but there was no sign of her.

Mrs. Abernathy walked by, glancing my way, nodding, just barely, and moving on.

A hearty "Ho, ho ho!" bellowed from the foyer. I poked my head in to see Will listening to a little girl recounting a long list of Christmas wishes. He *ho, ho, ho*ed again, Gracie tickled her cheek with the end of her ruffled scarf, Libby handed the girl a candy cane, and she was off. Another child climbed onto Will's lap and he let out another boisterous "Ho, ho, ho!"

"He's a good man," Mrs. Mcafferty said, coming up beside me. Her voice brimmed with emotions, her eyes turning glassy.

"And a good father." Not every man stepped up to the plate when it came to being a single dad, but Will certainly had, and he'd done a fine job raising Gracie.

"We talked, you know," she said after a beat. Her voice sounded steadier. "He introduced me to Gracie. They're going to come over tomorrow afternoon and spend a bit of their Christmas with us."

I took her hand, giving it a gentle, encouraging squeeze. "I'm so glad, Mrs. Mcafferty," I said, hoping that through their reunion, she'd keep quiet about the Cassidy charm. I still wasn't comfortable with the idea of our secret getting out to the whole town.

I spotted Raylene, and excused myself from Mrs. Mcafferty.

She still held Boone, clutching him in her arms as if she were afraid to let him go. I didn't blame her after she'd almost lost him. Arnie trailed behind her looking like a lost puppy dog. "Maybe she's in the kitchen," Raylene said.

Hattie. So Arnie had come back to make up to her. Good husband.

Mrs. Abernathy's voice drifted out from the parlor, the sound of it forcing a series of memories to the front of my mind. Abernathy Home Builders had taken the remodeling job of the Denison mansion even though it was small change. If anyone knew what might be hidden in this house that had Dan Lee on the hunt, it would be Mrs. Abernathy.

I listened to her tell stories about the quilts on display in the parlor. "The piecework on a quilt like this is detailed. Look how exquisite. Hand-stitching. Exacting work, and tedious. From what I . . ."

The talk of sewing gave me an excuse to go in and listen. I was like a moth to the light. I walked into the parlor and saw her talking to Josie, who looked exceedingly worn-out. All that strutting up and down the catwalk.

I pulled a chair forward for her and she sank into it, still listening to Mrs. Abernathy as she recounted the importance of quilts to women's history.

"My mom and grandmother can cook circles around anyone here," Josie said when Mrs. Abernathy paused to take a breath, "but they never did learn how to sew."

Another memory surfaced; this time, though, it wasn't about Mrs. Abernathy.

They kept talking. Somewhere in the back of my mind I heard my name.

"W-what?"

Josie leaned back in the chair, one hand on her swollen belly. "I said, I'm in awe of what you can create with fabric, Harlow."

I didn't respond. I couldn't. Something about what she'd said didn't make sense.

"There she goes again," Will said as he sidled up to me, still in his Santa suit. "Woolgathering."

"No. No, I was just thinking . . ." I trailed off as I tried to pinpoint what was bothering me. And then it came to me. "Oh!"

The three of them gawked at me. Well, Josie gawked. Will and Mrs. Abernathy looked, waiting for me to explain my outburst. "Oh, what?" Will asked.

"The quilt at the historical society."

His fake snowy eyebrows pulled together in a V. "What about it?"

"You said Josie donated it?" I turned to her for confirmation. She nodded, and I went on. "But you just said your mom doesn't sew. And neither does your grandmother, right?"

She reached up as Nate came into the parlor. Hattie, Arnie, Raylene, and Boone were in the foyer just outside the parlor, and Mama and Hoss were snuggling in Santa's chair. Mama gave an unconvincing, "Quit," followed by a giggle.

Ah, young love.

"They don't," Josie said.

"Who's 'they,' and what don't 'they' do?" Nate asked, moving behind her and gently rubbing her shoulders.

"Harlow was asking about the quilt I donated to the Historical Society."

"The one Pearl Denison made?"

Everything screeched to a halt as the pieces of this puzzle fit themselves together in my head. I could finally see the mystery in its entirety. "Pearl Denison made that quilt?" I remembered the faded letter from the signature. An *I* and two *N*s.

"She made this one, too," Mrs. Abernathy said. "It's been in this house all these years."

"So Pearl made quilts," I muttered, processing that

information. "And the Kincaids inherited those quilts when your great-great-grandfather won this house from Charles Denison?" I asked Nate.

He nodded as the front door slammed. Mama laughed again. And from where I stood I could see Boone crying in Raylene's arms. None of it stopped my mind from pulling together tidbits of information just like pieces of a quilt sewn together. Each fabric cutting by itself was just a scrap. But taken together, they made an entire story.

Goose bumps pricked on my arms as more ideas converged until finally one rose to the top. "Pincher's Jewelers," I said under my breath.

Josie stared at me like I was three sheets to the wind. "Pincher's—?"

"The jewelry store on the square," Nate finished.

"They've been there a long time, right?"

Nate nodded, his hands still rubbing Josie's shoulders. "Forever."

I whirled around to Will, grabbing his red velvet–covered arm, my words spilling out faster than I could even make sense of them. "There's an article in the courthouse about a Roosevelt coin from the U.S. Mint. It said something about Pincher's Jewelers."

"Yeah, the original Pincher—Jeremy, I think—came here from New Jersey. The story goes that Teddy Roosevelt wanted to make the American coins better-looking."

"I remember this story," Nate said. "My great-grandfather used to tell us about the artist the president hired and the double eagle design he created."

Will nodded. "Augustus Saint-Gaudens. It had the eagle on the front and the back. The mint changed the design to make it easier to strike."

"Weren't they all melted down?" Nate asked Will.

"No!" I exclaimed. "Not all of them. Two were put in a museum, but some were switched before the melting."

Now they all stared at me. "How do you know that?"

"Dan Lee Chrisson wrote an article about it," I said, remembering the Google search I'd done. "The mint produced the coins from 1907 to 1934."

Josie heaved herself up from the chair. "And one of them supposedly ended up in Bliss?" she asked.

Nate gave a single nod. "With Jeremy Pincher."

"Yes," I said, the goose bumps on my arms multiplying, "but Pincher's was robbed by Bonnie and Clyde."

All the chatter from the festival had vanished from my consciousness. The Christmas music faded away. Will folded his arms over his robust Santa chest. "Dan Lee Chrisson knew about the robbery. He must have thought Bonnie and Clyde hid the coin here in this house. That's what he was looking for."

A quiet sob came from behind us. Raylene. "D-did he find it?" she asked. "Is th-that why he was killed?"

Hattie appeared. When she saw her sister's tears, she handed her a wad of tissues. "Did he find what?"

"Some gold coin from the 1930s that's worth a lot of money. Dan Lee wrote an article about it. Harlow thinks he might have been lookin' for it."

"Worth a lot of money is an understatement," I said, shaking my head in disbelief. "Try about eight million."

The color drained from Mrs. Abernathy's face. "Eight million dollars?"

"For one coin?" Raylene choked out.

"For one coin," I said.

Raylene dabbed the clump of tissue against her nose. "We'll never know if he found it."

I was pretty sure he hadn't. "Someone's still looking," I said. "There's a hole in the wall on the widow's walk—"

"No there's not." Mrs. Abernathy's color had returned, but she looked stricken. "We had a crew come out and fix everything, and Barnett's did the finish work."

I shook my head. "The hole's there, and it's as big as my head."

Josie gasped, the realization of what that hole meant hitting her. "So someone else knows about the coin and is looking for it, too?"

"And they thought it was hidden in the widow's walk. Will showed me the original blueprints. The widow's walk was added on. Dan Lee might have thought the coin was hidden there because of the addition."

Silence fell over us. I studied each of them, considering. Nate and Josie were out, of course, and so was Will. Dan Lee might have told Raylene about the coin. Maybe her motive wasn't the divorce and the woman scorned at all. I wanted to clear her name, but I just couldn't.

Mrs. Abernathy moved away from our small group. The Abernathys, and her own family, went way back. Any of them might have known about the Saint-Gaudens coin. "Why'd you take this renovation job, Mrs. Abernathy?" I asked her. If she or her husband had known . . .

"We work closely with Barnett Restoration—" She choked, but managed to go on. "They won the bid, so we came on board."

Nothing made sense yet. I wandered to the window. Josie and Nate were called to the foyer by Madelyn. "Let me take your picture," she said.

Mama and Hoss got up from Santa's throne and Nate and Josie took their place. Madelyn started snapping.

Nana came through the kitchen, her cooler in tow,

Mrs. Mcafferty and Mrs. James in her wake. They spotted
Mrs. Abernathy and summoned her over. The clucking
started instantly.

"Woolgatherin' again, Harlow?"

"What?" I looked up to see Will, Hoss, and Mama all
watching me. "No, just thinking."

Hattie and Raylene sat in matching Queen Anne–
style chairs by the Christmas tree. The red and white of
the quilt in the parlor caught my eye and Mrs. Abernathy's talk about quilts came back to me. Quilting bees.
The Underground Railroad. Marriage quilts.

*The pieces by themselves don't tell a story, but put them
all together . . .*

"Oh Lord." That had to be it. I spun around and ran.

Chapter 33

Sheriff Hoss McClaine's boots crunched on the salted sidewalk behind me. He caught up with me at my car. Will was right by his side, ripping the snowy white beard from where he'd let it hang around his neck. "Where's the fire, Harlow?" Hoss said warily as Mama crashed through the gate.

"It's in the quilt," I said, breathless. "Just like the quilt Gracie got for Josie and Nate's baby."

They all stared at me. "What are you talking about, Cassidy?" Will asked.

"The Underground Railroad."

"The Underground Railroad," Hoss repeated.

"Yes! Bonnie and Clyde robbed Pincher's Jewelers, but they were run out of town before they could get their stuff." The image of a woman I'd gotten when I'd touched the dressing gown upstairs flashed in my mind. I'd seen the gold, but I'd thought it was a ring.

Mama put the back of her hand to my forehead. "You okay, child?"

I stepped back and her arm fell to her side. "I'm fine. Listen! Dan Lee's real name was Charles Denison. He must have known about the coin from stories his family

told way back when. Will," I said, looking at him, "you
told me that every time you came around, Dan Lee was
here. He must have thought that Bonnie and Clyde had
hidden it in the house before they had to skip town. He
was looking for it!"

"Go on," Will said.

"Quilts. They were a signal used during the Underground Railroad, but some folks also hid messages in
them."

"In a torn seam, you mean?" Mama asked, understanding dawning in her eyes.

The cold air blew through my clothes until I shivered,
my teeth chattering. "Yes! They would have hidden the
coin while they were here, expecting to take it when they
left, but if they didn't have time—"

"And you think it's in the quilt at the museum?"

Will stripped out of his Santa coat, draping it around
my shoulders. He had long johns on underneath his faux
belly. I'd never seen a man look so ridiculous . . . or so
attractive.

"An eight-million-dollar coin is sitting out in the open
over there?" Hoss said, shaking his head.

"Just like it has been for nearly a hundred years," I
said.

I hurried toward my truck.

"Cassidy!" Will called, coming after me. "Where the
hell are you going?"

I wrenched open the door, looking over my shoulder
at him. "To the courthouse."

"Who else knew? Who pushed Dan Lee Chrisson?"
Mama hollered.

That was the question I hadn't quite answered—

"I'll drive," Hoss said.

But as I turned to shut the door, I saw the half slip of goldenrod paper from this morning at the bakery. Cowtown Coin and Gun Show. One word popped out. "Numismatic," I muttered. The word was familiar.

And then it hit me like a big ol' bale of hay to the head. I grabbed for my bag and dug out the magazines I'd stuck inside to return to Hattie. A home-decorating glossy and *Numismatic News*.

Will caught the door. "What's that?"

"A coin magazine," I said slowly. I looked up at the house, the pieces of the quilt beginning to tell the whole story. Hattie had said that Arnie was going to Fort Worth to the Cowtown show.

"Dan Lee and Arnie were brothers-in-law," I said, realizing that a story about an eight-million-dollar Roosevelt coin was exactly the kind of thing two guys who were hobbyists would talk about. "Oh Lord." I turned to stare at the house again, as if I could see right through the walls to Hattie. I'd seen both her and Raylene in outfits perfect for a bed-and-breakfast. Because they only truly had each other?

I breathed out all the nervous air in my lungs. "It's Arnie Barnett."

The door. It had slammed earlier when we'd been talking in the parlor. He'd heard about the quilt and put it together.

I dashed toward the sheriff's car. Will's black Santa boots crunched against the icy cement behind me. I hit an ice patch just as I reached Hoss and Mama. My feet slipped out from under me and I went flying, but Will's hand grabbed my arm and he yanked me up before I hit the ground. "Darlin', you're going to get yourself killed."

I grabbed on to him to stay upright. "We have to get there before he does."

Hoss didn't even ask me to explain any more than I already had. He flung open the door to his patrol car, yanking out the handheld police radio. "Dispatch, get me Deputy McClaine," he demanded.

There was a blast of static and then Gavin McClaine responded. "Get over to the courthouse," Hoss snapped.

Gavin's response was muffled through the static.

"I'll explain later. Be on the lookout for Arnie Barnett."

We piled into the sheriff's car, Will and me in the back and Mama in the passenger seat.

The tires spun before catching. "Black ice," Hoss said. "Buckle up."

The car skidded at the corner of Mayberry and Maple, sliding through the light. Too bad Zinnia James hadn't bought enough salt to ice the road straight to the courthouse.

The car spun out in front of the limestone building; then we poured out of the car like a nest of agitated black water moccasins. Will charged ahead, plowing through the door, barreling past the visitors milling around. A minute later, the four of us slid to a stop in front of the empty quilt rack.

We heard the heavy, quick clomp of footsteps heading down. "He's got it!" I took off running, Mama and Will with me. From the corner of my eye, I saw Hoss head in the other direction. The back stairs. If he was quick, he'd be able to cut Arnie off at the door.

The courthouse door slammed open below us, the grunts and scuffling sounds of men fighting rising like hot air. We took the stairs two at a time, stopping short at the dog pile. Gavin was on top. Hoss rounded the corner by the stairs just as Will reached the bottom. After Gavin managed to stand, Hoss hauled Arnie up.

The courthouse door was flung open again, slamming against the wall. Hattie rushed in, Raylene and Boone on her heels. Hattie stopped short, Raylene crashing into her back with an "oomph!"

She spotted Arnie. "Lemme at him!" Hattie bellowed. The veins in her neck popped, her face turning the same red as Will's Santa pants. And then, like a snorting bull pawing the ground, Hattie hunched her shoulders and charged, careening into Arnie and Hoss. Hoss kept his balance, but Arnie fell to the ground like a gunnysack of flour. "You rat. You lying, thieving rat!"

"Jesus Christ, Hattie. I didn't mean to hurt him." He shook his head as if that one statement made everything all right.

She flung her arm out toward Raylene. "Boone's father is dead, Arnie. Dead."

His face contorted, his jaw trembling. "I told him to come in off that damn widow's walk. Those bolts were loose. You know how many times I tightened them," he said, looking at her with puppy dog eyes.

But Hattie was too smart to fall for that. "Because you loosened them, didn't you? And you let me sit out there. You killed that man for a stupid gold coin," she spit.

"An eight-million-dollar gold coin," he shot back.

"Reckon that didn't work out too well for you, pal." Gavin grabbed Arnie by the arm and led him outside, reading him his rights along the way.

Raylene sobbed, but she held Boone close. Her lifeline. Hattie wrapped her arms around the both of them, hugging on them like there was no tomorrow. I didn't have any new wardrobe flashes for them. So the bed-and-breakfast it was. I'd make them their outfits, and maybe some costume pieces for authenticity.

The truth. I'd discovered it and while it didn't right the wrongs, it filled me with peace.

They headed outside, Hattie to face the husband who'd betrayed her, and Raylene to face her new future. She was innocent, just like Meemaw had said. And no one would ever think otherwise.

Pearl Denison's quilt had flown out of Arnie's arms in the tussle. I grabbed it up by one corner. Mama caught the other end, and without a word we laid it flat on the courthouse floor and began working our hands down our respective edges. The gray and pastel calico prints had been painstakingly pieced together into a complex honeycomb pattern. Section by section, Mama and I felt for something hard hidden in the pattern. The pads of my fingers dusted over the old cloth. I remembered how I'd snagged them on a small section of broken thread when I'd looked at it before.

"Look at the stitches," Mama said. "So uniform. She did lovely handwork."

I moved on to the centermost section, feeling each piece of each hexagon. I found the torn seam. Stuck my finger inside. Will and Mama and Hoss held their collective breath. I dug around, but it wasn't there.

My shoulders sagged. "Maybe he did find it," I said, surprised at how disappointed I was. "It could be gone forever."

I folded the quilt in half, then picked it up and folded it in half again.

"But it was probably there." Will had stripped off his

faux belly. Black suspenders held up his pants. "You figured it out, Cassidy. You did good."

"You sure did, honey," Mama drawled. "Now we
oughta get back and start the cleanup—"

"Oh!" When I folded the halves together, my fingers
ran over something hard under the center hexagon of
one of the honeycomb shapes. "There's something here!"

The threads were loose, but I dug at the seam, pulling
the pieces apart enough to fit my fingers inside. Once
again, Will, Mama, and Hoss seemed to hold their breath.

My fingers grabbed hold of the cold, hard object with
the embossed picture. "It's here. It's here! I got it!" I
cried, finally extricating my fingers from the quilt and
holding up a twenty-dollar Saint-Gaudens coin worth
eight million dollars.

Chapter 34

On Christmas Eve, I hadn't thought Raylene or Hattie would ever be able to look at the courthouse without thinking of Bonnie and Clyde, Roosevelt's coin, Dan Lee who'd died searching for it, and Arnie Barnett who'd killed to make it his.

Pearl Denison had surely never imagined that the pattern of one of her quilts would hold the key to something so sinister.

But now, on Christmas Day, the same limestone building was lit up for the holiday, looking like it was straight out of a movie set. Full of hope. Maybe *that's* why I'd seen Raylene in the cheongsam dress. It represented hope and freedom from the burdens she'd been saddled with because of Dan Lee Chrisson's hunt for that outlaw gold.

My nephews, Cullen and Clay, all bundled up and high on Christmas cheer, ran across the courthouse green, their new handheld video games tucked in their back pockets. We were filled to the brim with the traditional Thanksgiving meal, which we always repeated on December 25, and a light snow was falling around us.

Mama and Hoss ambled a good ten yards ahead of me. Nana and Granddaddy fell behind, snuggling close to each other. Red and Darcie held hands as they walked, laughing at the energy their boys had.

"So Naomi McAfferty and Sandra James are cousins?"

Red asked a minute later.

"Distant."

"Very distant."

"Yup."

"And they're our . . . what?"

I shrugged. I wasn't really sure exactly what they were to us. Sort of cousins. Distantly. The connection was thin, and only through Butch Cassidy, but his blood—and his charm—was strong. "They're family."

"The Cassidy clan is growing," he said, giving Darcie a squeeze and a wink.

I knew that look. And I heard the playful note in his voice. I stopped short. "No."

They grinned and nodded, and Darcie's hand fluttered to her belly. "Yes."

I leapt toward them, wrapping them in a big hug. "Another C baby! Cullen. Clay. And . . . ?"

"A growing family," Red said.

A horn honked, snagging our attention. Will drove up Maple in his pickup truck. Gracie in the passenger seat. He pulled into a space in front of the courthouse. I left Darcie and Red to continue their walk as I hurried over to Will and Gracie. I couldn't stifle the smile tugging up the corners of my mouth, and I didn't want to. Seeing them both was the best Christmas gift I could get.

Will rolled down the window as I wrapped my scarf

tighter around my neck and rubbed my gloved hands together. I leaned my elbows on the window frame, the heat from the truck's cab warming my cheeks.

"Merry Christmas," he said, a sneaky grin on his face. I pushed my glasses up, smiling, but wondering just what he was up to. "Merry Christmas to you, too."

"We're heading to the McAffertys'," Will said, "but we have a little something for you."

I peered past him. Gracie giggled, bouncing in the passenger seat. She held something in her lap, but all I could see was an enormous red bow.

"Oh yeah?"

He turned to Gracie, blocking me so I couldn't see as she put something in his hands. "Close your eyes, Cassidy."

I obliged, grinning, and when I opened them, he held out the tiniest, and possibly the cutest, little creature I'd ever seen, sitting in an enormous red ceramic soup mug.

"What—?"

"It's a teacup pig!" Gracie squealed. "I picked it out for all of us," she said. "I thought . . ." She trailed off, hunching her shoulders nervously." "I thought . . . We thought . . ."

Will put his hand on hers and squeezed. "We figure we're kind of connected now, Cassidy, and we—"

"We want to share Earl because that way, we'll see more of each other. You and Daddy and me, I mean." She hurried on. "And Earl, of course."

I held back the laugh tickling my throat. "Earl?"

"Earl Grey," she explained. "Since he's a teacup pig and all. He's yours, and ours, because we're like family now."

"Bound together now by Earl Grey," Will said, a twinkle in his eye. "It was Loretta Mae's favorite kind of tea, right?"

"I reckon it was, Will Flores," I said, giving up on holding in my laugh. What Meemaw wanted, Meemaw got," I reckon it was."

Sewing Tips

1. When working with wool and silk, have the cleaners do a hot press of the fabric before cutting so when cleaning time comes, the garment won't shrink.

2. Use weights instead of pins to hold pattern pieces in place. Pins can cause fabric to stretch.

3. Always remember, cotton shrinks. Add one-third to three-quarters of an inch to the seam allowance to compensate for shrinkage.

4. Make your own pattern weights using a variety of large heavy washers, available in hardware stores, and use scraps of fabric to cover them.

5. When using pins, insert them carefully to avoid pushing fabric off the grain.

Cassidy Family Tree

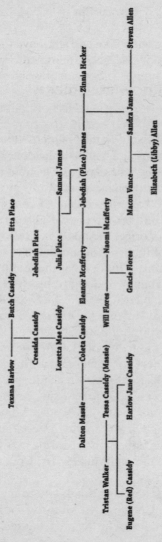

Acknowledgements

The story of the missing Saint-Gaudens double eagle coin, and its value, is real. Thanks to the deliciously dastardly outlaws Bonnie and Clyde, I was able to bring it to Bliss, Texas, and it became part of this story. Quilts, also, were often used as a real means of communication during the era of the Underground Railroad. Blending these and other historical elements in Harlow's world fascinates me, and I hope it fascinates you as well.

As always, there are a lot of ideas that contribute to a story as a whole. Thanks to Joe Strong from SMU for naming Nana's goat farm. Sundance Kids. Perfect! A huge thanks to Kym Roberts for her quick draw on the iPad, looking up information to help with a scene at just the right moment, and to the Book Carriage, my favorite indie bookstore, where so much brainstorming happens.

As always, thanks to Mom for teaching me the basics of quilting and sewing, and for passing on her love of fabrics, patterns, and trims, and to the women in the Bourbon, Massie, and Sears families for continuing to be an inspiration. Aunt Babe's disappearing acts were real.

A big thanks to the real Michele Brown, who is now my go-to girl for titles.

Of course, a huge ongoing thank-you to my family, to Holly, to Kathleen Cook, to Jan McInroy for her amazing attention to detail and little notes that make my day and make me smile, to Mimi Bark for bringing Harlow's shop to life on the Magical Dressmaking covers, and to Kerry for her continued support and love of Harlow's world.

And finally, thank you to all the readers who've become fans of the Magical Dressmaking Mystery series and Harlow Cassidy. The books are a joy to write.

—MBR

Read on for a preview of the next
Magical Dressmaking Mystery,

A CUSTOM-FIT CRIME

Coming in July from Obsidian

When I first came back home to Bliss, Texas, I thought my hometown would be just as peaceful as it was when I'd been a little girl. It was still sweet and Southern, sure, but death had found a way of creeping in between the seams, and too often, I'd been in the mix.

In New York, a knock on the door in the middle of the night would have been enough to send my heart into a frenzied pattern. But I was in Texas now, and a late-night *tap-tap-tap* on the front door of my little yellow farmhouse wasn't cause for alarm.

"Meemaw?" I rolled to my side, my voice sleepy. My great-grandmother had passed on before I'd come back home, but I'd learned that the Cassidy women didn't always cross right over to the other side.

Meemaw hung around the farmhouse her daddy had built, trying to communicate with me. Or playing jokes on me, depending on how you looked at it.

If Meemaw was tapping on the door downstairs, she wasn't letting on. "Meemaw, I'm sleeping," I murmured, but the sounds continued.

Suddenly, through my bleary eyes, I saw the red and gold curtains on either side of the window rustle, and then heard a louder *tap-tap-tap* from downstairs. But if Meemaw was up here with me, then who . . .

I lay still in my bed, listening, wondering for a second if I was imagining things.

But then it came again. *Tap. Tap. Tap.*

I peered at the clock. Two a.m. I was suddenly wide awake, my pulse zipping along like a sewing machine whose foot pedal was stuck. I jumped out of bed, stepped over Earl Gray, the sweet little pot belly pig Will Flores and his daughter, Gracie, had given me at Christmas, and padded barefoot across the cold wood floor and out to the landing, where I stopped to listen.

Tap. Tap. Tap.

Mama wouldn't knock. She'd just come on in. Same with Nana and Granddaddy, and *they'd* come into the house through the Dutch door off the back porch.

It could be Will, but he wouldn't be out at this time of night. "Oh no—Gracie?" I murmured. She'd run to me here once before, when she'd learned the truth about her mother leaving her when she was just a baby.

The sound at the door changed, became more of a scraping, and seemed to move off to the window. Surely it wasn't Gracie, I reasoned, darting a quick look around in search of a weapon. Just in case. An antique sidebar rested against the wall in the landing, a decorative metal dress form on one side, a bowl filled with handmade felt beads on the other. I could pelt the intruder with the little round balls of felt, but that probably wouldn't do me any good.

With nothing but my wits, I descended the stairs. They were even colder against my bare feet, but I made it down, turned left into the part of the house that doubled as my shop, Buttons & Bows, and stooped to snatch up one of my red Frye harness cowboy boots. Not much in the way of defense but better than nothing.

The scraping turned back to knocking and I had another thought. Nana's goats! Maybe it wasn't an intruder at all. Nana and Granddaddy's property was directly behind mine, and Thelma Louise, the granddam of Nana's herd of dairy goats, managed to escape more frequently than not. She was as mischievous as all get out, and she seemed to pick on me.

"Harlow?"

I froze, my elbow bent, the boot cocked behind my head. Nana's goats didn't speak. Neither did Meemaw, for that matter.

With my ear up to the door, I held my breath and listened.

"Harlow, are you there?"

The voice was familiar. It was a woman. Speaking in low tones, as if she didn't want anyone to hear her calling my name, which was silly, since it was the middle of the night and how else was she going to get my attention?

The doorknob jiggled and I jumped back. "Who's there?"

The doorknob jiggled again. "It's Orphie."

Orphie? I dropped the boot, turned the lock, and pulled open the door.

Dark, curly, shoulder-length hair. Tall and thin like a model. Bronzed skin. It really *was* my former roommate and friend Orphie Cates.

I squealed, rushing onto the porch, wrapping her into a bear hug. "I can't believe it! You're really here?" I pushed her back, stared at her, and then drew her in for another embrace. I hadn't seen her in a year and a half, although we'd talked on the phone and had a constant stream of e-mails back and forth.

"In the flesh," she said after I finally let her go. A wry smile graced her perfect lips. We'd worked together for a top New York designer, but really, Orphie should have been on the runway. She was *that* beautiful.

And she was right about the flesh part, too. The dress she wore had a low-cut scoop neck that draped at her cleavage. Two thin spaghetti straps went over her shoulders and crisscrossed in the back. The pattern had been cut on the bias and hung in silky waves over her body. It was her own design, I knew, utterly sexy and absolutely out of place in a town like Bliss.

But Orphie was Orphie, and she had style in spades.

She looked over my shoulder at the shop. I grabbed her by the wrist and pulled her into the house, shutting and locking the door behind her.

"So this is where the magic happens, eh?" she said, a playful grin on her face.

That one little sentence made me gasp. Only a handful of people knew about the Cassidy charm: my family, of course, since they were all charmed, too; Madelyn Brighton, the town photographer and a good friend; and Will Flores, the man I'd recently started dating. His daughter was charmed, too, but didn't know it yet. So many secrets in such a small town.

But Orphie didn't know, and she wasn't referring to my magic. She was talking about my dressmaking. "This is it," I said.

She wandered around, looking at the antique armoire that held stacks of fabric, the custom designs hanging on a freestanding rack against the back wall, and a bulletin board with my favorite sketches pinned to it, oohing and ahhing the whole time. Finally, she made her way to the French doors dividing the front room of the shop and what had once been Meemaw's dining room, which I'd turned into my workroom. Her gaze took in the cutting table sitting in the middle, a wooden pulley contraption for fancy gowns affixed to the ceiling, Meemaw's old Singer and my Phaff, my Babylock serger, dress forms, and a shelf unit with Mason jars of buttons, baskets filled with trim, and every other sewing supply I might need as I developed Cassidy Designs.

"It's really great, Harlow," she said, stopping at my newest purchase, a commercial sewing machine. "And look at this!" She lovingly brushed her fingers over the top.

"Business has been getting better," I said. I'd made custom designs for a few of Bliss's most prominent matrons. I'd worked on several festivals, including the local debutante pageant and ball and the town's holiday extravaganza. Word was getting around about my designs and how they made people feel. I could make people's wishes and dreams come true through the clothes I sewed for them.

"And you're sewing for your mother's wedding now?" She looked around, searching for a wedding dress.

"The gown, if you can call it that, is put away for now. I'm finishing my fall collection first," I said. "It's for *D Magazine*, and kind of outside the norm for them."

She trailed her hand across the cutting table, looking longingly at the length of fabric stretched out and ready to be cut first thing in the morning.

"They're usually so Dallas-centric," I continued, "but for this issue, they're featuring up-and-coming designers." I notched my thumbs toward myself, smiling. The exact words of the journalist who'd contacted me were committed to memory. *We'd like to do an article featuring Dallas-area fashion designers who offer a unique perspective in the industry. We'd like you to be one of the designers, Ms. Cassidy.*

My newest collection was "Country Girl in the City," and I'd been working round the clock to flesh out the collection, finalize my lookbook, and make sure every piece had a cohesiveness both in textiles and presentation, and also reflected my voice and what I brought to the fashion world. "They're featuring me, along with Midori—"

Orphie's mouth gaped. "Midori? I love what she does with pattern and cut."

I did, too, and to have my designs next to hers made my skin prickle with excitement. The Japanese perspective she brought to her designs made her unique, and although it wasn't a competition between us, I wanted my clothes to show well in comparison.

"And the third designer is Michel Ralph—"

"Beaulieu?!" she exclaimed.

"Yes." I nodded gravely. "Beaulieu."

She collapsed onto the red velvet settee in the seating area of Buttons & Bows. "That's right," she said, realization dawning on her. "He's in Dallas now."

"Moved here before I came back." We both knew Michel Ralph Beaulieu from our days at Maximilian.

She frowned but not even that marred the perfect, unlined silk of her skin. "The magazine should feature Jean Paul Gaultier, not Beaulieu," she said, shaking her head. "*He's* the original. Beaulieu is just a cheap imitator."

It was true. The haute couture fashion statements of Jean Paul Gaultier were in a league of their own, his brilliance drawn from the world around him, from different cultures, cinema, and rock music, for starters. His designs were worn by Madonna and Lady Gaga, among other fashion-forward celebrities, and he brought something utterly new to the fashion world.

"And Beaulieu only does the cheap prêt-à-porter stuff." Orphie stretched her long legs out on the settee, stifling a yawn. I hid my own, suddenly reminded that it was now nearly two thirty in the morning.

"I do some ready-to-wear pieces, too, Orphie," I said. She'd glanced at some of the clothing on the portable rack. I preferred couture, like any designer, but the town of Bliss didn't have much use for stagelike costuming or artistic statements through bold clothing. My Country Girl in the City collection was unique, practical, and truly represented my hybrid perspective. It wasn't boudoir or urban jungle like Beaulieu, and it wasn't Japanese punk or metropolis like Midori, but it was me, and I was proud of it.

I sank down on the loveseat opposite her, the coffee table that had been repurposed from an old door between us. My lookbook and another bowl of felt beads I'd been working on for my collection's accessories sat in the middle of it. I stifled another yawn. I plumped a pillow under my head, and it suddenly felt like we were back in Manhattan in our minuscule loft apartment.

"Orphie," I said, "why are you here? It's the middle of the night."

"You said your mom's getting married to that cowboy sheriff," she said drowsily.

I followed her lead, letting sleep slip over me like a

veil. "Right." My mother and Hoss McLaine were getting hitched, and it was going to be a really eclectic Southern wedding. I'd already made her dress and a dress for my sister-in-law, Darcie, who was to be a bridesmaid. I just had to make my own maid-of-honor dress and I'd be done, but I hadn't come up with the right design yet.

Orphie's eyes had begun to drift closed, but she pried them open again, her gaze falling on the red and black suitcase she'd set by the steps to the little dining area. "And you have the big photo shoot with your collection. I haven't seen you in ages, and I figured you could use a little help with all of it."

She was a true friend, and she sounded sincere, but there was a terseness to her voice, and I knew there was something she wasn't telling me. Southern women had a slew of rules they lived by, one of which was being well-versed in double speak. True, Orphie wasn't Southern—she was as Midwestern as they came—but she'd picked up some tricks from me over the years we'd spent together, and I suspected there was a little subtext under her statement. "Orphie?" I prompted, stretching out her name.

"Harlow," she replied.

"What's going on? You did not show up on my doorstep in the middle of the night unannounced to help me with my sewing, although, don't get me wrong, I'm glad you're here."

She sighed, sitting up and propping her pointy elbows on her knees. I mirrored her, but then she got up and trudged, as much as a five-foot-ten-inch lithe woman can trudge, to her suitcase. She plopped it down flat, unzipped it, and lifted a book off the top of the neatly folded clothes.

I recognized that book. Hard, black cover. Crisp white interior pages. Maximilian logo embossed on the front. I jumped up and backed away as if it were a coiled snake. "Orphie, what are you doing with that?"

"I never told you the reason I left Maximilian," she said, her voice slow and tired.

I didn't like the sound of that simple statement. The fact was, she'd just up and quit. Packed up one day and left with no explanation. "Family," she'd said later when I'd pressed her.

"Why'd you leave?" I asked, not entirely sure I wanted to hear the answer.

She strode to me, book outstretched in her arms. "This is why," she said solemnly.

And with those three words, I knew that Orphie hadn't come to help me with Mama's wedding to the sheriff, and she hadn't come to be my assistant for the *D Magazine* photo shoot. No, she'd come because she'd stolen one of Maximilian's prized design books in which he jotted down his ideas, sketches, and, if the rumors in New York were true, kept track of celebrity secrets and tidbits of information he'd gathered over time that he held over people. And Lord knew what else. From the grave look on her face, I knew it couldn't be good.

Also available from

Melissa Bourbon

Pleating for Mercy
A Magical Dressmaking Mystery

When her great-grandmother passes away, Harlow leaves her job as a Manhattan fashion designer and moves back to Bliss, Texas. But soon after she opens Buttons & Bows, a custom dressmaking boutique in the old farmhouse she inherited, Harlow begins to feel an inexplicable presence...

One of her first clients is her old friend Josie, who needs a gown for her upcoming wedding. But when Josie's boss turns up dead, it starts to look as if the bride-to-be may be wearing handcuffs instead of a veil. Suddenly, Josie needs a lot more from Harlow than the perfect dress. Can Harlow find the real killer—with a little help from beyond?

Available wherever books are sold or at
penguin.com

facebook.com/TheCrimeSceneBooks

OM0062

Also available from
Melissa Bourbon

A Fitting End
A Magical Dressmaking Mystery

Business is booming at Harlow Jane Cassidy's
custom dressmaking boutique—even with her great-
grandmother's ghost hanging around the shop.
But when a local golf pro is found stabbed with
dressmaking shears, the new town deputy suspects
Harlow. Now she has to clear her name before the
next outfit she designs is a prison jumpsuit...

**"The Cassidy women are naturally drawn to mystery
and mischief. You'll love meeting them!"**
—Maggie Sefton

Available wherever books are sold or at
penguin.com

facebook.com/TheCrimeSceneBooks

OM0085

Molly MacRae

LAST WOOL AND TESTAMENT

A Haunted Yarn Shop Mystery

When Kath Rutledge comes to the small town of Blue Plum, Tennessee, to settle her grandmother Ivy's will, she learns she's inherited Ivy's fabric and fiber shop, The Weaver's Cat. She also winds up learning the true meaning of T.G.I.F.—Thank Goodness It's Fiber. That's the name of the spunky group of fiber and needlework artists founded by Kat's grandmother, who now are determined to help Ivy run the shop and carry on her grandmother's legacy.

But when Kath learns her grandmother was also the prime suspect in a murder, solving the case becomes the most important thing on her "to do" list. Luckily, she won't have to do it alone. She's got the members of T.G.I.F. to lean on—and she's about to get some help from a new friend from beyond the grave...

Available wherever books are sold or
at penguin.com

facebook.com/TheCrimeSceneBooks